ELIZABETH GILL
THE CRIME COAST

ELIZABETH GILL was born Elizabeth Joyce Copping in 1901, into a family including journalists, novelists and illustrators. She married for the first time, at the age of 19, to archaeologist Kenneth Codrington. Her second marriage, to artist Colin Gill, lasted until her death, at the age of only 32, in 1934, following complications from surgery.

She is the author of three golden age mystery novels, *The Crime Coast* (aka *Strange Holiday*) (1931), *What Dread Hand?* (1932), and *Crime de Luxe* (1933), all featuring eccentric but perceptive artist-detective Benvenuto Brown.

By Elizabeth Gill

ELIZABETH GILL

THE CRIME COAST

With an introduction
by Curtis Evans

DEAN STREET PRESS

INTRODUCTION

THE DEATH OF Elizabeth Joyce Copping Gill on 18 June 1934 in London at the age of 32 cruelly deprived Golden Age detective fiction readers of a rapidly rising talent in the mystery fiction field, "Elizabeth Gill." Under this name Gill had published, in both the UK and the US, a trio of acclaimed detective novels, all of which were headlined by her memorably-named amateur detective, the cosmopolitan English artist Benvenuto Brown: *Strange Holiday* (in the US, *The Crime Coast*) (1929), *What Dread Hand?* (1932) and *Crime De Luxe* (1933). Graced with keen social observation, interesting characters, quicksilver wit and lively and intriguing plots, the three Benvenuto Brown detective novels are worthy representatives of the so-called "manners" school of British mystery that was being richly developed in the 1930s not only by Elizabeth Gill before her untimely death, but by the famed British Crime Queens Dorothy L. Sayers, Margery Allingham and Ngaio Marsh, as well as such lately rediscovered doyennes of detective fiction (all, like Elizabeth Gill, reprinted by Dean Street Press) as Ianthe Jerrold, Molly Thynne and Harriet Rutland.

Like her contemporaries Ianthe Jerrold and Molly Thynne, the estimable Elizabeth Gill sprang from a lineage of literary and artistic distinction. She was born Elizabeth Joyce Copping on 2 November 1901 in Sevenoaks, Kent, not far from London, the elder child of illustrator Harold Copping and his second wife, Edith Louisa Mothersill, daughter of a commercial traveler in photographic equipment. Elizabeth--who was known by her second name, Joyce (to avoid confusion I will continue to call her Elizabeth in this introduction)--was raised at "The Studio" in the nearby village of Shoreham, where she resided in 1911 with only her parents and a young Irish governess. From her father's previous marriage, Elizabeth had two significantly older half-brothers, Ernest Noel, who migrated to Canada before the Great War, and Romney, who died in 1910, when Elizabeth was but eight years old.

Elizabeth's half-sister, Violet, had passed away in infancy before Elizabeth's birth, and a much younger brother, John Clarence, would be born to her parents in 1914. For much of her life, it seems, young Elizabeth essentially lived as an only child. Whether she was instructed privately or institutionally in the later years of her adolescence is unknown to me, but judging from her novels her education in the liberal arts must have been a good one.

Elizabeth's father Harold Copping (1863-1932) was the elder son of Edward Copping--a longtime editor of the *London Daily News* and the author of *The Home at Rosefield* (1861), a triple-decker tragic Victorian novel vigorously and lengthily denounced for its "morbid exaggeration of false sentiment" by the *Spectator* (26 October 1861, 24)—and Rose Heathilla Prout, daughter of watercolorist John Skinner Prout. Harold Copping's brother, Arthur E. Copping (1865-1941), was a journalist, travel writer, comic novelist and devoted member of the Salvation Army. Harold Copping himself was best-known for his Biblical illustrations, especially "The Hope of the World" (1915), a depiction of a beatific Jesus Christ surrounded by a multi-racial group of children from different continents that became an iconic image in British Sunday Schools; and the pieces collected in what became known as *The Copping Bible* (1910), a bestseller in Britain. Harold Copping also did illustrations for non-Biblical works, including such classics from Anglo-American literature as *David Copperfield*, *A Christmas Carol*, *Little Women* and *Westward, Ho!* Intriguingly Copping's oeuvre also includes illustrations for an 1895 girls' novel, *Willful Joyce*, whose titular character is described in a contemporary review as being, despite her willfulness, "a thoroughly healthy young creature whose mischievous escapades form very interesting reading" (*The Publisher's Circular*, Christmas 1895, 13).

Whether or not Harold Copping's surviving daughter Joyce, aka Elizabeth, was herself "willful," her choice of marriage partners certainly was out of the common rut. Both of her husbands were extremely talented men with an affinity for art. In 1921, when she was only 19, Elizabeth wed Kenneth de Burgh Codrington (1899-1986), a brilliant young colonial Englishman then studying Indian archaeology at Oxford. (Like Agatha Christie, Elizabeth made a marital match with an archaeologist, though, to be sure, it was a union of much shorter duration.) Less than six years later the couple were divorced, with Elizabeth seeming to express ambivalent feelings about her first husband in her second detective novel, *What Dread Hand?* After his divorce from Elizabeth, Codrington, who corresponded about matters of religious philosophy with T.S. Eliot, would become Keeper of the Indian Museum at the Victoria and Albert Museum, London, and later the first professor of Indian archaeology at London's School of Oriental and African Studies. Codrington's "affection and respect for Indian culture," notes an authority on colonial Indian history, "led him to a strong belief in a mid-century ideal of universal humanity" (Saloni Mathur, *India by Design: Colonial History and Cultural Display*)—though presumably this was not to be under the specifically Christian banner metaphorically unfurled in Harold Copping's "The Hope of the World."

In 1927 Elizabeth wed a second time, this time to Colin Unwin Gill (1892-1940), a prominent English painter and muralist and cousin of the controversial British sculptor Eric Gill. As was the case with his new bride, Colin Gill's first marriage had ended in divorce. A veteran of the Great War, where he served in the Royal Engineers as a front-line camouflage officer, Colin was invalided back to England with gas poisoning in 1918. In much of his best-known work, including *Heavy Artillery* (1919), he drew directly from his own combat experience in France, although in the year of his marriage to Elizabeth he completed one of his finest pieces, inspired by English medieval history, *King Alfred's Longships Defeat the Danes, 877*, which was unveiled with fanfare at St. Stephen's Hall in the Palace of Westminster, the meeting place of the British Parliament, by Prime Minister Stanley Baldwin.

During the seven years of Elizabeth and Colin's marriage,

which ended in 1934 with Elizabeth's premature death, the couple resided at a ground-floor studio flat at the Tower House, Tite Street, Chelsea--the same one, indeed, where James McNeill Whistler, the famous painter and a great-uncle of the mystery writer Molly Thynne, had also once lived and worked. (Other notable one-time residents of Tite Street include writers Oscar Wilde and Radclyffe Hall, composer Peter Warlock, and artists John Singer Sargent, Augustus John and Hannah Gluckstein, aka "Gluck"—see Devon Cox's recent collective biography of famous Tite Street denizens, *The Street of Wonderful Possibilities: Whistler, Wilde and Sargent in Tite Street*.) Designed by progressive architect William Edward Godwin, a leading light in the Aesthetic Movement, the picturesque Tower House was, as described in *The British Architect* ("Rambles in London Streets: Chelsea District," 3 December 1892, p. 403), "divided into four great stories of studios," each of them with a "corresponding set of chambers formed by the introduction of a mezzanine floor, at about half the height of the studio." Given the strongly-conveyed settings of Elizabeth's first two detective novels, the first of which she began writing not long after her marriage to Colin, I surmise that the couple also spent a great deal of their time in southern France.

Despite Elizabeth Gill's successful embarkation upon a career as a detective novelist (she also dabbled in watercolors, like her great-grandfather, as well as dress design), dark clouds loomed forebodingly on her horizon. In the early 1930s her husband commenced a sexual affair with another tenant at the Tower House: Mabel Lethbridge (1900-1968), then the youngest recipient of the Order of the British Empire (O.B.E.), which had been awarded to her for her services as a munitions worker in the Great War. As a teenager Lethbridge had lost her left leg when a shell she was packing exploded, an event recounted by her in her bestselling autobiography, *Fortune Grass*. The book was published several months after Elizabeth's death, which occurred suddenly and unexpectedly after the mystery writer underwent an operation in a West London hospital in June 1934. Elizabeth was laid to rest in Shoreham, Kent, beside her parents, who had barely predeceased her. In 1938 Colin married again, though his new wife was not Mabel Lethbridge, but rather South African journalist Una Elizabeth Kellett Long (1909-1984), with whom Colin, under the joint pseudonym Richard Saxby, co-authored a crime thriller, *Five Came to London* (1938). Colin would himself pass away in 1940, just six years after Elizabeth, expiring from illness in South Africa, where he had traveled with Una to paint murals at the Johannesburg Magistrates' Courts.

While Kenneth de Burgh Codrington continues to receive his due in studies of Indian antiquities and Colin Gill maintains a foothold in the annals of British art history, Elizabeth Gill's place in Golden Age British detective fiction was for decades largely forgotten. Happily this long period of unmerited neglect has ended with the reprinting by Dean Street Press of Elizabeth Gill's fine trio of Benvenuto Brown mysteries. The American poet, critic, editor and journalist Amy Bonner aptly appraised Elizabeth's talent as a detective novelist in her *Brooklyn Eagle* review of the final Gill mystery novel, *Crime De Luxe*, writing glowingly that "Miss Gill is a consummate artist. . . . she writes detective stories like a novelist. . . . [Her work] may be unhesitatingly recommended to detective fiction fans and others who want to be converted."

THE CRIME COAST

Elizabeth Gill's *The Crime Coast* (aka *Strange Holiday*), the first of her three known detective novels, opens tantalizingly with a newspaper account of a paradoxical double crime committed against a pair of guests at a London hotel: the Countess of Trelorne, whose world-famous jewelry collection was purloined, and the Signora Luela da Costa, a wealthy Argentine beauty and favorite subject of "modern" artists, who was found smothered to death on her bed, wrapped in an eiderdown and beneath it clad only in a dazzling array of magnificent jewelry (not the Countess of Trelorne's). Next we follow a young Oxonian, Paul Ashby, as he travels from London to the French Riviera, partially on behalf of Major Kent, a frail old man who has begged him to attempt to locate his vanished painter son, Adrian. Paul Ashby's quest in southern France brings him into contact with a number of striking individuals, including Adelaide Moon, a lovely young artist and reader of André Gide; Don Hernandez de Najera, a handsome and tempestuous Argentinian; Herbert Dawkins, a colorful if dubious individual better known by the appellation "the Slosher"; and Benvenuto Brown, greatly gifted both as an artist and an amateur sleuth. Soon enough Paul Ashby finds himself playing ingenuous Watson to Benvenuto Brown's incisive Holmes.

Benvenuto Brown is described in detail by Gill as he for the first time falls under Paul Ashby's scrutinizing gaze at a café in the coastal artists' colony of St. Antoine:

> His clothes were rather eccentric, consisting of a very wide pair of almost white corduroy trousers, liberally bespattered with paint, a vividly checked shirt open at the neck, and a black beret. He looked between thirty and forty, obviously an Englishman, with a humorous, deeply-lined face, rather a big nose and a long upper lip. Surveying the company through half-closed eyes, he waved a vague greeting in answer to shouts from the various tables. . . . Evidently a popular figure and an interesting looking chap, Paul thought.

Later in the novel, Adelaide Moon provides some important background information on Brown, revealing that the perspicacious painter is something more than a mere dabbler at daubs, being, like Dorothy L. Sayers's universal genius Lord Peter Wimsey, a man of many parts:

> During the war I didn't see much of him—I was only ten when it ended. He was in the secret service, you know; he did simply brilliantly and got covered in

decorations. . . . he was offered a marvelous job in the Foreign Office after the war, but he refused, and took up painting and has wandered about all over the world since then. He's always had a passion for elucidating mysteries....if he hadn't been such an independent creature he'd have been a terrific success—in the F.O. or the Diplomatic Service or the Police, or anything he'd chosen to take up. But he never would—he's got a perfect passion for flying his own flag. As things are, he's making himself a reputation as a painter, and he sells awfully well in Paris and the States. . . .

In *The Crime Coast*, a novel which Bruce Rae in the *New York Times Book Review* deemed a "first-rate story all the way through," Benvenuto Brown scores his first of three recorded investigative triumphs. A delighted Rae avowed that "If Miss Gill does as well in subsequent efforts as she has in this, her first, she will quickly find her place in the front rank of mystery writers. There is not a trick in this particular type of craftsmanship that she does not employ completely and to good advantage—suspense, plausibility, characterization and a fast tempo that carries the reader to an ingenious conclusion." Readers who go on to peruse Elizabeth Gill's detective novels *What Dread Hand?* and *Crime De Luxe* will see just how amply the talented author confirmed this laudatory judgment.

Curtis Evans

CHAPTER I
FROM A MORNING PAPER

DOUBLE CRIME AT LONDON HOTEL

—

Body of Woman Found wrapped in Eiderdown

—

COUNTESS'S JEWELS STOLEN

—

A TRAGIC DISCOVERY was made at Bishop's Hotel last evening when a maid, on entering the suite of Signora da Costa, a rich Argentine guest at the hotel, found her dead body on the bed wrapped in an eiderdown.

An extraordinary feature of the crime is that the body had on nothing but a number of magnificent jewels. Other jewels of great value were strewn on the dressing table, and so far nothing appears to be missing. The unfortunate woman had been smothered.

Half an hour after this tragedy was discovered the Countess of Trelorne, on returning from a drive in her car, found that her room in the same corridor had been ransacked by thieves who had made off with her famous collection of jewels including the well-known Trelorne pearls.

Scotland Yard officers are at work on the scenes of both crimes, and are anxious to get in touch with a young man who is known to have lunched with the Signora yesterday, and a woman who visited her later in the afternoon.

The Signora arrived from Paris on Monday night. She was a woman of great beauty and had been painted by many artists of the modern school.

CHAPTER II
P. L. M.

"DIJON, MAÇON, Lyons, Valence, Avignon, Marseille!" shouted the conductors. Paul Ashby, standing on the platform at the Gare de Lyons, thought that no poem could please him better. His place was booked and his luggage stowed away in his sleeping car, and he walked up and down watching the tremendous bustle and excitement that attends the departure of a French train—rather as if, he thought, a great experiment were about to be made in transport, and the first steam-driven vehicle were starting on a hazardous journey across France. Porters shouted, whistles blew, bells rang, and passengers rushed madly up and down, losing and finding their places, their luggage, and their children. Everyone but Paul appeared to be travelling *en famille*. The third class was already crowded to bursting point and through the windows he could see perspiring faces of every nationality and every hue, peasants, soldiers, and sailors; Moors, Turks, Lascars, Chinese, and French; brown, black, and yellow faces, white faces, painted faces. Paul caught sight of the gold teeth and flashing eyeballs of a Negro, and then the pale face and black hair of a French woman who had taken off her hat and was putting a shawl over her head for the night. The barrows of foodstuffs were doing a brisk trade with long loaves of bread and bottles of Vichy and wine, and the air was full of the smell of sulphur and smoke and, more intimately, with the odours of humanity, garlic, and French cigarettes.

The noise and excitement increased until the great iron girders of the Gare de Lyons seemed to vibrate with it, and then a bell rang with more determination than usual. Paul looked at his watch and walked towards his carriage.

"En voiture, m'sieurs, dames, en voiture!" yelled the porters with the enthusiasm that Englishmen reserve for a football match. Paul got into the train; doors banged, the whistle blew, and with a tremendous jerk the train started.

With every revolution of the wheels Paul's spirits rose. His acquaintance with the Continent extended at the moment no further than a view of Boulogne, with grey houses huddled together in the rain; a rather dull countryside of wide green fields and grey stone villages seen from the windows of the train, all of which looked surprisingly English, he thought; a remarkably good lunch in the restaurant car where it had been a relief to find his first order, spoken a little gruffly, in French, unhesitatingly obeyed; rain and more rain driving against the carriage windows and through it glimpses of long straight roads planted endlessly with plane trees which together with advertising signs imparted a faintly foreign air to the landscape. *"Byrrh,"* he read, *"Savon Cadum," "Thé Lipton."*

At last Paris, its outskirts shabby and rather sordid, lightened with an occasional view of the Seine, and finally the Gare du Nord where he was outraged at being taken for an Englishman by an officious Cook's man. Three hours to spare—what could one do in three hours?

Deciding to damn the expense, he took a taxi and drove endlessly through the wet streets. Perhaps because of the weather, it was not quite the Paris he had expected—a glittering city of fountains and flowers, chic, elegant, and faintly sinful. Instead he found it a trifle sinister, old, and heavy with history, half expected a tumbril to clatter down the grey streets, and to see the full gutters flowing with blood. In the Place de la Concorde the city surprised him again; here it was austere, intellectual, and grave, and then in a flash it changed and seemed to flutter a skirt at him as he drove down the Rue de Rivoli and saw through the arcades bright windows of pearls, flowers, and scents. There on his right were gardens and statues and a great palace which must be the Louvre. He decided to have a drink before seeing anything more, and tapping on the window told the man to drive to a café.

Here he paid him off, sat down, ordered a *bock*, and listened to a bearded gentleman explain to another with a good deal of passion how to mix a salad. He wondered if the animated conversations going on on each side of him were equally trivial, then, suddenly feeling lonely, he finished his drink and left. He was glad when his sight-seeing was over—if Brian and Evans had been with him it would have been different, but exploring cities alone was dreary work. They had planned this trip together, the three of them, standing over a map of France in Paul's rooms during their last term at Oxford. Then during the summer an unexpected job had sent Brian off to India, and as for Evans, he had suddenly, inexplicably, got engaged to be married. Paul could make nothing of it, and feeling distinctly bereaved, he had decided on carrying out the holiday alone—partly from a temperamental dislike of altering his plans, partly to satisfy a craving for adventure which existed somewhere in the secret places of his soul. Once in the train he forgot to feel lonely—he was heading south, to a strange country, and unexpectedly on a stranger quest.

The day before London had been in a particularly bad mood. It was the end of a long heat wave, and on this particular July evening the city lay sinister, tense, and expectant, not a breath stirring. In Bloomsbury the leaves of the plane trees hung limply, the Georgian houses looked shabby and discouraged. Paul, sitting in his rooms in Great James Street, surveyed his pile of neatly strapped and labelled luggage and wondered if he'd made a fool of himself. To go south in this weather . . .

He stared out of the window, where the edge of a purple thunder cloud had rolled into view, got up, stretched his long legs, and mixed himself a drink. "At least," he thought, "I shall be able to swim in the Mediterranean, and go about in shirt sleeves. I wonder if I've packed enough shirts"—and, his thoughts reverting to his luggage, he sat down again and began to write in his neat, rather academic hand an extra label for his largest suitcase:

PAUL ASHBY PASSENGER TO MARSEILLE VIA BOU-
LOGNE AND PARIS

He blotted the label and paused, listening. Footsteps were passing his door and ascending the staircase, and in the tense atmosphere of the hot evening every sound had a peculiar significance. He wondered who it could be, for the top of the house was occupied only by the offices of a private inquiry agency which had closed for the night half an hour earlier.

The footsteps hesitated—stopped—there was a crash, and the sound of something slithering down the staircase.

Paul rushed to the door and opened it to find the body of a man lying at his feet. He appeared to be just conscious and was breathing fast, his face distorted with pain. Paul managed to get him onto his sofa and propped him up with cushions, looking down at him anxiously. It would be discouraging on the eve of a summer holiday to have an unknown man fall into one's rooms and die on one—and while half Paul's mind was engaged upon a picture of himself as chief witness at an inquest, the other half was taking in details of his precipitate guest. The man was elderly and white-haired, with a sensitive, distinguished face. His clothes were beautifully cut and there was a nice harmony between shirt, socks, and tie. He looked pathetic lying there in his fine clothes.

"How about a whisky, sir?" said Paul nervously, rather at a loss as to how to deal with the situation.

"Thank you—no—a little water," gasped the old gentleman, his hand going feebly towards his breast pocket.

Paul brought him a glass of water and saw a couple of little white pills disappear into his mouth.

He didn't like to stand there watching the old man, so he strolled across to the window to await developments.

There was no car outside; who on earth could he be? A scholarly soldier or a gentleman of leisure who dabbled in the fine arts? Certainly one who would look more at home in a club in St. James's than in the offices of a private inquiry agency.

Presently Paul heard a movement behind him and turned to find his guest, shaky but obviously recovering, sitting up and dusting his trousers.

"Came rather a crash," he said apologetically. "Most good of you to pick me up. It's my wretched heart, you know, gets me like that sometimes. I do hope I didn't give you a shock. I'll be getting along now—and many many thanks."

"You mustn't think of it, sir. Please sit down and rest, and I'll get you a taxi later. It must have given you a nasty jar, coming down those stairs. Won't you drink a glass of sherry with me?"

"Well, really, my dear fellow, you're very good—and if you're sure I'm not putting you out I will stay a few minutes longer."

He subsided on to the settee with an air of relief, and Paul went to fetch sherry and glasses. When he came back he found a card lying on the table, and read: "Major E. W. Kent, Black's Club." He introduced himself as he poured out the drinks, and as he sat there, glass in hand, felt the situation becoming more normal.

"Pleasant rooms you've got here," said Major Kent appreciatively, looking at the green painted walls lined with bookshelves, the neatly framed etchings, and curtains of faded Indian red silk that hung from the high Georgian windows.

"I'm afraid it looks like a left-luggage office at the moment," apologized Paul. "As you see, I'm just off for abroad."

"Are you staying in Marseille long?" asked Major Kent, looking at the label on the nearer suitcase. "You'll find it a bit hot just now."

"I've no idea. This is the first time I've been able to go abroad since I was a kid and I'm off into the blue for a month or so before starting work. I've no plans and very little money, but the idea of seeing the Mediterranean makes me feel as adventurous as though I were about to explore darkest Africa. I want to stay in France because I know the language pretty well and I believe it's cheaper than Italy. I suppose, actually, the French Riviera is about as exciting as Bath or Tunbridge Wells?"

"That depends where you go. I have a son—" Major Kent hesitated, and a look of sadness crossed his face—"who is a painter and who has spent a good deal of time down there since he left the Slade. Before my heart went groggy I used to travel about with him, and I could give you the names of a good many delightful places off the beaten track if you'd care to have them."

"I say—that would be awfully good of you, sir."

"I don't know what you're after, of course, but you'll find most of the so-called gay places like Monte Carlo and Cannes with their dust covers on at this time of year. Now what was that little place Adrian was so fond of?—I have it—St. Tropez." And for the next half hour Major Kent described to Paul the life of the Southern fishing ports, with their floating population of painters, writers, and *étrangers* from all parts of the world, while Paul, intensely interested and a little startled, listened and made some methodical notes in his notebook.

Major Kent talked well, choosing his words with fastidious care and speaking from a slightly impersonal angle, as though his interest in life was from the observer's point of view; though whenever he mentioned his son a note of warmth and gentleness came into his voice.

He appeared to be still suffering from his fall, and when he rose to go Paul, who began to feel a sincere liking for him, said:

"Look here, sir, you'd be doing me a real favour if you'd care to stay and dine with me. I was feeling thoroughly bored when you—er—dropped in, and I'm in the desolate state of having nothing whatever to do till my train goes to-morrow morning. If you don't mind a rather scratch meal I'd be really grateful if you'd stay."

After a slight hesitation, Major Kent accepted and Paul telephoned to the near-by restaurant that sent up his meals. They were soon seated over an excellent sole, a bottle of Beaune and a roast chicken, and as the meal went on Paul felt he had known his guest for years. Major Kent talked a lot, and on a variety of subjects, yet all the time Paul felt that one half of his mind was engaged on some personal and acute problem.

When the waiter had cleared away and left them with coffee and liqueurs, Major Kent said hesitatingly:

"That place upstairs—d'you know anything about it?"

"The inquiry agency? Can't say I do, except that I don't much like the look of the chap that runs it."

"H'm—I was a fool. I went there on the impulse of the moment." Then abruptly: "I have been wondering as I talked to you whether I should put to you a rather extraordinary proposition. It must be on the clear understanding that if you don't like the sound of it you turn it down."

"But of course, sir, carry on. If there is anything I can do . . ."

"Then I'll take you at your word, and ask you to listen to what is for me a tragic story."

CHAPTER III
PRIVATE INQUIRY

"I DON'T WANT to fatigue you with my whole family history," commenced Major Kent apologetically, "so I will tell you as briefly as I can how things stand.

"You heard me speak just now of my son Adrian. Twenty-five years ago my wife, with whom I was very deeply in love, died in giving birth to him. We'd been very happily married for two years, and when she died I felt—well, I needn't go into that. I retired from the army and left England, leaving the child in the care of an old woman, a cousin of mine. I could hardly bear to set eyes on him, feeling that his birth had caused my wife's death. For ten years I wandered about the earth, doing nothing in particular, leading a life that was adventurous and not specially creditable. I had no wish to marry again, and my chief interest was in starting to make a small collection of paintings, which is still my hobby.

"At the end of ten years I heard that the cousin to whom I had intrusted my son had died, and I returned to England to make new arrangements for him, but with no particular interest in seeing him again.

"On arriving in England I went to the small country town where my cousin had lived. I found her house, which was a large gloomy Victorian affair surrounded by a garden full of depressing-looking shrubs and gravel paths. An elderly parlourmaid informed me that Master Adrian was in the garden, and feeling a little conscience-stricken at the idea of a child living in such an atmosphere, I went in search of him. He was sitting, dressed in deep black, in an ivy-covered arbour with a drawing book on his knee, and when he raised his head he showed me a face of such strange intelligence and faunlike beauty, a face which bore so strong a resemblance to that of my dead wife that I stood silent and afraid in front of him. However, he was very polite, and got up and shook hands with me with a kind of Victorian courtesy, saying that I must be his father, and had I had any tea?

"I took him away from that horrible house the same night, and we spent three months together on the Norfolk Broads in a yacht. We had a good time, and I was very happy watching him gradually throw off the influence of his upbringing and develop into a creature of great physical bravery and spontaneous gaiety, combined with remarkable intelligence for a child of his age. He had a talent for drawing which was unmistakable, and which I determined to encourage.

"From that day onward we were seldom separated, never willingly, and I think the fact that we met as strangers helped us to be friends in a way that father and son seldom are."

Major Kent was silent, and Paul felt that his own presence was forgotten. He sat quietly waiting, until with an effort the old man went on.

"Six months ago we quarrelled, with a bitterness only possible for people as close to each other as we were. My son had been commissioned to paint the portrait of a certain woman. I never met her, as she did not come to my son's studio, preferring, he told me, to be painted in her own surroundings. One day he came to me and told me that he had fallen passionately in love, and was anxious to marry her. He had brought her finished portrait to show me, which he unwrapped and placed carefully on an easel. He took my arm and led me up to it, full of pride and enthusiasm, and trembling with excitement. Can you imagine my horror when I saw that the original was a woman whose photograph had been in every newspaper about ten years ago as the chief character in a particularly unsavoury divorce case? I had reason to remember her, for this case had involved the disgrace and ultimate suicide of a man in my old regiment, a great friend of mine. My revulsion of feeling was so great that I was speechless. When I turned to my son I saw him gazing at the painting with such adoration that I lost my head and heaped abuse upon this woman. I told him all I knew about her, sparing no detail, and then suddenly realized as I caught sight of his face that he did not believe a word I was saying. It nearly broke my heart and I continued more and more fiercely, trying to justify myself. We said terrible things to each other—he accused me of trying to poison his mind against her.

"The end of it all was that he rushed from the house and I have not seen him since.

"Soon after my son disappeared I had the first of a series of bad heart attacks, and my doctors tell me I may have only a year to live. I have made every possible effort to trace my son, with no success, and as I am forbidden to travel I feel almost despairing, for I am convinced he is not in England. A week or so ago I believed I had a clue to his whereabouts. I had a letter from the Leinster Galleries asking me to come round and see some paintings which had just arrived from Paris, the work of a young English artist named Adelaide Moon, which they thought would interest me. I went along, and in looking through the paintings I saw one of a group of people at a café table in the south of France. It was dated July of this year—only a month ago—and one of the figures I felt certain I recognized as that of my son, from the very typical attitude in which he is seated. I immediately got into touch with Miss Moon's Paris dealer, only to hear that she had gone off on a painting expedition in France and Italy, leaving no address. They have promised to let me know immediately she returns, but apparently she is erratic, and sometimes goes off for months at a time.

"Then, this morning I received a typewritten envelope, posted in London, and inside it another envelope addressed in my son's handwriting."

Major Kent felt in his pocket and brought out a letter, which after a moment's hesitation he handed to Paul.

"Perhaps you'll read it," he said. "As you will see, it gives me no clue as to where he is. It explains better than I can the terrible mess the boy has got into."

Paul read:

DEAR DAD:

I find it very hard to write to you, for I don't see that anything can make any difference now after the awful things I said to you before I went away. Sometimes I think we will forget about it one day and our life will go on as it used to.

Of course you were absolutely right about Luela. I loved her for months and was terribly unhappy most of the time. I couldn't leave her for a long time, even after I was unhappy. She seemed to make me mad, so that I forgot everything. She wouldn't let me paint, except sometimes she would want me to paint her. I used to think she was interested in my work, but I realized after a bit she would have much preferred nude photographs of herself. One day we had a terrible row and I went away. For a month I was very happy—I felt as if I'd recovered from some horrible disease. I started to work again, and made up my mind I would stay abroad for a few months painting until I had done some decent things I could bring back to you. I hadn't any money, but I was able to pawn my cigarette case and a few other things. Then one day I got very low and I sold that jewel Luela had given me when I was painting her portrait. By bad luck the jeweller I sold it to recognized it, and knew Luela and wrote to her. She immediately came to see me and begged me to come away with her. It was all horrible and disgusting, and I refused. She continued to come and see me, and then one day got into a terrible passion and said unless I would come she would denounce me to the police as a jewel thief. She went away and I didn't hear any more for several weeks. Yesterday I had a letter from her saying she would give me one last chance to come to her, and if I didn't she would carry out her threat. I am going to see her about it, and if she won't relent I shall disappear for a few months, by which time she will have started a new *affaire* and forgotten. So please don't try to get in touch with me. I am not coming back until this business is all over and done with. And then—if you can possibly forget it all—how about that trip to the Pacific we promised ourselves?

All my love,

ADRIAN.

Paul finished reading, and sat for a few moments sucking at his pipe and staring at the letter in his hand. He felt puzzled and embarrassed, profoundly sorry for the old man whose story he had listened to, yet both shy and hesitant of offering sympathy or advice. He glanced up and caught the wistful and eager eye of Major Kent, who leant forward.

"You must forgive me for inflicting on you the troubles of an absolute stranger," he said. "I was feeling rather desperate this evening and felt that the only thing left for me to do was to go to an inquiry agency and employ a man to look for my son. Much as I loathed the thought of it, I felt I couldn't go on any longer in a state of suspense. By an accident I find myself instead in your rooms, just as you are starting for that very part of the world where I feel my son to be, or at least where news of him could be had. You've been so very good already in entertaining a perfect stranger and allowing him to take up your whole evening, that I am almost ashamed to go on."

"Look here, sir," said Paul earnestly, "if you think there's anything I can do, please go ahead and don't hesitate for a moment."

"Find the boy for me!" said the old man, stretching out his hand in a kind of vague appeal. "I must see him—I must—and if he is in any danger from the police, as he imagines, I must help him. He does not know I am ill, and unless I get in touch with him soon I may never see him again."

He pulled himself together, and continued more quietly: "Could you possibly look upon it as a job to combine with your holiday? It would give you an object, and might lead you into places you would not otherwise see. Let me pay all your expenses; go and make inquiries among the colony of painters in different villages in the South for my son and for this Miss

Adelaide Moon. You may fail, in which case there's no harm done, and meanwhile—well, I should feel a different man if I knew a real effort was being made. And I don't believe you would fail. . . ."

Paul stood in the doorway, with his hands in the pockets of his Burberry, watching the tail light of Major Kent's taxi disappear down the road through a deluge of rain. The storm had burst, and Paul sniffed the rain appreciatively, watching the skyline of Great James Street, the Georgian fronts and plane trees illuminated by great flashes of lightning, with a loud accompaniment in the bass. It was glorious after the dusty, sunbaked days and stuffy nights and Paul felt wildly exhilarated. He was committed to all kinds of adventure, he felt, and grinned as he thought of himself in his new character of sleuth. His holiday, which until now he'd thought of as an opportunity for doing a lot of reading, walking, and swimming, had taken on new and exciting colours. What was more, it wasn't going to cost him a penny, for Major Kent had insisted on paying all his expenses, and was seeing him off at Victoria in the morning with a large check, a letter to Adrian, and a photograph whereby Paul might identify him.

He went in, shut the door, and ran upstairs in the best of spirits. His foot kicked against something as he reached the landing, sending it flying with a clink of metal. He groped on the floor until he found it. It was a key. He stood looking at it for a moment. Then he said aloud: "When we notice the brass tab attached to the key, my dear Watson, we realize that our fellow detectives up above have been making investigations in an hotel." He slipped the key into the pocket of his Burberry, thinking that he must remember to give it to the caretaker in the morning, and went off to bed feeling that his career as a detective was launched.

CHAPTER IV
P. L. M. CONTINUED

PAUL STOOD in the corridor and watched Paris slip by, rain-swept under a leaden sky. The storm had followed him across the Channel and had broken over the whole of the north of France. The rain looked as though it would never stop, and he rather enjoyed the dreary landscape, knowing that every moment he was nearing a sunny coast he had never seen. How did the poem go—Dijon, Mâcon, Lyons, Valence, Avignon, Marseille—the very names were full of sunlight and the smell of wine—it couldn't be raining in Valence or Avignon. His meditations were interrupted by the dinner steward and he took a ticket for the *premier service*. He went along to his sleeper to clean up for dinner, and realized with a shock as he opened the door that he was to share the compartment with another.

A very stout person was seated on the lower bunk. He was clad in a light grey suit covered with the largest checks Paul had ever seen, and on the floor beside him was an extremely pointed pair of light tan shoes. He was engaged in wriggling his toes, freed from their *glacés* prisons, with exquisite satisfaction, and mopping his face with a flowered bandana. As Paul came in he paused and looked out from the folds of flowered silk. The small eyes fringed with sandy lashes were set in a pink face. He was thick-necked and heavy-jowled, and his head being almost bald appeared to go up to a point, like some gleaming and highly coloured egg. Paul thought of a bookie he had once seen on Brighton Race Course.

"Evenin'," he said.

"Good-evening," replied Paul rather shortly.

"Whew! Bit warm, ain't it? Glad to see you ain't one o' them Frenchies—can't get on with their lingo myself. 'Ave a cigar—Coronas, they are." And he offered Paul an enormous Corona from his pocket.

"Er—thanks awfully but I think I'd rather have a cigarette if you don't mind—I'm just going to have dinner."

"Oh, well—just as *you* like. Pity though—good cigars, they are." He lit one himself and leant back with his thumbs in his waistcoat.

"'Aving dinner on the train, d'you say? You're wrong, you know, you're wrong. I 'ad a slap-up meal in Paree before starting, and jolly good it was; cheap, too, only fifty francs for a bottle of 'Eidseick—and everything of the best." To add point to his remarks, he removed his cigar and got to work with a toothpick. Paul lit a cigarette and stared at him coldly. His companion was rendered temporarily speechless, but having brought his excavations to a triumphant conclusion he went on: "You got the top bunk, I see. Just as well, p'raps—I ain't built for Alpine sports meself." He laughed wheezily. "Stayin' in Marsails?" he asked.

"No," said Paul, "I'm going straight through to a fishing village along the coast."

"Very nice, too," said his companion. "Very nice indeed, I should say. I'm stoppin' in Marsails for a while, just to see a bit of night life—and then I'm for the seaside meself. Come in for a bit of the best lately," slapping his pocket, "so I thought I'd 'ave a look at the Sunny Sarth, as they say."

The dinner bell came as a welcome interruption and Paul got up hurriedly.

"Well, I hope you'll like it," he said. "Er—care to have a look at my papers while I'm at dinner?"

"Well, that's very kind of you. I don't mind if I do. 'Ere—take a cigar to 'ave with your dinner—you'll like it reelly—five bob a piece, they are."

And Paul found himself in the corridor, Corona in hand. He started on a perilous journey to the restaurant car, the train lurching and shaking. Having navigated two coaches without accident, he saw Nemesis approaching in the form of a very large lady bearing down on him from the opposite direction. As he stepped backwards into a carriage to avoid her the train gave a particularly violent spring, jerking him off his balance. He felt his foot come down on something, and heard a small shriek behind him. Turning hurriedly round, he saw a tiny black felt hat bent in anguish over a pair of exquisite silk-clad legs, and a small hand clutching a patent-leather shoe. Paul blushed scarlet and addressed the top of the hat.

"Madame—je vous demande pardon—qu'est-ce que j'ai fait—" he stammered, bending down over her, and just then a face as exquisite as the legs was raised to his own. He caught a glimpse of brown eyes in a fine oval face and a small scarlet mouth twisted into an expression half of pain and half of amusement.

"It's all right," she said. "I don't think I'm permanently damaged. But you took me rather by surprise."

Paul blushed again, and renewing his apologies in English he turned to go on his way when a voice called him back.

"I say, is this yours?" she said, and Paul saw her face round the door of the carriage now definitely laughing at him, and her hand holding out a battered Corona-Corona. He went back to retrieve it, conscious of the fact that the whole carriage was looking on with delighted interest.

"Thanks awfully," he said. "Someone just gave me the wretched thing—how absurd!" and he caught her eye and laughed, and went on to dinner feeling he'd cut a figure that was far from heroic. And such a lovely girl. . . . Paul wondered if she'd had dinner—if he'd see her again—if he could possibly go back later to inquire about her foot.

Sitting down to dinner, he found himself entirely unable to concentrate on the copy of *Life and Letters* he'd brought with him to read. What extraordinarily nice legs she'd got. Paul wasn't an expert on legs, but frequent visits to the British Museum to study the Greek vases made him recognize that hers really were the most classic shape. He sighed and ordered his food and wine, and found himself wishing he was the sort of chap who'd have the courage to ask a girl out to dinner. The empty chair opposite wasn't very good company, and Paul, stimulated by the happenings of the past twenty-four hours, was bursting to talk. The restaurant car was packed, mostly with English and Americans, and above the rattle of the train there was a cheerful sound of conversation, the clatter of plates, and the popping of corks. Paul made another determined attempt on *Life and Letters*.

"Par ici, madame, s'il vous plaît," and then a voice said, "Oh—d'you mind if I sit at your table?" It was the girl he had trampled on.

She settled herself opposite him, placed a yellow-covered copy of André Gide on the table, and taking up a large flat handbag she held it in front of her and began to powder her nose.

What a fool she must think him, with his pompous Corona and his weak French; a tourist, a schoolmaster on holiday— horrible! That, he thought, looking at her covertly, was what she did *not* look like, a tourist. She seemed very much at home and Paul envied and admired her. She was something quite new to him, as exciting as a new flower discovered in a foreign land. Her face hidden, he noticed her hands, darting in and out of her bag with first a puff and then a lipstick, small, incredibly bronzed, with scarlet-enamelled nails. She lowered her handbag and frowned slightly into the mirror, which seemed to Paul extraordinary considering that it reflected a bronzed oval face with a flowerlike scarlet mouth and enormous brown eyes that looked frank and childish in spite of their heavy make-up. She was beautiful, she was startling, but to Paul she was a problem about which he had no data.

Could she possibly be a lady of Uncertain Virtue?

She summoned the waiter and ordered a cocktail and her dinner in faultless French.

"Aren't these trains positively *filthy?*"

Paul gave a slight start and said: "Er—yes."

She polished her glass, plate, knife, and fork with a napkin and smiled at him. The waiter brought her Martini and she leant across the table.

"Won't you have a cocktail, too, to wash away our stormy encounter?"

Paul gave in gladly; she was making a party of it, and, damn it, why not? After all, wasn't he in France? He summoned the waiter and ordered another.

"I must explain about that cigar," he said. "I don't generally carry them in my hand, but an awful fellow in my compartment pressed it on me. I don't smoke the things myself."

"Certes, vous n'avez pas l'air d'être banquier," she retorted, nonplussing him for the moment. "We all hate bankers, don't we? Perhaps your expensive friend is one. Let's make him buy us some champagne. Isn't this soup almost *too* P. L. M.? I suppose you're going to India or somewhere from Marseille?"

"Oh, no," replied Paul. "I'm going to St. Antoine along the coast. Do you know it? I say, by the way, would you really like some champagne?"

"Oh my *dear* no. I was only joking. But thanks very much. St. Antoine! Why, it's my home town."

(She had called him "my dear," and was going to St. Antoine.)

"If you've never been there before you'll like it," she went on. "Of course everyone's quite mad, or pretends to be. Lots of bright young people in bright young jumpers. They talk and drink and bathe at midnight and have amusing parties, but it's all froth, you know. Just a few really hard workers like myself go there every year."

She was speaking seriously, and Paul, who hadn't enough courage to ask her what she worked at, concluded she was probably a journalist, or perhaps a professional dancer. Yes, very likely she was a dancer and he would see her in pearls in some Casino.

"Do you paint, too?" she asked.

(Good God! and he'd thought of her foxtrotting!)

"No, I'm afraid I can't do anything like that. I'm a barrister. I say, do you really paint?"

"Why do you look so astonished?" she laughed.

"Well, I don't know but—I've got a cousin who paints and she goes about in a sort of hand-woven bathrobe—like Burne-Jones, you know," he added vaguely. She gave a peal of laughter.

"Sandals and no sex appeal—I know. Funny old-fashioned thing. I don't see why one should dress the part, do you? And anyhow it's a far cry from Morris to Matisse."

"No, I don't—that is, I mean," he stumbled, "I think you look awfully nice as you are."

She smiled into her coffee cup.

"We shall get swept out with the crumbs if we stay here much longer. Why not come and have a cigarette in my carriage if you don't want to talk to your banker friend?"

So Paul followed the entrancing creature along the lurching train, and they sat down in opposite corners of the carriage. She gave him a French cigarette from her case and then said: "Is that to-day's London paper you've got? May I look at it? I crossed over last night, and forgot to get a *Daily Mail* in Paris."

She subsided behind it and Paul tried to bury himself in a magazine. He was rather proud of himself, for he'd insisted on paying for her dinner. And she'd asked him to dine with her in St. Antoine. What a marvellous holiday he was going to have. With a sense of guilt he suddenly remembered Major Kent, and the quest he was on. By Jove—if she was a painter she would probably know Adelaide Moon—even Adrian himself. He would ask her. He leant across and addressed the *Daily Mail*.

"I was wondering—do you know anyone called Adelaide Moon—or—"

The paper dropped from her hands. She stood up, and her face was white.

"I—I—Good-night—I'm going to bed." And she disappeared into the corridor.

Paul sat staring at the empty seat in front of him. What had happened? Why had she rushed away? Could it have been his question—or something she'd read in the paper? He picked it up and scanned it.

The Premier to visit America. Murder in a London hotel. Cricket results. There was nothing there. Could he have offended her?

Puzzled and miserable, he went along to his carriage.

Paul told afterwards of the strange effect that his first view of the South had on him that morning, after rattling through the night from the grey rain-swept North:

"I woke up about half-past six, dressed and went out into the corridor. I suppose I was a bit sleepy still, and didn't have time to dissect things and look at them like a tourist. I know I felt, as I leant out of the window, that I had suddenly come to life in a new world—a world that really had been created by the sun. It was brilliant, hard, dry and clear, extraordinarily arresting and exciting. There was a great plain stretching away to the distant mountains under a pale clear blue sky, and peasants ploughing with teams of white oxen. I could see far away towns and villages, white and sharply defined in the clear morning air. Then some low hills of crumbling yellowish rock with a little green scrub on them, some of them cut away into terraced vineyards. I remember a square stone house looking as though it had grown out of the side of the rock, with tiny slits of windows like a Moorish fort, and an old peasant woman dressed in black sitting under a vine minding some goats. The whole country was dried with sun so that the colours of the earth, sky, houses, and vegetation were pallid and full of light. I felt frightfully stimulated and excited, as though all kinds of adventure were waiting for me in this vital pagan land. Near Avignon I saw my first silvery grey olive trees—and then, as we drew in, the Palace of the Popes. I was torn between its castellated Italian towers and the smell of steaming bowls of coffee they were selling on the station. The coffee won!"

CHAPTER V
LA FÊTE COMMENCE

PAUL STROLLED out on to the quay after dinner. It was his first night in St. Antoine and he was feeling very good after a couple of *apéritifs*, a *cuisine bourgeoise* dinner, and a bottle of white wine.

The sun had disappeared behind the old houses round the port, and lights were coming out in the cafés. The whole town seemed to be out for a promenade, and Paul thought it all looked very like the scene in a ballet or an opera. Girls in bright-coloured shawls were walking up and down arm-in-arm, talking and laughing and very conscious of the *matelots*, smart in their flat white hats with red pompons and blue-and-white suits, who were standing about in groups with the fishermen. The high masts and crossed rigging of sailing boats moored right up to the town made patterns against the twilit sky.

Paul went into a big café with its tables spilling across the pavement, sat down and ordered coffee and a *fine*. He looked round hoping he might see his friend of the train who had disappeared so abruptly the night before; for though he'd looked for her among the crowd on Marseille station that morning, he could not find her, nor had she been on the afternoon train to St. Antoine. Whether she had already come here or was staying in Marseille he did not know, and worse still he did not know her name. There was no sign of her in the café—though, sure enough, here were the "bright young people in bright young jumpers." Everyone seemed to be burnt the colour of mahogany, and wearing what to Paul's inexperienced eye was fancy dress. At the next table a stout figure in a little pair of shorts and a pale blue-and-white sleeveless *tricot*, surmounted rather surprisingly by a square-cut beard, a ferocious expression, and a monocle, was engaged in earnest conversation with a slim-hipped blond whose mouth was painted to match her scarlet béret. As Paul watched them they were joined by a brunette in black pajamas and a young man whose costume appeared to be in faithful imitation of Tom Mix. Amid a babel of talk he could distinguish English, Russian, American, German—very little French.

Waiters rushed about between the crowded tables performing feats of balance with drink-laden trays.

Outside, someone was playing a guitar.

Paul turned to look at a long yellow-and-black Hispaño-Suiza which had just drawn up in front of the café with a gentle purr of its engine. Most of the people at the tables seemed to know the occupants, and conversation died down while greetings were shouted to them. A man got out of the driver's seat. Dressed to match his car, he wore a saffron-yellow *tricot* tucked into beautifully creased black trousers. He was tall and lithe, and Paul caught a momentary glimpse of almost jet-black eyes in an olive-skinned face, before he turned to speak to someone in the car. He had evidently been dining extremely well and swayed a little on his feet. A man who got out the other side and strolled round the bonnet, patting it nervously as he passed, presented an extraordinary contrast to him. His clothes were rather eccentric, consisting of a very wide pair of almost white corduroy trousers, liberally bespattered with paint, a vividly checked shirt open at the neck, and a black béret. He looked between thirty and forty, obviously an Englishman, with a humorous, deeply lined face, rather a big nose, and a long upper lip. Surveying the company through half-closed eyes, he waved a vague greeting in answer to shouts from the various tables, before turning to a girl who was getting out of the car. Evidently a popular figure, and an interesting-looking chap, Paul thought. But his attention was immediately concentrated on the third person, who stepped on to the pavement and slipped her hands into the arms of the two men. Very young and slim, she was hatless, and her chestnut-brown shingled hair, disordered by a drive in the open car, was blown back from her face. Her fresh white linen frock was moulded to her figure and was short and sleeveless, showing up the startling tan of her arms and legs. Paul stared at her small oval face with its flowerlike mouth and half rose from his chair. At last, it was the girl of the train. But he sank back again; she seemed to know everyone in the place and was laughing and talking with people at the tables round her.

"We represent Brueghel's picture of the Blind leading the Blind. Imitation, very *difficile!*" he heard her say. "My dears, I'm so glad to be back from the land of fogs and savages. It was raining, as usual."

She disentangled one of her hands to receive the kiss of an immaculate youth who bent over it, saying, "I salute thee, O Moon of my delight! Did you survive the perils of the P.L.M.?" (Paul could have killed him.)

"Barely," she smiled. "I arrived completely shattered, but Ben and I have been dining at the Rich Man's Table and he stayed us with flagons and comforted us with caviar."

"Talking of flagons—" said the Englishman in the check shirt, and started to pilot her across to a vacant table. Halfway over she caught sight of Paul in his corner. She stopped dead. All the laughter went out of her face, she paled and flushed, and then suddenly making up her mind she murmured an excuse to the two men with her and crossed over to Paul's table. She held out her hand with a friendly smile. Paul stood up and greeted her eagerly.

"I say, it is nice to see you. I've been looking for you all the evening," he said, and was puzzled to see the curious expression that seemed very like fear flash across her face. It was quickly replaced by a smile as she sat down in the chair he offered her. (Of course he'd been mistaken.)

"I think it's very nice of you to say so after the appalling way I rushed off last night," she said. "As a matter of fact, I was—I was terribly afraid you were a journalist on my tracks when you asked me if I knew Adelaide Moon because—well, I am Adelaide Moon myself, you see."

Before he could speak she rushed on: "I don't mean that I'm suffering from delusions that the whole of Fleet Street is hanging on my lips—but I have just had a show in London now, and I do so *loathe* being interviewed. You've no idea how humiliating it is to read things like 'Girl Artist thinks women should use lipstick,' just because some of one's miserable canvases are hanging in a well-known gallery. I assure you!" as Paul laughed.

"Why, last year the Cube Gallery bought one of my paintings; it was one I did down here of a Provençal farmhouse and there happened to be a woman and a child sitting there while I was working so I put them in—rather a good design it made. My dear, would you believe it—the *Ladies' World* wanted my views on Motherhood! When I come down here to paint I never tell anyone where I'm going or even leave an address for letters. It makes me feel absolutely free—and this place is so personal and absorbing that I forget all about any other life, and then I can begin to paint."

"Yes, I can absolutely understand that," said Paul. "It is amazingly full of character and flavour down here—London seems quite a vague memory to me already. As a matter of fact, until you came in I was feeling rather like a disembodied spirit, not knowing a soul here. Everyone seems to know everyone else."

She laughed. "We'll soon put that right," she said. "I want you to come over and meet a great friend of mine, Benvenuto Brown. Yes, over there in the check shirt. He's a perfect darling—I've known him for ever," she added, and refusing his offer of a drink she led him across to the table where the two men were sitting. They stood up as she approached. Judging by the drinks on the table, they had not been idle.

"Ben, I want to introduce you to a friend of mine, Mr.—" She hesitated, looked at Paul and laughed.

"Paul Ashby," he said, shaking hands with the Englishman, thinking as he did so that it would take him a long time to catch up in the matter of drinks. The Englishman was looking mellow and amiable, while the man in the yellow jumper had apparently reached the morose stage. Adelaide introduced him.

"Don Hernandez de Najera, Mr. Ashby," she said. "He's got a lot of other names as well, but that's all I can manage at the moment."

De Najera bowed stiffly and then smiled down at Adelaide in a way that Paul found himself very much disliking.

"What are you two going to drink?" asked the Englishman as they seated themselves; and as he leant back to order brandies and sodas Paul turned to Adelaide.

"Er—did you say his name was Benvenuto Brown?" he asked her quietly. She laughed.

"It really is," she said, and then, confidentially, "I do hope you're going to like him. He's a most frightfully nice and frightfully interesting person—but he's just a little bit drunk to-night." She leant across the table. "Ben, Mr. Ashby wants to know if you were really christened Benvenuto."

He was surveying the world through half-closed eyes from behind a cloud of smoke, a pipe in the corner of his mouth, his chair tipped back, and wearing an expression at once dry and benign. He nodded gravely. "I had that honour," he said. "Possibly it does merit explanation. I understand my parents were drawn together in the first instance by a mutual enthusiasm for the Fine Arts which eventually led them to Italy on a honeymoon, Ruskin and Baedeker in hand. It appears that they discovered Florence to be their spiritual home and decided to settle there. When I burst on an astonished world about a year later my mother, having determined to give birth to an artist, decided to call me Benvenuto. I understand she dallied with the idea of Fra Angelico for a time, but a nice ear for alliteration finally decided her choice."

He paused and they raised glasses.

"Oh, Ben, I would *love* to meet your mother," laughed Adelaide. "She must be a perfect pet."

"I'm afraid there isn't a hope, my dear," said Benvenuto. "She is, as you say, a pet—but having practically raised me in the Uffizi she cannot bring herself to forgive me for being conscious of the existence of Picasso. You see, painting, or Art as she prefers to call it, is her religion, and she thinks my mild efforts with the brush are positively blasphemous. She's always been rather a vague person and I think she tries to forget that she brought someone into the world who has turned out an exponent of cubism, dadaism, vorticism, or what not. She's accused me of each in turn."

He drained his glass and called for more drinks, and the talk became general. De Najera, however, remained silent, drinking hard, with a sullen expression on his handsome, rather vicious face. Benvenuto Brown also appeared to be getting extremely drunk, and Paul looked with some disgust at his vague smile and half-closed eyes. He was trying to draw De Najera into a conversation, but the latter either could not or would not respond.

Suddenly a rather prim-looking woman at the next table got up and, followed by her husband, left the café, glaring at them as she did so. Adelaide laughed.

"Ho, I ses, and swep' out," she murmured. She turned to Paul.

"I can't think why people like that come down here. Those people have been here for weeks, disapproving violently of the whole place. They hate our costumes, manners, and customs— so why not leave us alone? I do so resent the cold breath of disapproval on our innocent pleasures."

Benvenuto put down his glass with a crash and, rising with as much dignity as his unsteady legs would muster, addressed the café.

"My friends," he said, "we must all have noticed from time to time a dishthreshing tendency amongst the bourgeoisie— *hic*—of all nations to regard the artist," drawing himself up, "as a creature of strange habits and unbridled passions." He turned round to frown at the author of a feeble cheer, and continued.

"I feel that the time has come to dishpel this illusion and to show ourselves to the world as we are—as we have been— from Tintoretto to Tonks—gentle creatures of domestic habits, moderate drinkers—*hic*—fond of children and dogs."

He paused amid loud cheering and drained his glass. He turned and shook his fist at a mild-looking little man who was silently sipping his lemonade.

"You tell me Van Gogh cut off his ear and sent it to his mistress when she betrayed him. Now I put it to you—wouldn't a business man have cut off *hers?*"

He glared fiercely round. "Can anyone here tell me of a single instance of an artist who has committed a social scholeshism greater than being late for meals?" He happened to catch Paul's eye, who grinned nervously and said:

"What about Adolphus Smith?"

Benvenuto wrung him by the hand.

"My dear sir, a thousand thanks. The crowning point to my argument. The great modern example of the artist's craving for domesticity, developed to such an exshtent that the man begins to found a family wherever he goes."

Benvenuto subsided into his chair amidst laughter. By this time the whole café had gathered round them and people were standing on chairs and tables. Tom Mix had the black pajamaed girl perched on his shoulder, where she was screaming with laughter, and the bearded man in his infantile blue-and-white costume was listening with his mouth open while his blond companion translated Ben's speech into his ear.

"Quel type," he said, looking at Ben.

De Najera was at last roused from his apathy. He put his arm across Benvenuto's shoulders.

"You will drink with me, my friend," he said thickly. He stared round at the crowd of people and summoned the patron, who hurried up all smiles, evidently knowing his man. De Najera went on: "You are all my friends—you will all drink with me," he indicated the company with a wide sweep of his arm.

"I will give you music, dancing, wine—you will come with me."

Adelaide pulled at his arm.

"Not to-night," she whispered. "Another time."

He seized her hand and kissed it.

"Lady, I obey, but to-morrow—to-morrow night, I invite you all to Les Palmiers and we will dance and drink."

He passed his hand across his forehead, evidently trying to remember something. "Yes, I will come back from Cannes in time. Tomorrow night at nine."

He looked round. People were whispering to one another, but they all accepted with enthusiasm.

"You must come," Adelaide murmured to Paul. "Hernandez's parties are always marvellous. You and I and Ben will go together—dine with me first."

Paul thanked her and agreed eagerly. This place was exceeding his wildest expectations.

Meanwhile trays of drinks were arriving and people were settling down at their own tables, some talking in low voices and casting covert glances at De Najera, who drained his glass and relapsed into a stupor. Paul wondered what they were saying. He thought he'd take advantage of an interval and ask a question that he'd had on the tip of his tongue for some time. Even Benvenuto seemed to have got past talking and was blinking down at a vague drawing he'd made on the table top. Paul turned to Adelaide.

"What I've been wanting to ask you all the evening is—do you know a man called Adrian Kent?"

De Najera's chair went back with a crash as he leapt to his feet. Paul looked at him in amazement.

The man's eyes were flashing, his face was dark with fury.

"Adrian Kent?" he shouted. "He murdered my sister!"

Before Paul could open his mouth he felt a hard grip on his arm, and a voice said: "Don't take any notice of him. He's drunk. Help me get him out of here, quick!"

Paul felt as if he were going mad. For it was Benvenuto Brown speaking. The blinking half-closed eyes were wide open, amazing eyes, of steely clear blue that changed his entire face as he looked at Paul commandingly, urgently. The amiably smiling mouth had set in a hard line, and he issued curt directions to Paul under his breath. The man was dead sober.

De Najera had slumped across the table. As they went to help him out Paul looked round for Adelaide. She had disappeared.

CHAPTER VI
BENVENUTO BROWN

"HALF A MINUTE, till I find the switch. That's better."

Paul found himself in a square tiled hall, as Benvenuto closed the heavy front door behind him. There were enormous wine casks along the wall, and a strong sour-sweet, rather yeasty, smell.

"Smells good, doesn't it?" remarked Benvenuto, pausing on his way to the stairs. "My landlord's a wine grower—that's his cave down those steps where he keeps the stuff. He's a great character, a marvellous old chap. Spends most of his time in his cave, and you can never get through this hall in the daytime without a hoarse voice from below inviting you to *un peu de vin blanc*. He calls it the Café des Hommes. Come on up and I'll make some real coffee."

Paul followed Benvenuto up an arched winding staircase with carved stone balusters. "Amazing place you've got," he said. "These stairs remind me of that German film, *Dr. Caligari*."

Benvenuto laughed. "Come and see the studio," he said, and they went into an enormous whitewashed room with a shining red-tiled floor. Paul sank into a settee while Benvenuto went off to make coffee. He lit his pipe and looked round him. It was a delightful room, furnished with a few pieces of carved Provençal furniture, two easels, one holding a half-finished canvas, and some red flowers on a table. The long windows were hung with silver-grey curtains in a modernistic design, beautiful with the red floor and white walls. The rest of the room seemed to be furnished almost entirely with books. From the kitchen came the hiss of an expiring Primus, and Benvenuto appeared with bowls of coffee.

"By Jove, this is nice," said Paul. "Very decent of you to ask me up here at this time of night. I love your house."

"Very decent of you to help me send that drunken fool home," replied Ben, "particularly as you must have thought I was blind to the world myself. I shall feel extremely hurt if you say you didn't," as Paul protested, "after my praiseworthy imitation of a drunken man. I feel I owe you an explanation, but I wonder if you'd mind telling me first why you were asking for Adrian Kent?"

Paul made up his mind to take Benvenuto into his confidence.

"Are you prepared to listen to a long story? I don't know the chap myself, and my connection with him is rather extraordinary."

"Go ahead."

And so Paul told him about Major Kent's dramatic entry into his room, and the curious mission with which he'd been charged. Benvenuto, leaning back in an armchair, regarded him steadily and put in one or two questions. He sucked at his pipe for a few minutes when Paul had finished and then said: "Thanks. I'm glad you've told me all that because now I know more where I am. This boy Adrian Kent is a great friend of mine, and of Adelaide's. You heard what that Argentine fellow said about him to-night? Well, unfortunately he isn't the only one who thinks so, and the boy is in very great danger. Now, I've taken it on myself to do a bit of investigation on his behalf, and it seems to me that this is where your job and mine link up. I may as well say at once that I believe the chap is perfectly innocent, but at the same time it may be a tough job to prove it. If you'd care to come in with me . . . ?" He looked at Paul inquiringly.

"Of course I will—this is terrible. Do you know where Kent is?"

Benvenuto didn't answer directly. "I can tell you this much," he said. "If you'll stick around here for a bit, and we succeed with some quiet sleuthing, so to speak, I can promise that you shall meet Adrian before long."

"That's a bargain then. Tell me, when was this woman murdered and who—Good Lord! Is she the woman Adrian Kent got in such a mess over?"

Benvenuto nodded. "I expect you've read about the case in the paper. Three days ago she was found smothered on her bed in Bishop's Hotel in London. What makes everything so difficult is that the police know that Adrian lunched with her that day in her rooms. According to the evidence in the paper, some woman also called on her in the afternoon, but at present they don't know who she was, nor what time either she or Adrian left. Of course, if they get hold of her it may clear the whole thing up. Did you notice a quiet-looking little chap in pince-nez who was sitting in the café to-night drinking lemonade? Well, that's Detective Inspector Leech of Scotland Yard. Fortunately I know him a bit, because I was once able to give him a hand over one of his cases. He's told me he's down here after Kent, and also after another chap, an old lag, commonly known as the Slosher, who he knows is somewhere along this coast, and who I believe he thinks may have something to do with this case. He was a bit close about that though, and I couldn't get much out of him.

"I think I'd better tell you something about this unfortunate woman Luela da Costa, who was done in. She's lived down her for some years on and off, with her brother De Najera, whom you met to-night. No one seems to know much about Da Costa, but rumour hath it that they were divorced some year ago. De Najera and his sister own the Château les Palmiers, a colossal affair along the Corniche that looks like a pastry cook's conception of an ancestral hall, all turrets and white icing. You'll see it tomorrow when we attend the party. They appear to be rich enough, their possessions—or his, I suppose I should say now—including a speed boat and a perfect fleet of cars, one of which you saw to-night. Almost indecent, isn't it?

"Luela was a remarkably beautiful woman, a bit too fierce for my taste—all hips and flashing eyes, you know—but still very fine in her way. Anyhow, she succeeded in completely turning young Kent's head, although she must have been at least fifteen years older than he, and he followed her about in a highly lovesick condition for some four months. He told me he wanted to marry her, and was only waiting till he'd made enough money to ask her. Well, I hate butting into other people's affairs of that sort, and anyhow he was too far gone to listen to advice, so I avoided discussing the thing with him as much as possible. He realized I didn't like her, and things cooled off a bit between us in consequence. While this was going on she had a terrific row with De Najera, and rushed off to Paris or London or somewhere. I don't know what it was about but it must have been pretty serious because she hasn't stayed at Les Palmiers since, putting up at the Continental when she came down once or twice. There is a story to the effect that they quarrelled over Adelaide, on whom, as you may have noticed, De Najera is casting a lustful eye, curse him!

"Adrian was still doing the moth to her candle at that time and went off after her, but he reappeared at a village near here shortly afterwards and started to paint like mad. We became as good friends as ever and he told me he was completely cured. Evidently he'd had a bit of a shock and found out something highly sinister about her—but he never told me what it was. Just as he was getting back his usual form and starting to work really well (he's a damn good painter by the way), she descended on him, and like Diana she pursued him. Luela wasn't as young as she had been, and had got to the stage when she couldn't stand the idea of losing her power over a man. Adrian became a kind of obsession with her, I think, and when he presented a blind eye to all her allurements she turned savage and started to threaten him over that jewel business. If only the young fool had told me about it I might have been able to do something, but at the time I hadn't the least idea he'd quarrelled with his father or was short of cash. I believe he'd actually been pretty near starving before he sold that jewel, and though I knew him as well as anyone I hadn't the least idea of it. The end of it was she went off in a huff, and then started bombarding him with letters ending with the one threatening to put the police on his track unless he went over to London immediately. He left a note for me telling me he'd gone to see her and would be back in a day or two, and then, as you know, the balloon went up."

Paul broke in, rather hesitatingly:

"Of course—you know Kent, and I don't—but on the face of it, it really does look as if he may have lost his head, and—"

"I know it does. That's the devil of it. But wait a minute. Enter the second murderer. I've got a theory about the thing that I haven't told you yet, and that's where *you* come in. If Adrian is innocent, as I believe, it's going to be damned hard to prove it unless the real criminal is produced. Now, the only other person I know of who was on bad terms with Luela is— De Najera. And by a fluke I hit on something the other day which may be interesting in that connection.

"On the afternoon Luela was murdered, last Tuesday, at least fifty people in St. Antoine must have seen De Najera rushing up and down the coast in his speed boat, dressed in his usual yellow-and-black outfit, and waving to people on the beach. It so happened that that afternoon I'd gone for a pretty long swim, and was lying on some rocks a good way out having a breather. I must have been practically invisible because I'm burnt pretty dark, and my bathing pants are a dull reddish colour much the same as the rocks round here. The speed boat came tearing along quite near my rock, and I was just going to hail De Najera when I saw to my surprise that it wasn't him at all, but his valet, who is an Argentine chap of much the same build and colouring—*wearing De Najera's clothes*—and waving to De Najera's friends on the beach. Presently, after going up and down the coast several times, the boat went back into the small private harbour which belongs to Les Palmiers. I puzzled lazily over the thing for a bit as I lay in the sun, and then dismissed it from my mind. After all, it wasn't my business if the chap pinched his master's clothes for the afternoon. It seemed funny though, because I know De Najera brought him over from the Argentine and trusts him implicitly."

"Looks very fishy to me," said Paul.

Benvenuto went on. "There's more to come. As soon as I heard about Luela's death and Adrian being suspected I determined I'd cultivate friend Hernandez rather more than usual, and this incident coming back to my mind, the next day—

Wednesday, that was—I said to him while sitting over a drink, 'How's the boat going?'

"'Better than ever,' he said. 'I nearly touched seventy when I had her out yesterday.' That was the day of the murder, mark you. It's a perfectly sweet little alibi, isn't it?"

"What time on Wednesday did you see him?" said Paul, feeling like the complete detective.

"It was Wednesday evening, after I'd heard the news, that I asked him about the boat. But—he was down on the quay between nine and ten on Wednesday morning,"

Paul's face fell.

"Well then—he couldn't possibly have been in London on Tuesday. The night train doesn't reach Marseille till ten-thirty."

"Wait a minute," said Benvenuto. "There are more ways of getting about than are dreamed of in the P.L.M. philosophy."

"That's true, I hadn't thought of a plane," said Paul, feeling rather dashed.

"Don't you worry about that. I've already got an idea as to how I can check his movements. Meanwhile, I'm rather interested to know what he's up to to-morrow. He told me he was going into Marseille for the day to see the British consul about his sister's death, which is quite as it should be. But—he doesn't generally keep me posted in this touching way as to his whereabouts, and I thought it might be worth keeping an eye on him. What's more—to-night, when I'd got him thoroughly tight, he mentioned he was going to *Cannes* to-morrow—d'you remember?"

"Yes, of course—when he was issuing his princely invitation. You're right, he is worth watching. How are you going to manage it?"

"Would you care to come along? Right, then be sitting in the Café de la Phare over your morning coffee to-morrow at nine, and I'll pick you up. Let's see—you're a bit conspicuous like that, aren't you?" looking at Paul's essentially quiet grey-flannel suit. "Fit yourself up in a few glad rags from the Marine Store—they keep everything the human frame requires—and wear some green glasses. I don't want him to spot either of us."

Paul laughed.

"Anything you say. I was contemplating a sartorial change anyhow. I can't promise I've got the makings of a great detective, but if I can help you catch that swine out, well, I should love to be Watson to your Holmes."

"Don't talk rot—two heads are better than one in a business of this sort, and I'm damn grateful to you for coming in on it."

Paul got up to go. "Till to-morrow then. And thanks for the coffee." He got as far as the door and turned back.

"Look here," he said. "If this chap De Najera *did* kill his sister, and it looks very like it, surely he wouldn't be going about giving parties and drinking in cafés? He'd be certain to put up an appearance of profound grief, I should have thought."

Benvenuto studied the interior of his pipe for a minute. Then he looked up with a smile.

"That's the perfect reaction, isn't it? I'd thought about it myself—and as they were known not to have been on good terms, it seems to me that De Najera, being far from a fool, might have decided on a double bluff."

CHAPTER VII
THE ADVENTURES OF A TAXICAB

PAUL WOKE UP and looked at his watch. Only seven o'clock. He'd time for another snooze; and pulling the sheet over his head as protection from an importunate mosquito, he turned lazily over and closed his eyes. But sleep eluded him, and instead the events of the last two days came crowding into his mind. A procession of figures walked through his brain, people of whose existence he'd been entirely ignorant three days before and who had taken their places with an urgent reality in his life. Adelaide Moon's laughing face; was he wrong in feeling that laughter had once or twice been the camouflage of fear? The gentle features of Major Kent towards whom Paul felt somehow responsible; Benvenuto Brown, a definite and eccentric personality, very reassuring; the Argentine, whom Paul now thought positively loathsome, with his sallow handsome face; and mixed with them all a chorus of strange tongues and curious clothes.

This was no time for sleep. Paul jumped out of bed and went to the window. His hotel was on the quay, and when he threw back the shutters he found a glorious blue-and-white world glittering in the sun. Across the bay motorboats were coming in with the morning catch, leaving white trails in the vivid blue, their engines *plop-plopping* over the water. Below his window a group of fishermen was collected round a boat that had just come in. They were discussing an enormous swordfish that lay on top of a rainbow-coloured haul, their rich Provençal accents interspersed with words of Italian, and as different from Parisian argot as Devonshire is from Cockney. They all appeared to be filled with a passionate conviction about something or other, and Paul grinned as he listened to the rapid deep-voiced argument emphasized with oaths and gestures. Magnificent-looking chaps, he thought, with their muscular sunburnt arms and bare feet, set off by clothes that were washed and bleached to every conceivable shade of blue.

What a morning—and what a marvellous sea. In the best of spirits Paul shaved rapidly, and slipping on a bathing suit under his shirt and trousers he hurried off for a swim. Halfway along the quay the Marine Store, already open, caught his eye, and remembering Benvenuto's instructions he went in, to be profoundly embarrassed by the keen personal interest that the *patronne* at once took in his toilette. Linen trousers, check shirts, coloured bérets, and *tricots*, being tight-fitting, short-sleeved jumpers of woven cotton and dyed in every tint, met his eyes, and he found himself being led to a mirror in front of which the enthusiastic *patronne* used him as a peg on which to hang all her wares in turn, keeping up a running comment the while.

"Ah! *Que c'est jolie, ça!*" and then, "*M'sieur va très bien comme ça.*"

Discarding a vermilion jumper as being a little conspicuous for a detective, he finally picked on one in broad stripes of blue and white, which besides toning, he felt, with the landscape had the advantage of being repeated all over the port. A black béret and a pair of rope-soled shoes laced across the instep, called, he discovered, *espadrilles*, completed his toilette. Firmly resisting offers of coloured trousers and clinging, metaphorically speaking, to his grey-flannel bags as a drowning man to a straw, he left the shop with a bundle under his arm amidst a chorus of "*Au revoir, m'sieur*" from the *patronne* and her family, all of whom had by now drifted in to offer words of encouragement and advice. Next door he found green sun spectacles and then continued on his way to the beach, feeling rather proud of his efforts.

The beach was deserted, though the sand was already hot in the sun; the sea, almost motionless, stretched before him like glittering blue glass. He took a running dive and found himself borne to the top instantly. Feeling like a cork floating in blue soda water, he swam on his back, crawled, dived to the bottom, stood on his head, sent up mountains of spray, and then came out feeling tremendously exhilarated, and lay on the hot sand. His white skin looked terribly nude, he thought, as he lay stripped to the waist, and he wondered how long it would take him to get a rich veneer of sunburn. A pleasant process—he could feel his skin coming to life in the sun and air. Presently pangs of hunger drove him into his clothes, and feeling odd but comfortable in the unaccustomed *tricot* and soft shoes, he stood up, pulled on his béret, shook the sand off his clothes, and went back to the town.

He ran up to his room to drop his other shirt and shoes before having breakfast, and started back in amazement at the stranger who looked at him from the mirror. Most modest of human beings though he was, he had to admit he really looked rather nice; these *tricots* certainly showed off one's shoulders if one had any—and not wearing a coat did reveal the fact that one had small hips. He tried on the green spectacles, and deciding that his dearest friend wouldn't recognize him, he put them back in his trouser pocket and went down to the café.

Choosing a table on the pavement in order to look out for Benvenuto, he ordered coffee and *brioches*, and consumed them contentedly as he watched the life of the port. The early-morning activities were over and fish nets were spread out on the cobbles in long trails of dark brown. Some sailors were polishing the brass of a private yacht that had come in the night before. Paul paid for his coffee and lit a cigarette.

Suddenly the yellow-and-black Hispaño-Suiza went past driven by De Najera and disappeared at a good speed. Immediately afterwards a closed Renault taxi drew up alongside the café and the driver looked about. He caught sight of Paul and leant out saying, "*Pardon, m'sieur—vous avez fait rendezvous avec M. Brown, n'est-ce pas?*"

"*Oui, c'est ça,*" replied Paul.

"Well then, hop in," returned the taxi man. "I'm Brown, and don't look so startled!"

Paul climbed obediently into the back. They didn't exchange a word until they were out of the town following the Hispaño-Suiza down the Marseille road. Then Paul slid back the windows between himself and the driver.

"Congratulations," he said. "I should never have known you in that peaked cap and wearing that little moustache. Simply amazing the way it alters you."

"Well, you're looking rather dressy yourself, aren't you? I was a bit uncertain when I first caught sight of you. Ah—look at that!"

Paul looked ahead and saw the tail of the Hispaño-Suiza disappearing off to the right up a small track through the wood. Benvenuto immediately reversed his taxi and shot back in the direction from which they'd come, going through St. Antoine on to the Cannes road. About four kilometres beyond St. Antoine he stopped just before a small road that entered the Route Nationale from the left, and turned round to speak to Paul.

"Unless I've made a fool of myself we shall see our friend reappear out of that turning in a minute or two. We're certain to be ahead of him in time because the forest road makes a big circle at the back of the town, and it's a bad surface too—impossible to speed on. Didn't bring my own car—he knows it too well. Hired this taxi from a pal of mine."

"Jolly good way to hide your identity, too. But for God's sake put the flag up—all those francs totting up are making me nervous," said Paul. Benvenuto suddenly held up his hand, listening, then got out and buried his head in the bonnet, as the Hispaño-Suiza turned into the road and headed for Cannes at a tremendous speed.

"Enter through gap in hedge," murmured Benvenuto in pleased tones. "Conduct's pretty suspicious, isn't it?"

Before Paul could reply he had let in the clutch, and they started down the road at a hair-raising speed. On one side were high walls of pink rock, on the other a big drop to the sea, and Benvenuto went tearing round the hairpin bends with complete unconcern while Paul was shot from side to side of the car. To Paul's horror Benvenuto turned round to address him.

"Afraid we can't catch him up, but if he's going to stop in Cannes it ought to be quite easy to find him with that super-shiny Hispaño-Suiza. Vulgar, I call it, what?"

Paul's only answer was to point frantically at an enormous lorry that had appeared round a corner and was crashing down on them. They avoided it by a hair's breadth, and Paul decided to look at the scenery instead of treading on imaginary brakes. He realized as he looked about him what Homer meant by the "wine-dark sea," for the blue was so intense as to appear almost purple at the foot of the rocks. There was, however, little else to remind him of the classic coast, for as they approached the chic part of the Riviera he saw on the landward side, dotted amongst pine and palm trees, the hundreds of hotels and white villas of the cosmopolitan rich whose coming has created probably the most highly artificial landscape in the world. Swinging round a corner, he caught sight of the massed white buildings of Cannes—like lumps of sugar spilt on the edge of a blue bowl, he thought. They had long since lost sight of the Hispaño-Suiza, and another half hour's furious driving brought them into the town itself. Calling to Paul to keep a weather eye open, Benvenuto drove along the water front, raised his hat politely to Edward VII in yachting costume, so perpetually unconcerned with the nude lady in bronze at his feet, and then turned back along the main street. There was no sign of their quarry and Benvenuto drew up for a consultation.

"Judging by Hernandez's condition last night, I think we may safely say he's suffering from a decided thirst by this time," he said. "How about going along to the Rendezvous Bar? I could do with a drink myself, and Louis the barman's a great friend of mine—one of the few people I know who would accept my present costume without blinking. If Hernandez has been in, Louis *may* know where he's lunching."

Paul assented with enthusiasm and they started off. Seeing no Hispaño outside the Rendezvous, they went in to find the place empty, it not yet being the hour of cocktails. Behind the bar a white-coated individual, whose face took Paul back with a rush to his native land, was delicately arranging some olives in a dish.

"Good-morning, Louis," said Ben.

"God bless my soul, sir, good-morning. Haven't been in to see us lately, eh? Good-morning, sir," to Paul. "And what shall we do this morning?"

"Oh, two of the usual, I think, Louis." He turned to Paul. "Will a champagne cocktail suit you, Ashby? Louis's are the best in Europe."

"Sounds all right to me," replied Paul.

"Very good, sir, thank you, sir," and he began the rite of mixing them with the air of a true artist. Perched on a high stool, Benvenuto chatted with him until, sipping his drink, he said casually, "Seen anything of Mr. de Najera lately, Louis?"

"Funny thing you should say that, sir—why, he went out not five minutes before you came in."

"Oh, sorry I missed him. Did you manage to nail him for lunch? What is it now, grouse?"

Louis raised his eyes to heaven. "Wonderful birds, sir, wonderful. Just you look at these." And bustling across to a Frigidaire, he produced two little carcasses on a plate and eyed them with affectionate pride. "Came over by plane yesterday, they did. Absolutely prime—just you smell 'em, sir. No, Mr. de Najera he wasn't in no mood for grouse. Generally lunches at one of them big hotels, I think. Now, can I tempt you, sir?"

"Afraid not to-day, Louis, I've got other fish to fry. Next week, perhaps. Well, we must be getting along. Er—by the way, I've not been in here this morning."

The barman permitted just a flicker of curiosity to cross his face as he eyed Benvenuto's moustache. "Quite, sir, quite—*entendu*—good morning, sir, and thank you very much."

"Now for 'them big hotels,' " said Benvenuto, climbing into the car, and they started off again. After going the round of several shining examples of comfort *moderne* they finally to their great delight located the Hispaño in the garage of the Hotel Luxuria, and Benvenuto drew up his taxi at a small restaurant opposite.

"Afraid you'll have to see how the poor live to-day, since you're hob-nobbing with a taxi driver," he said. "And anyway

I bet we get a better meal here than Hernandez does in that whited sepulchre."

Seated at a small table behind a bay tree, they ate an excellent lunch, washed down with red wine, taking it in turns to keep an eye on the hotel entrance.

During Benvenuto's shift which occurred in a pause in the meal Paul pulled a notebook and pencil from his pocket.

"I wonder if you'd mind," he said, "running over very quickly the facts of the crime as you know them from the newspapers and from the Scotland Yard man, together with the comings and goings of De Najera which I'm still not entirely clear about, and I'll jot them down. I feel it would straighten things out in my mind. That is, if it wouldn't bore you."

"Good idea," remarked Benvenuto, gazing abstractedly across the road. "Fire away. I'll begin from the day of the murder—last Tuesday.

1. "Inspector Leech tells me Adrian lunched with Luela on Tuesday at one o'clock in her rooms. *We* know that he had gone there to make a last attempt to part from her on good terms and dissuade her from taking vengeance on him through the police over the sold-jewel affair. Time of his departure unknown.

2. "He also tells me that a woman called on her later in the afternoon—chambermaid thinks it was about five o'clock. Name and business unknown. Time of departure unknown. Description of back view which might apply to anyone.

3. "Luela had given her maid Annette the afternoon off. This was unusual, according to Annette, and we presume Luela had hopes of subjugating Adrian.

4. "Annette comes in at six-thirty. Unlocks door of suite with her own key. Goes in, finds Luela dead on the bed smothered by an eiderdown. Body has no clothes on but is covered with jewels. Scarlet silk dressing gown lying on floor beside bed. Bathroom in disorder, looking as though Luela had taken a bath shortly before.

5. "It is known that a big jewel robbery took place in the hotel the same afternoon. Luela's jewels are, however, intact, although those she was not wearing were found strewn about the dressing table. Maid is uncertain about a diamond brooch which is missing, but the police don't attach much importance to that as it had no very great value compared with other things in her collection, and Luela may have lost it or given it away.

6. "Inspector Leech is down here in search of Adrian. He is also keeping an eye open for one known as the Slosher, who I imagine he thinks committed the jewel robbery.

7. "De Najera accuses Adrian of murdering Luela, and has, I believe, told Leech something about the affair of the jewel which Adrian sold, and Adrian's former infatuation for Luela.

8. "I know De Najera to have quarrelled with Luela and to have been on bad terms with her at the time of her death.

9. "On Tuesday afternoon last when the murder was committed De Najera establishes an alibi by sending his valet out in speed boat disguised as himself. Valet waves to De Najera's friends on beach. I, owing to an accident, spot the fact that it is not De Najera.

10. "De Najera is seen on the quay on Wednesday morning at ten o'clock.

11. "I hear of the murder on Wednesday, and becoming interested ask De Najera how boat is going. He tells me direct lie, saying he'd had it out on Tuesday afternoon.

12. "De Najera tells me he is going to Marseille for the day on *Friday* to see British consul about Luela's death. We follow him and find he starts for Marseille and doubles back to Cannes.

"You notice that the end of De Najera's alibi is established at ten o'clock on Wednesday. Now I saw him myself late on Monday night, so what we've got to find out is what time he left St. Antoine, how he left, and if possible where he went. I've got an idea about it that I'm going to test when we get back this evening. Meanwhile Entry No. 13 ought to prove interesting—here he comes." Paul looked up to see De Najera walk down the hotel steps and stroll along the Promenade des Anglais. Hurriedly paying their bill, Benvenuto and Paul got into the taxi and started in pursuit. They saw De Najera glance at his watch and turn up a side street where he entered a very chic hairdresser's and perfumery shop. Benvenuto whistled softly, and drawing up to the curb he turned round to speak to Paul.

"I know this place by reputation," he said. "Very shady. More things go on upstairs than meet the eye. Now unless he comes out very soon or is having his hair cut he's here to meet someone. Convenient place, you know. Man goes into hairdresser's shop for an hour—what could be more natural and even commendable?" He got down from the driver's seat, signing to Paul to stay where he was, and walked past the shop. Returning immediately, he said, "No, he's not having his beauty improved. *But*—there are two vacant chairs. We go in. You have a face massage and I'll have a haircut. If anyone comes out who looks to me suspicious I will follow him, or her. You will follow De Najera because he's seen you only once when he was dead drunk. They obviously won't come out together. We'll meet as soon as we can, where we had lunch. *Compris?*" Paul nodded and they went in. "*Liberté, Fraternité, Egalité,*" murmured Benvenuto. "Thank God, this isn't London or my clothes might prove awkward." They settled themselves in the two empty chairs, which faced a mirror giving them a good view of anyone passing behind them to the door. Benvenuto entrenched himself behind a copy of *La Vie Parisienne* and ordered a haircut, warning the barber to avoid his moustache which, he explained, he was bringing up by kindness. Meanwhile Paul delivered himself unwillingly into the hands of an animated gentleman who proceeded to blind him with a wet pad and then attack his face in a businesslike fashion with towels dipped in hot water. Paul submitted himself as philosophically as possible to being patted, pummelled, and tapped, to the application of strange smelling creams and stranger lotions, until, with the pad still over his eyes, he heard De Najera's voice saying good-bye to someone upstairs, followed by heavy footsteps descending. The next moment Benvenuto's voice in his ear said, "Even better than I'd hoped. I'm off—goodbye, and good hunting." Tearing off the pad from his eyes, Paul saw Benvenuto hurriedly pay the bill and leave, and he resigned himself to the rest of the operation, which unfortunately came to an end before De Najera appeared. With a glowing face he stood up and glared angrily at his tormentor. *"Combien?"* he demanded, and insult added to injury, found he had to part with an enormous sum. Feeling thoroughly martyred, he lingered in the shop, buying shaving materials he didn't want, until at last De Najera came down the stairs, and muttering a word to the proprietor went out. Paul followed at a discreet distance, feeling reasonably secure with his pink face and sun glasses.

CHAPTER VIII
CORONA–CORONA

DE NAJERA walked rapidly into the main street and entered a Bureau de Change, while Paul stationed himself at a shop window opposite in which he could see his prey reflected. It was a moment or two before he realized that the shining glass separated him from a delectable display of the more intimate garments worn by females, and blushing hotly he strolled on to the discreet establishment of a watchmaker. After about ten minutes, by which time he was beginning to fear that the Bureau had a back entrance, De Najera reappeared and set off briskly down the road, Paul following. He next went into an imposing-looking building which on inspection proved to be a bank, where he remained for some time. This was beginning to get boring—the man appeared to be going about some perfectly ordinary and legitimate business and Paul felt rather a fool. However, his interest revived somewhat when he saw that the third port of call was another Bureau de Change, and rose to fever heat by the time De Najera had repeated the proceeding eight or nine times, calling at every bank and *bureau* as he came to it. At last he went back to the hotel, got his car from the garage, and disappeared rapidly in the direction of St. Antoine. Paul hurried back to his rendezvous with Benvenuto, feeling he had some really valuable news to impart, only to find to his disappointment that his confederate had not yet returned. Paul sat down at the table where they had lunched and ordered some tea, pondering over his discovery. Was De Najera planning a getaway? He must have been handling a lot of money to have divided his patronage between so many places—and must also have been anxious to conceal the fact. Paul gave it up, and looking at his watch began to feel a little anxious about Benvenuto. It was nearly two hours since they had parted at the hairdresser's, and though he felt the extraordinary man was more capable of looking after himself than most people, still—it would be reassuring to see him turn up.

Paul sat back and began to sort out his impressions. It was peculiar, when one came to think about it, the way he had placed complete trust in Brown after knowing him for only a few hours, and found it the most natural thing possible to take the lead from him in the whole affair; particularly as Benvenuto was by no means a transparent or easily comprehensible character. It was impossible to fit him in with the popular conception of an artist, which Paul had previously to some extent shared, the word calling up a vague mental image of some highly eccentric and impractical being whose concerns lay wholly in the realms of imagination. Eccentric, yes—his odd, rather puckish face and oblique turns of phrase fitted that; imaginative he certainly was, for, apart from his painting, his attitude towards the problem they were tackling proved that, but impractical he definitely was not. His appearance that morning in a false moustache and a taxicab, which at the time Paul had privately felt to be a little like an incident in a detective serial for boys, now seemed to be the merest common sense, and his conduct at the wheel of the aforesaid taxicab certainly proved he had judgment and nerve control. Paul was wondering what part he had played in the war when the object of his meditations drove up to the entrance of the café, looking hot, tired, but triumphant. He got down and joined Paul, flourishing a hundred-franc note in his hand.

"A little tip from my fare," he said with modest pride. "I'd no idea taxi driving was so profitable."

"What happened?" asked Paul.

"Well, quite a lot. It was a shame you were temporarily blinded because he wasn't the sort of thing one sees every day. Quite the last person one would expect to find hob-nobbing with De Najera in a scent shop. The Blackfriar's Ring would be a much more sympathetic setting. He was obviously in an opulent condition, oozing with food and glittering with rings and tie pins. I hopped into the Renault and followed him down the street, drove slowly past him, touched my cap, and said in my best broken English, 'Taxi—you want taxi, milord?' He did, it seemed, and on hearing his native tongue an expression of such childish joy illumined his fat red face that he quite charmed me. 'That's right, mate,' he said. 'Half a mo' and I'll give yer the address to go to.' He brought out a slip of paper from his pocket with the name K. Paleidos and an address in Cannes on it, in De Najera's handwriting, which I know well. Good enough, I thought, you're my man. I don't know Cannes too well, but by going into a garage, ostensibly to get some water, I learnt the direction, and the address turned out to be a dim little bric-a-brac shop near the port, with the name K. Paleidos, *propriétaire*, over the door, and looked like the sort of place where sailors get rid of things when they come ashore. Another establishment that doesn't wear its heart on its sleeve, I thought. My fat friend went inside, but reappeared in a minute or two and beckoned me to come in.

"'Ere,' he said, 'can you make out what this Jane is talking about? I want Mr. Pilidos and keep telling 'er so.'

"There was rather a pretty girl in the shop who explained to me that the *propriétaire* had a little colic and was at home at his villa, *'pas loin six kilometres derrière la ville sur la route de Grasse.'* We got the address from her and went along to the Villa Sphinx, which turned out to be a most palatial affair with nude ladies (in stone, of course) climbing about the façade.

"My profiteer rang the bell and was let in, and presently I wandered round the shrubbery which came close up to the house to see if I could come upon anything interesting. As luck would have it, there was an open window and from it came the sound of my fare shouting at the top of his voice, more in sorrow than in anger, in a way the English have when trying to make a foreigner understand them. I kept below the level of the window sill and had not the slightest difficulty in overhearing the conversation.

"'Well, if yer won't, yer won't,' he was saying disappointedly, and then I caught the chink of metal or glass. A suave voice replied, 'M'sieur, I am *désolé*, but it is for me too *dangereux*. I like not to not oblige, but what will you? The affair is too recent; but if M'sieur will go to Marseille to my *confrère*, every satisfaction is assured to him.' Then in a lower voice, 'M'sieur will understand that here at Cannes I am municipal councillor, yes, friend with the police, but I cannot take such risk. At Marseille my *confrère* is more friend with the police, she has—how you say?—a graft. I give to you her address, *enfin?*' Apparently he had to be content with this and tried, as far as I could make out, to tip Mr. Paleidos, who was much shocked. The door opened and shut and their voices died away. In a second I was in the room, and luck was with me again, for on a bureau in the corner was a little writing pad for notes. I tore the top sheet off, slid out of the window, and appeared round the corner doing up my buttons just as my fare and the discreet Mr. Paleidos came out of the door. They seemed to have got quite matey and were both smoking enormous cigars. They parted with mutual compliments, and I took Flash Fred back to his hotel, where he gave me a couple of cigars of similar proportions and a hundred-franc note, saying, '*Au revoyer*, mate, keep the change.' "

Benvenuto felt in his pocket and brought out a silk handkerchief which he unwrapped with care. "Corona-Coronas—and of the largest size," he murmured reverently. "Here you are—we share the spoils."

Paul wiped his brow. "I suppose it's inevitable," he said weakly.

"What's inevitable?"

"That I should learn to smoke these things. It's the second time in three days I've been given one. Last time it was a terrible fellow who came down in my sleeper who gave me a Corona and wouldn't be denied."

Benvenuto's hand, which at the beginning of Paul's speech had shot out towards the cigar, was arrested in mid-air.

"Ginger eyelashes?" he said sharply.

Paul started.

"Yes—and a bald head."

"Check suit and tan shoes—looked like an ex-pugilist?"

Paul nodded vigorously.

"That's it—but Brighton Race Course, I thought."

Benvenuto beamed. "The very man! What did you learn about him?"

"Practically nothing, I'm afraid—I escaped as soon as I could and didn't go back till he was peacefully snoring."

"Great mistake, you know. Always talk to people in trains—I do. They'll tell you things in the intimacy of a railway carriage that they wouldn't breathe to their dearest friend. Most interesting. That chap would have told me how many gold teeth he'd got, what his income was, and where he'd bought his boots, which would have been a revelation in itself."

"Now I come to think about it," said Paul, "he *did* tell me he'd come into some money lately."

"Oh, he did, did he?" Benvenuto jumped up. "Let's get to hell out of here. I want to think. And I want to hear what Hernandez does when he's alone."

They climbed into the taxi.

CHAPTER IX
COOKERY AND CRIME

As THE RENAULT left the outskirts of Cannes Paul leant across to the driver's seat, and began to recount to Benvenuto his discoveries while trailing De Najera. When he had finished, Benvenuto was silent, driving rapidly along the tortuous road and apparently devoting all his attention to the car. Suddenly he drew into the side, stopped the engine, got his pipe from his pocket, and having lit up turned round to Paul. He frowned. "Can't make it fit," he said. "It's got all the elements of a neat little story in the usual tradition, only unfortunately everything contradicts everything else. What are your conclusions about all this money changing?"

"Don't you think it looks as though he were planning a getaway?" Paul asked.

Benvenuto shook his head.

"I don't think that's likely to be his game. Far too dangerous. If he did go to London last Tuesday and has covered his tracks as neatly as he thinks, why attract attention to himself by disappearing? Let's suppose for a moment that he didn't do the job himself, but employed our boy friend of this afternoon, who is, as we know, fresh from England, to do it for him. Why then, in heaven's name, was De Najera receiving money from him instead of paying it to him? For it seems obvious from his visits to all these money-changing establishments that he'd just received a pretty handsome sum of foreign money, presumably English, from the fat man and was anxious to change it into French without attracting notice of the amount. It won't fit—it isn't even as though there'd been a motive of robbery, for Luela's jewels were found intact." Suddenly Benvenuto sat up, his eyes wide open, and stared at Paul. "'The Countess of Trelorne on returning from a drive found her room ransacked and her jewels stolen.'" A seraphic smile spread over his face. "The Slosher," he said. "I've spent the afternoon with the Slosher and never knew it. How annoyed Leech will be."

"Good Lord—d'you really think it was?"

"Of course—and our Mr. Paleidos is obviously a jewel fence. It begins to shape—but does it though? For I don't see where Hernandez comes in. Whatever his source of income may be, I'm pretty certain he's not a jewel thief, or he wouldn't have his headquarters in the seclusion of St. Antoine. Those sort of gentry lose themselves in big cities." He clutched at his hair. "It's all so beautifully suggestive and I can't get any shape into it. I shall have to do a painting to-morrow, I know I shall."

"A painting?" asked Paul in surprised tones.

Benvenuto nodded. "I always paint best when I've got a problem to work out, likewise always work a problem out best when I'm painting. It seems to get the two sides of my mind free to work independently. I suppose that's why I took up criminology." He laughed. "One ought to be able to project a world's masterpiece out of this affair. Meanwhile we shall be late for dinner if we don't get on, and so invoke the wrath of Adelaide. That girl's cooking doesn't deserve a slight, I assure you." He kissed his fingers to the air and turned to the driving wheel, and they were soon racing towards the setting sun.

Paul settled back in a corner of the taxi and surveyed the world contentedly. It was beautiful beyond words, the sea pale green in the evening light, and turning he could see the mountains behind touched to burning rose by the sun. The air grew cool after the hot day, and as they swept past a village he could see far below on a sandy beach people in gay-coloured clothes returning from their day's sun bathing. The sound of voices singing floated faintly up to him. It was very peaceful. Paul thought suddenly of Adrian, in hiding and in fear of his life possibly somewhere along this sunny coast. It was something to feel that their day's work might help towards clearing him, and the prospect of spending the evening at the house of De Najera was a stimulating one. With rising spirits Paul remembered Benvenuto's remark about dining with Adelaide— apparently the invitation still held. His life was pretty good, he thought, and lay back, letting his thoughts slip in and out of his mind, lazily conscious of things round him, until Benvenuto deposited him at the door of his hotel. Arranging to meet him in the café in half an hour, Paul went up to bathe and change.

Twenty minutes later, leaning out of his bedroom window with a cigarette, he saw Benvenuto down on the quay, dressed in his corduroys and minus the moustache, in earnest conversation with a fisherman. They were too far away for him to overhear what they were saying and he stayed there leaning out of the window until he saw them part with a tremendous handshake. Benvenuto came striding along, looking pleased with himself, and glanced up at Paul's window as he went by. He waved a greeting. "Joshua fit de battle of Jericho and de walls came tumbling down," he said mysteriously, and passed on.

Paul pondered over this statement and decided it was an optimistic one. Smiling to himself, he completed his toilet and went down to the café where Benvenuto soon joined him. "Hullo—I take it you've been putting in some good work."

Benvenuto nodded. *"Ça marche,"* he said. "I'll tell you about it later. We'd better get along to Adelaide's now or we'll be late. There's no time for a drink, but she'll give us a cocktail when we get there. Come on—it's just along the port."

Beyond the cafés and the Marine Store Benvenuto stopped opposite a blue-painted door and pushed it open. He shouted up the stairs, and Adelaide's smiling face peered down at them. She waved a spoon.

"Well met," she said. "The cocktails are cold and the soup's hot, so enter. I've been wanting to show you my house," smiling at Paul.

Bending his head, he entered the low doorway, followed by Benvenuto, to find Adelaide in a white frock, her cheeks flushed with cooking, against the background of a rose-and-blue room. As she turned to a cocktail shaker on the table, he looked about him. Long windows hung with curtains of transparent white material looked over the port. The walls, faintly washed with pink, were bare except for a Marie Laurencin flower piece in a silver frame, and cushions and divan were covered in faded blue silk. On the floor of polished red tiles was a modernistic rug in greys and blacks. It was all very simple, and never, Paul thought, had he seen a more charming room. He told her so and she smiled with pleasure. Giving them each a cocktail, she led him to the window. "Come and see my view which I'm extremely proud of. I wish you'd been here earlier and seen the sunset. The cliffs looked as if you could toast bread on them."

Outside in the blue night he could see the houses of St. Antoine in a half circle round the port, their lights spilling reflections in the dark water. Above the mass of headland stars were coming out.

Benvenuto joined them. "My dear, it's high time you went to live in Clapham Junction," he expostulated. "Like Mrs. Aldwinkle of *Barren Leaves*, you're developing a proprietary interest in the beauties of Nature. You're beginning to believe you're responsible for all this"—he indicated the night with a sweep of his arm.

Her eyes twinkled.

"At least I'm responsible for the fact that you can look at it through white curtains, with a moonshine cocktail inside you. And there's no need to be catty because you live up a nasty back street without a view. Come and have your savage breast soothed with soup and tell me what you've been doing with Mr. Ashby all day."

"Les affaires sont les affaires," he replied darkly as they seated themselves at the table. "As a matter of fact, we've been out hunting—and it's quite possible that before long I shall invite you to join in the chase. Meanwhile I am preserving an enigmatic silence."

She looked at him curiously.

"Has the Open Season for Crooks recommenced?" she asked. She turned to Paul. "I don't know if you've discovered already—but Ben is quite the most brilliant detective outside fiction."

"Quel blague!"

"It *is* so useful," she went on. "He can produce the lost umbrella or the missing heir within twenty-four hours. It's a little trying of course in private life, for I can never deceive him about the simplest thing. Ben, do give a public performance and tell me what is in the soup?"

"The result is nectar and ambrosia—my felicitations. Chestnuts allied with white burgundy and cream were a pretty thought—and do I detect the least trace of Bacardi rum?"

She looked at Paul despairingly. "You see? One can have no reserves—no delicate mysteries. All one's subtleties lie naked under his pitiless gaze."

Paul laughed.

"Cookery is one of the holy mysteries to me," he said, "though, believe me, I appreciate the results."

Benvenuto was tenderly apportioning some sauce-enveloped fish onto a plate. "You should take it up," he said. "One of the most interesting of all the arts. I place it above painting, and below music, though of course it rides hand-in-hand with them. One has only to try the effect of a Bach concerto after a good dinner and the same work after a meal of canned salmon to prove that." He handed Paul his plate. "Adelaide, who practises both arts with extraordinary distinction, is the only woman I know who can give one pleasure in a Mediterranean fish. Her still-lifes are second only to her *sole Normande*. Have you noticed that on this coast the fish are the most beautiful and the most unpalatable in the world?"

"Judging from the present example, I should never have suspected that. The sauce is marvellous," said Paul. "You people are full of surprises. I always thought painters lived on canned salmon and gin from the top of an orange box, and that Bohemian life consisted of a highly coloured disorder. All this is as startling as finding a painter interested in detection. Have you ever thought of taking it up as a profession? I should have thought you'd get more scope from within the walls of the C.I.D."

Benvenuto shook his head. "Neither have I seriously considered taking up crime as a profession. To me both the one and the other are, generally speaking, conventions. The full-blooded criminal who terrorizes society because he is Evil is a sufficiently rare phenomenon for us to ignore. Ninety per cent of crimes are in the same gallery as petty larceny; they are committed from over-developed motives of greed or lust which are present to a small degree in all of us; they always have been and they always will be. The criminal who would poison his aunt for her war-savings certificates or hold up a jeweller's shop is not, to me, interesting, and this type of crime the police deal with effectively, one case being as like another as two peas. There remains the subtle motive—the criminal who is actuated by something obscure, even praiseworthy. In cases like this the crime is possibly quite justified, or at least inevitable, and as far as I am concerned I should hate to be part of the machinery that inflicts the same punishment in the one case as in the other. The English have invented a system of punishment that probably fits crime in general as well as any convention can. But it is difficult to forget that it *is* a convention, and that in Basutu land, for instance, it is an offence not to go out and slay the man who has run off with your wife. You see, a woman is worth three cows in that country, and they are a logical people. Likewise a hungry man has the right to go into whoever's house he likes to take food—whereas our logic would retaliate with three months' hard in a similar case."

"But surely," Paul objected, "you don't deny the necessity of protecting the individual's property? Speaking as a lawyer—"

"I neither deny it nor uphold it. Mine not to reason why. I only know that by instinct I prefer knocking the man down whom I catch stealing my watch to handing him over to a policeman. At the same time we all admire and respect the policemen who protect our old mothers. The reasons that would keep me out of the C.I.D. are purely illogical, and spring from an inherent desire to sit on the fence. Put yourself one side or the other of it and you never know the truth about anything. Take the case of murder now: When a murderer is brought to justice he has to pretend he did the bloody deed because he was inflamed with jealousy or because the victim had a £10 note on him, the real reason being that he didn't like his face or that his conversation was intolerably boring. But he can't say so at his trial—there are conventions to be observed. I am perfectly serious; I have never felt any desire to murder for money, but often I have been on the verge of shooting someone out of sheer irritation. If I had, I should of course have pretended that he had run off with my wife. *Noblesse oblige*—one must have some consideration for the corpse."

Paul's desire for a logical argument vanished in laughter led by Adelaide, and dinner being finished they moved over to the divan for coffee.

"Make yourselves comfortable, you two, and I'll bring you your cups over there. Mr. Ashby, will you have some of my Spanish brandy? It's really rather nice, and you'll need a fortifier before Hernandez's party."

"I'd love some," said Paul, and came towards her. "Let me—"

She was pouring brandy into beautifully shaped goblets, when Benvenuto's voice came from the divan.

"Talking of Hernandez's party—I've a favour to ask you, my dear."

She paused and looked at him, glass in hand.

"You can help me immensely in—something I'm trying to puzzle out—if you'd, well, repel his advances rather less than usual this evening. Let him drink—and let him talk. You were in London last Tuesday—" He stepped forward and bent to pick up the scattered fragments of the glass which had slipped from her hand.

"Bad luck—but at least it wasn't full. Sit here and I'll get you another."

He went across to a cupboard in the corner, and when he came back Adelaide was lying among the cushions smoking a cigarette, Paul in a chair opposite her. Benvenuto gave her a drink, and taking one himself sat down beside her. He went on.

"I want you, if you will, to pull his leg gently, and ask him what he meant by cutting you dead in London last Tuesday."

Adelaide gave him a startled look.

"But he wasn't—I didn't see him—"

Benvenuto looked at her reproachfully. "Don't you call it to mind—just outside the Piccadilly Hotel?"

She laughed, a little shakily.

"Very well, O man of mystery—but can't we make it the Ritz?"

"The Ritz be it. Don't press the point—just note what his reactions are. Furthermore, I want you to be animated by an intense desire to go up in an aëroplane, and tell him so—and try to gather if possible whether he can pilot a machine himself. I feel rather a pig asking you to do this, because I know how you feel about the fellow, but—well, we've worked together before, haven't we? And this time you may be helping someone we're both very fond of—I mean Adrian."

Adelaide sat up with a little cry and clutched his arm.

"Ben—Ben, what do you mean? He's not—in danger?"

Benvenuto looked at her gravely.

"I'm sorry to say he is," he answered, "and I'm doing all I can to get him out of it. He is suspected of the murder of Luela, and by an abominable bit of bad luck things look pretty black against him. I didn't want to tell you about it because I knew how it would worry you, but now every scrap of information I can get hold of will help, and you can help me to-night by doing this."

She was staring straight in front of her, and Paul was horrified to see tears running down her pale face. Benvenuto patted her hand.

"My dear," he said gently, "of course I'm absolutely sure he's innocent and it's only a question of time and hard work before we can prove it. It may not be so difficult after all, because, as you've no doubt read in the papers, some woman went to see Luela on the afternoon of her death, and if she comes forward her evidence will probably clear up the whole matter, so don't worry."

She snatched her hand away from him, and suddenly bursting into a fit of sobbing, she ran out of the room.

Benvenuto got up quickly and went across to the window. Paul sat still and silent in his chair, fear and doubt and misery closing in on him. He thought of Adelaide in the train, the newspaper dropping from her hands, fear in her white face as she left him; Adelaide in the café, fear again in her face when she saw him and her hurried, too-quick explanations; Adelaide gone so suddenly after De Najera's accusation of Adrian; Adelaide here to-night. With a feeling of terror himself, he looked quickly at Benvenuto to see him strolling back from the window, and braced himself to conceal the suspicions that came half formed into his mind. Benvenuto sat down and poured out some drinks, handing one to Paul. He looked worried and unhappy.

"Poor kid," he said, "it's unlike her to let herself go, but she's as fond of Adrian as I am. Blasted fool I am to go frightening her like that. Better let her alone for a bit. Cigarette?"

Paul took one, and they talked desultorily for a time, Paul trying to appear intelligent with questions beating in his brain. What was she hiding?—what was there that she couldn't tell them?

"Ben, will I do?"

He turned with a start to see Adelaide pirouetting in the doorway, vivid as some tropical bird, in a scarlet frock, her feet in scarlet shoes showing below her long full skirts, and a scarlet flower in her hair. Though she was still pale, she had painted her lips and they were parted in a smile. His heart thumped as he looked at her. She flew across the room and caught Benvenuto's hand.

"Darling, forgive me for being an idiot. I've changed my manners with my frock and now behold! The complete vamp, at your service."

She swept them a curtsey.

CHAPTER X
THE PARTY

ADELAIDE SANG softly under her breath as she swung in his arms. She was very gay, dancing lightly, with her head thrown back, and Paul, in a confusion of fears and strange happiness, held her tightly and tried to forget the tune would soon be over. They paused for a moment to avoid contact with a gleaming sunburnt arm.

Why had she cried?—why did he seem to see an expression of desperate misery in her small face as she laughed up at him now? For a moment their eyes met and held and he tried dumbly to ask her confidence and reassure her. Her smile faded, she half shook her head, and then the floor cleared and they went on. They danced in silence until the music ended and then she laughed again.

"Two more exhibition dancers lost to the world," she said. "Wasn't that good? I shall insist on somebody giving a party every night you're here. No men can really dance except Englishmen, you know. You notice to-night. The Germans are too precise, the French take too short steps, Argentines crouch over one like panthers, Americans wear their shoulders too high. Letts and Finns I've never experienced. Come and join Ben among the trophies of the chase—he's looking pretty good."

The object of her last remark was seated on a pile of purple silk cushions that were heaped over a tiger skin. A bottle under one arm and a glass in his hand, he wore a beatific smile and was dividing his attention between the stuffed head of the tiger and a scantily clad little flapper who was lying beside him, gazing at him adoringly, holding his hand and talking in swift bursts of French. She greeted Adelaide with a bright smile and made a place for her, then, catching sight of Paul, she pulled him down beside her and climbed on to his knee.

"Engleesh boy," she remarked, "nice."

Putting her arms round his neck, she commenced to sing in a curious husky voice:

> *"'E's got bright blue eyes,*
> *I nevaire caire for bright blue eyes,*
> *But 'e's got bright blue eyes,*
> *Et maintenant j'adore ça."*

She peeped round at Benvenuto for applause.

"Bravo, Tina!" he said, while Adelaide shook with laughter, looking at Paul. Profoundly embarrassed, he groped for his cigarette case, and furnishing his newly found friend with a cigarette tried to achieve an air of complete nonchalance. Hurriedly casting round in his mind for a suitable conversational opening, he was more than relieved when Benvenuto despatched the amorous Tina for some glasses. He looked at Paul gravely.

"You've been received into St. Antoine society," he said. "You must cultivate Tina."

"Her methods are rather—er—direct, aren't they?" Paul said.

"Well—possibly. But she's a cheerful little piece and part of the tradition of this place. Curse her—she's forgotten about those glasses. I'll go and hunt some up."

A circle had formed round Tina, in the middle of which she was dancing, her diminutive body shaken by an ecstatic Charleston, entirely abandoned to the feverish rhythm that was being stroked and torn from a ukulele by an American boy. He sang as he played:

> *"Oh, sister, shake that thing . . ."*

His fingers thrumming and flying, his fair hair tumbled over his sunburnt forehead, his foot beating the ground, and his body jerking in time to the Negro syncopation that he struck from his instrument, he played faster and faster, his eyes fixed on Tina's writhing body:

> *"Oh, sister, shake that thing . . ."*

Hands and feet marking time all around her, she had forgotten her audience, and with her dark curls flying, her thin brown arms and legs twisting and stamping to the music, her hips swaying under the thin silk of her dress, she looked like a small negress from a Harlem cabaret. Some forgotten strain of dark blood was alive in her. Paul counted a dozen nationalities amongst the people round her, all intent on her, all swaying a little in rhythm to the curious half-savage dance. One immobile figure seated on a cushion, his arms folded in a tense stillness, was that of a Japanese painter. His Oriental face expressing neither pleasure nor interest, he kept his eyes fixed on her, and when at last she flung herself exhausted onto a divan amidst shouts of applause Paul saw him rise with startling suddenness and cross over to her.

Someone put a record on the gramophone, and in a moment the floor was crowded. Benvenuto reappeared with bottles and glasses and Paul, who was longing to dance again with Adelaide, waited for a drink before asking her. The noise of ice clinking as Benvenuto poured out brandies and sodas was good in the hot room, and he passed Adelaide a drink. The next moment De Najera was bending over asking her to dance, and they moved off together. Paul, looking after them blackly, was forced to admit he was a perfect dancer as he steered her easily over the crowded floor. His head bent, he was talking to her earnestly, and Paul wondered what he was saying.

"Good Lord, look at that," Benvenuto's voice interrupted his thoughts; and following the direction of his glance he saw a curious couple pass them: the man slightly bald on top with pince-nez perched on his nose and wearing an ill-fitting pair of plus-fours, the girl Tina giggling delightedly up at him as he held her awkwardly and looked down at her with ill-concealed nervousness.

Paul chuckled as he looked at them.

"By all that's holy—it's Leech," murmured Benvenuto. "He'll need a detachment from the Yard complete with truncheons to protect him if Tina's got designs on his virtue. Why in God's name did he come here?"

"I suppose he took advantage of De Najera's general invitation and decided to combine pleasure with business—though I don't detect signs of very reckless abandon yet awhile. It must be the polka he's dancing. Can I have another drink?"

"Pardon, *mon vieux*. And when you've finished it—unless you feel like receiving the advances of the lady over there—perhaps you'd come on an expedition with me. I want to go up to Luela's room and explore. Not the height of good manners perhaps—but I feel all's fair just now."

Hastily averting his eyes from a languorous-looking lady in a Spanish shawl, Paul got up and put down his empty glass. He felt curiously unlike devoting himself to practical things. The brandy was good—it was perhaps his sixth—the summer night was hot, and scented breezes blowing in at the open windows made him long for a stroll. Later he would take Adelaide out there. Meanwhile the violins wailed and the saxophone spilled its plaintive notes through the room. In the dim light of shaded lamps couples locked in each other's arms swayed to the rhythm. Through the crowd he caught a glimpse of Adelaide's scarlet frock and her face lifted, smiling, to De Najera. Paul turned quickly and followed Benvenuto to the door.

He found the latter mopping his brow and leaning against a gilt cupid in a highly ornate marble-tiled hall. Palms and flowering shrubs filled a well in the centre round which the staircase rose to the floor above. Stucco ornaments and painted decorations covered every conceivable space in an orgy of depraved Baroque. Paul shuddered slightly as he looked about him.

"This is considered extremely chic in the neighbourhood, let me tell you," remarked Benvenuto. "People have been known to come from miles round to catch a glimpse of it. I have a distinct weakness for it myself—don't you admire the allegorical painting of Hope following Appetite? Come on, there's some more up the staircase."

Past overgrown ladies wallowing in a confusion of fruits and ruined towers against a blue sky, they mounted to the corridor above.

"If questioned, ask for the bathroom," said Benvenuto, but they met no one, and on coming to some large double doors he went in followed by Paul. The room was in darkness, but after a moment's pause Benvenuto found the switch, the light revealing a large bedroom of a luxuriant and rather exotic character, with other doors leading out of it.

"Luela's suite," Benvenuto explained. "This room and her boudoir look over the sea, and there is the bathroom. I'll open the shutters, and if anyone comes in I'll explain that I was showing you the view, which is colossal." He unshuttered a long window and Paul went out onto the balcony to find a marvellous moonlit panorama and a sheer drop to the sea below his feet. On his left the lights of distant coast towns twinkled. Les Palmiers was built on a rock and had a staircase carved out of the cliff down to a small natural harbour below, Benvenuto explained. They came in and went through to the boudoir. Both rooms seemed to have been untouched since they were last occupied, a heavy scent was in the air and photographs littered the tables. Benvenuto looked through the photographs with care until he came to one of a man, obviously taken a good many years before. Uttering a slight exclamation, he took it to the light and looked at it in a puzzled way, afterwards putting it in his pocket. Paul watched him curiously.

"I feel rather like a ghoul," he said, "but that reminds me of someone and I can't think of whom."

Frowning, he walked about the room and then went back to the bedroom, where Paul followed him and sat on the bed. Watching lazily, he thought Benvenuto looked rather like a well-bred pointer as he moved swiftly about examining furniture, cupboards, and knick-knacks. He finally disappeared into the bathroom and was absent so long that Paul thought he must be trying to reconstruct the crime in that other suite. Getting impatient, he followed him in, and was somewhat irritated to find him sitting on a cork-covered bathstool gazing earnestly at a pile of powder boxes.

Benvenuto looked up at him queerly.

"Half a dozen brand new boxes of Loty's bath powder— enough to flour a regiment—only they're all empty."

Only mildly interested, Paul looked them over.

"Notice anything peculiar about them? No? Well, look at the labels—the sticky ones which they use to seal the top to the bottom. They've all been carefully steamed open—not torn in half as one would expect." He rubbed his chin, and then jumping to his feet he took Paul's arm and propelled him out of the room.

"On with the dance—let joy be unconfined," he said, and closing the shutters and switching off the lights they went into the corridor and down the stairs. There was still no one about, all the life of the house being confined, apparently, to the big salon which they re-entered and there helped themselves to drinks. A haze of cigarette smoke filled the room; for a moment the party was in repose as if in the interval between two acts of a pantomime.

A sense of unreality took possession of Paul; he felt that at any moment something magical might happen, and by association of ideas looked about for Adelaide. She was lying on some cushions with Hernandez and talking lazily to him, his arm round her shoulders. Suddenly the rich twang of a guitar filled the room. A Spaniard dressed in blue jeans with one foot on a gilded chair began to sing an Andalusian love song, fierce and earthy. The jazz beginning of the party was over, and the Spaniard had timed his song for the altered mood of the guests, who were becoming quarrelsome or amorous or merely sentimental, according to their natures. As for Paul, he felt unnaturally heroic, and found himself, rather to his surprise, wanting both to sing and to hit someone. Controlling these unusual emotions, he went and sat on the floor by himself, and watched a couple dancing slowly a kind of elemental tango. He felt very much out of it all and became extremely, but exquisitely, sad: a mood which changed suddenly to morbid softening of the heart as he received an unexpected wink from Adelaide.

The song went on, and suddenly through it he caught the sound of sobbing behind him. Turning round, he saw Tina lying on a divan crying as though her heart would break, and kneeling beside her the bald and pince-nezed Leech, who was trying valiantly to mop her tears up with a large pocket handkerchief, a worried look on his face. A few feet away sat the Japanese, expressionless as ever, staring at them. Tina continued to sob with unabated violence and Paul began to feel extremely concerned about her. Not liking to intrude himself, he went off in search of Benvenuto, whom he found talking to a group in a corner. He attracted his attention and Benvenuto rose and came towards him quickly.

"What's up?" he asked.

"Well, it's about Tina—I'm afraid she's got into trouble of some sort. She's over there with Leech, crying bitterly. Oughtn't we to do something? What d'you suppose is the matter?"

Benvenuto caught sight of her and grinned.

"Alcoholic remorse," he said briefly, and walked across to her.

As they reached the divan Leech looked angrily at the Japanese, whose immobile stare seemed to infuriate him.

"What the devil do you want?" he demanded.

A bland smile spread over the Oriental's face.

"I want to dance like a flea," he replied.

Uttering an exclamation of rage, Leech turned his attention to Tina, when Benvenuto, who had been an amused spectator, intervened.

"Tina, my little one, you've been at the gin again," he said in French. "Silly child, you're washing your make-up all over your face—just look at it."

Taking a mirror from her handbag he held it in front of her, and checking a sob she directed a blurred gaze towards it. A look of concern came through her tears and the next moment she was busy with a puff and a lipstick. Having completed the picture, her mood changed instantly to one of extreme gaiety, and presently she was dancing with the American boy. Benvenuto got up and looked at his watch.

"I don't know about you, Ashby, but I'm going to push off," he said. "The night is yet young—it's just one o'clock—so if you want to stay here and shake a leg, do, and come along to my rooms later for a drink."

Paul looked uncertainly across at Adelaide. She seemed very much occupied with De Najera.

"What about Miss Moon?" he said.

"I don't expect she'll come away yet. I'll go and say good-bye to our host and see."

Together they did so, and to Paul's intense disappointment he heard her say to Benvenuto:

"No—I've promised to dance the next one with Hernandez. I'll go back to town with some of the others. Yes—I'd love to come along for some coffee. I'll be with you in an hour—two o'clock."

"Good-bye," they said.

CHAPTER XI
THE DARK HOUSE

A LOG BROKE in two and tumbled over the hearth, sending a shower of burning fragments into the room. With a muttered curse Benvenuto stooped forward to brush them back, and built up the fire with a fresh supply of fuel. It blazed high, lighting the room with its dancing flames, picking out the facets of polished wood, recreating itself in the surface of mirrors and china. The coffee pot on the hearth gleamed cheerfully, the logs crackled, but the two men sat in uneasy silence. Paul pulled out his watch for the twentieth time. Three-thirty—and still no sign of Adelaide. Suddenly he jumped to his feet.

"I'm going up there," he said, his voice sounding queer and loud after the silence.

Benvenuto stood up more slowly.

"You're perfectly right," he said. "God knows I feel every kind of a swine for leaving her with him—a chap who is to the best of my belief a murderer. But it never occurred to me there'd be any danger in it. But it's all *right*, you know—why, there were thirty or forty people we know there. We shall find the ball still rolling and Adelaide dancing without a thought for her miserable confederates—you'll see."

But his assurance sounded a bit thin, and Paul looked at him grimly. Suddenly he realized that Benvenuto's tone had somehow conveyed an apology to him—Paul—and something seemed to light up inside him. He crammed on his béret and marched out, shoulders well back. If that fellow had been up to any tricks he'd—The rest of his resolve became blurred but none the less determined.

The silence of St. Antoine by night was suddenly broken by the sound of singing, and Benvenuto, hearing it, turned quickly down a side street that led to the port. They emerged to find a band of revellers straggling along arm in arm past the shuttered cafés, singing a little unevenly: *"Auprès de ma blonde.*" The party halted in front of a café and the singing died down.

> *"Arise, O woman, and let me in,*
> *Whisky—Johnny—"*

came the voice of the American boy, and then Benvenuto tapped him on the shoulder.

"Seen anything of Adelaide?" he asked.

The American boy clapped his finger to his nose and looked at him sharply.

"Sh!" he said, and began to get on with his song. Benvenuto shook him roughly, and he paused with his mouth open. Recovering from his surprise and adjusting his balance, he commenced to peel off his coat.

"You guys get ready to witness the middleweight championship of Europe—Big Ben Brown versus the Colorado Chicken—purse 100 francs and may the best man win, as Carnera said to Tunney." He grasped Benvenuto's hand, looked at him fondly, and attempted to kiss him. The latter moaned with rage, and sent the boy sprawling into the arms of his companions.

The road up to Les Palmiers was dark, for the moon was down and the town lighting had been cut off. Benvenuto set off quickly, and Paul was thankful he knew the road. The squat shapes of olive trees loomed up as they passed, and the only sound was the occasional clanking chain of some goat disturbed by their footsteps. A few minutes' walk brought them to the château which they found in complete darkness, grim and sepulchral-looking with its mass of white stucco. Benvenuto pushed at the front door which gave to his touch, and in a moment they were in the heavy flower-scented atmosphere of the hall.

"Damn the lights—they won't function," said Benvenuto, fumbling with the switches. "Got a match, Ashby?" Paul struck a light and they made for the door of the salon. It was dark inside except for the first pale glimmer of dawn that showed through the windows. They were open and the early-morning wind blew the curtains towards Paul. He shivered and the match went out, and then Benvenuto said:

"Come on, I'm going up to De Najera's rooms. There's nothing here."

Paul struck another match and was turning to follow him when his eye caught something sticking out from below the curtains of an alcove close beside him. It was a hand, a very small hand, lying palm uppermost on the carpet. Was it the light of the match—or had it a horrible deathly pallor? Perfectly still, Paul stood staring at it until the match burnt his fingers. Then he felt himself trembling violently so that he could not speak. At last: "Brown—come here—come here—" he said, and fumbled for his match box. His fingers shook so that it seemed to him an eternity before he struck a light. Benvenuto was beside him.

"What the devil—" he began, and caught sight of it, lying there. "God," he whispered, and his hand shot out to the curtain, dragging it back.

The next moment Paul heard himself giggling weakly, while Benvenuto, uttering an oath that was strange to him, directed a kick at the prostrate form of the Japanese. He, beyond stirring a little and folding his arms across his breast, gave no sign that his slumbers were disturbed and continued to wear an expressionless smile on his immobile face.

"Eclipsé," muttered Benvenuto, and then with nervous fury: "Why the devil does he want to go leaving his hands about the place?"

Somewhat shaken, they got out of the room and felt their way up the staircase. "Follow me," whispered Benvenuto, "and don't make a noise. I'm going into De Najera's rooms, which are up on the next floor. When we get in, if there's no light and no sound, strike a match."

They climbed another flight, and then Benvenuto silently opened a door at the top and they slipped inside, shutting it behind them. Their backs against the door, they stood in tense silence staring into the inky blackness, till Paul struck a match. The room was empty, the bed unslept in.

"Stay where you are—I'll open the shutters and let in some light," murmured Benvenuto in his ear, and Paul heard him creep across the room. The sound of a latch slipping, a creak, and things became faintly visible in the cold glimmer of early dawn.

Benvenuto gave a muffled exclamation as he leant out of the window.

"Come and look at this," he whispered, and Paul joined him. A balcony over the sea ran along past the window, and where it ended an extraordinary sight met their eyes; for perched on the top of the white stone balustrade three or four feet up were a thin pair of legs protruding from plus-fours, standing perilously on tiptoe. The head and upper part of the figure were hidden by a flying buttress round which the man's arm was clinging for support, but it was unmistakably Leech. He was watching something or other with interest, and they could hear faintly the murmur of voices from above him. Paul and Benvenuto slid out into the balcony and went towards him. Hearing a sound behind him, his head appeared round the buttress, and recognizing the two men he climbed gingerly down.

"Looking for cat burglars?" whispered Benvenuto.

The little detective looked somewhat sheepish.

"The fact is," he answered, "I was keeping an eye on Miss Moon. I've been trying to get a word with her all the evening, and . . ."

Without waiting to hear the rest of his sentence, the two men clambered up onto the balustrade, and were able to see through some stone tracery the flat roof garden above.

Although the early light had brightened, Paul at first could see nothing but a large telescope mounted on a tripod which occupied the centre of the flat roof; but a voice, the silky voice of De Najera, was evident enough. He was talking earnestly to someone in the farther corner, someone who had backed against the balustrade and whose silhouette against the deep mauve sky was Adelaide's.

"Let me go now, Hernandez. Let me go, you hurt me. I must go—I've got to meet Benvenuto."

"May he be damned in hell." Then, less fiercely, "Come with me, my turtle dove, my little one. See, I only kiss your hand. Listen, I am rich, very rich now that Luela is dead. In Argentina I have a palace by the sea where we shall live, in country more beautiful than you have ever seen. My house is in a garden where fountains play and flowers bloom all the year, and birds sing among the peach groves."

Paul could see him now, bending forward over her, talking with all the rich inflections of his voice, persuasively and passionately. He bent farther forward still over her shrinking figure; she turned her head from side to side like a bird looking for a way of escape.

"*Madre de Dios*, you are beautiful," he murmured, and caught her in his arms.

Adelaide's shriek and Paul's climb onto the balcony coincided. For a sickening moment he saw far below him the black sea, then pulled himself over the parapet and he and his enemy were facing one another.

The pale light on De Najera's face showed it distorted with rage, and as he saw Paul's threatening attitude he drew a knife from his belt and walked lightly forward, his thumb on the blade. The moment for Paul was critical. He knew that if his first blow failed he was in for it. De Najera crouched. Both men leapt at the same moment—the Argentine with an upward sweep of the knife was a fraction late. Paul's left hand, with all the inhibitions of his evening behind it, caught his opponent very neatly on the jaw, and man and knife lifted for a second, then crashed backwards onto the floor.

Paul bent down to make sure he was unconscious, picked up the knife, and glowing all over started to rush back to Adelaide. Then he stopped—for she was in Benvenuto's arms, while he patted her shoulder and murmured words of encouragement. Paul stood quite still and went very cold.

The next moment a sound beside him made him look down, to see the face of Leech, pink with exertion, his pince-nez askew on his nose, emerging through a trap door in the floor.

"Ah!" he said. "Excuse me intruding, but I've been wanting to get a word with Miss Moon all the evening, and this seems quite an opportunity."

"Just so, Leech," returned Benvenuto, "cozy little spot for a chat. But supposing we defer it till we get back to my rooms."

By now Adelaide had pulled herself together and was wrapping her shawl round her. Benvenuto walked over to the unconscious man.

"He'll wake up with a headache, that's all," he said. He bent down and grasped the limp hand.

"Thanks so much for a delightful evening," he murmured politely. Then straightening himself, *"Allons y.* Sheath your sword, Ashby, and come along."

Paul looked down at the knife in his hand and blushed, feeling suddenly rather a fool. He threw it into the sea and followed the others down the staircase and through the dark house.

CHAPTER XII
A WORD WITH MISS MOON

ALMOST IN SILENCE they walked back to the town. In the east red streaks were appearing in the sky, which was a pallid translucent green by contrast, and though Leech remarked that it was the best part of the day and it was a pity you didn't see the sun rise more often, no one seemed disposed to enlarge upon the subject.

Back in the studio the fire still burned, and they were grateful for it and for the hot coffee which Benvenuto soon produced. Seated round the fire they felt tired, nervous, and ill at ease. Adelaide, very pale in her scarlet frock, avoided Paul's eye, and he on his part was suffering from a reaction after the events of the night. Benvenuto puffed rapidly at his pipe and stared into his coffee cup. Leech was the only person who appeared to be entirely at ease, and enjoying himself rather than not. He stirred his coffee vigorously and took a large gulp, then sitting back with his feet to the blaze he turned to Adelaide.

"As I was saying, Miss Moon, I've been wanting to get a word with you all the evening," he said. He looked at the other two.

"Mr. Brown is an old friend of mine. Ahem—I take it I can speak quite frank in front of the other young gentleman?"

"By all means—certainly," said Adelaide and Benvenuto together, and Paul, who had made a movement towards departure, sank back in his chair.

The detective rubbed his hands together.

"Well, since we're all friends present, I'm going to ask you, Miss Moon, to give me some help about a little matter I'm engaged in. Now, I want you to tell me in your own words—take your own time, mind—the events which took place on the afternoon of last Tuesday the 24th when you were present in the suite of the late Signora da Costa at Bishop's Hotel, London."

Paul felt as though his inside had turned completely over. Looking at Adelaide, he saw her paler than ever, but perfectly calm. She was about to speak when Benvenuto addressed Leech.

"On what grounds do you state—" he began, when she interrupted him.

"It's all right, Ben," she said. "I was there, and I've been a fool not to tell you about it, but I was afraid—" She looked at Leech.

"That's right, Miss Moon," he said. *"We* know you were there, so there's no use in wasting time, is there?" He produced a notebook and pencil from his pocket and cocked his head at her expectantly.

"I went there because Signora da Costa wished to buy one of my paintings from the Leinster Galleries," Adelaide began quietly. "The show ended before she decided which one she wanted, and she wrote me a note asking me to call and see her if I came to London."

Inspector Leech was scribbling in his book. He paused.

"Can you let me see that letter?" She looked at him, startled.

"I don't know—I may have it somewhere—I—"

"Quite so. I should like to see it if possible. Purely a matter of routine, Miss Moon. Go on, please."

"I rang her up at Bishop's Hotel about half-past four on Tuesday afternoon and arranged to go round and see her at half-past five. She explained her maid was out, and asked me to come up, telling me the number of her room. When I got there she was having a bath, and I talked to her through her bathroom door."

"How did you enter her room?"

"How—? Oh, the key was in the door, and she called out to me to come in."

"I see. Did you actually see her before you left?"

"Oh, yes—she came out when she'd finished her bath."

"Can you remember how she was dressed?"

"In a silk wrap—a purple one. She excused herself, saying she was tired and was going to lie down."

"Did she say why she was tired—whether, for instance, she had had a tiring day, or what she had been doing?"

"No. She told me nothing, nothing at all."

"You are sure?"

Adelaide stiffened. "Quite sure."

"Just so, Miss Moon, just so. Did she mention she was expecting a guest?"

"I have just told you—she said she was going to lie down."

"No mention at all was made of anyone coming to see her later in the day?"

"None—none at all."

He looked at her.

"I see. And what did you two ladies talk about?"

"My paintings. She arranged to buy one, and I was to send it to her, and then I left."

"What time was that?"

"Five minutes to six."

"Excuse me—how do you happen to remember the time? This is important."

"I looked at my watch so as to get away before—while there was still time to go back to my hotel and get some food before leaving for Paris. I was staying at Green's."

"Did you see anyone when you left her room—in the corridor, for instance?"

"No—not that I remember. I think there was a chambermaid coming out of one of the rooms."

"But no one you knew by sight?"

"Certainly not. I should remember that"

"Now, about the telephone call that came through while you were in the room. Please tell me all you can remember about that."

"But there was no telephone call."

"You are sure?"

"Quite sure."

"Be careful, Miss Moon. The telephone operator says she put a call through between five forty-five and six when, by your own showing, you would have been in the room."

"It must have been later, when I had gone. There was no call!"

Her voice sounded strained under the continued questioning, and she looked deadly tired.

The inspector nodded. He made a few notes and closed his book.

"I am very much obliged to you, Miss Moon—very much obliged, I'm sure. I hope I shall not have to trouble you again, but I must ask you to let me know your movements should you think of leaving St. Antoine. Purely a matter of routine, Miss Moon, but until the inquiry is over I must ask you to keep in touch with me."

She looked at him quickly.

"I am not going away," she said.

"Well, perhaps that is wisest." He got up. "And now, Mr. Brown, allow me to thank you for some very pleasant refreshment, and very welcome, I'm sure." He smiled genially round at them and rubbed his hands.

"Well, my little white sheets are calling me, so allow me to wish you all a very good night—or morning, should I say? Ha, ha!" He shook hands all round and Benvenuto took him downstairs.

"Can I get you some more coffee? You must be dead beat," said Paul. Adelaide started to laugh hysterically.

"His little white sheets . . ." Her voice trailed off into something very like a sob. She smothered it and looked up at him.

"Sorry," she said. "It's been so awful all night." She put her hand out to him impulsively.

"I don't know how to thank you—it seemed like a miracle when you came. I don't know what I'd have done—"

"Thank God _he's_ gone," said Benvenuto, walking in. "Hullo—all silent and all damned? How about some more coffee—and your excellent dinner, my dear, is now so much a thing of the past that there'll be no offence offered if I suggest kippers."

"Ben, you are a genius sometimes. Have you been extracting them from the Mediterranean?"

"Got them in Cannes, and I've waited in modest pride all the evening for the right moment to produce them. Ashby probably doesn't realize the exile's craving for them, being as he is fresh from an English breakfast table. Anyone want to come and smell them cooking?"

They repaired to the kitchen, where Adelaide, an apron over her frock, fanned the charcoal to a glow and insisted on grilling the kippers herself. Paul ground the coffee while Benvenuto laid the studio table, and they were soon seated at an excellent meal, telling Adelaide their adventures of the evening. Somewhat to Paul's surprise, Benvenuto made no reference to her revelations to Leech, nor did he ask her what she had been able to get out of De Najera. At last with an effort she spoke herself.

"Ben, couldn't you reproach me a bit?" she said. "I should feel less of a criminal if you did. I have been such a fool, and I felt so bad about not telling you I was in Luela's room. But you see, I thought the Missing Woman—if she remained a mystery to everyone—would be a point in Adrian's favour. I still don't know how Leech found out I was she. You must both think I was being a frightful coward."

"On the contrary."

"I think it must have taken a tremendous amount of pluck not to tell the truth before," said Paul admiringly.

Benvenuto looked at him for a minute. Then: "Ah, young man," he said portentously, "what *is* Truth?" He turned to Adelaide, leaving Paul puzzled. "Don't you think it's about time, my dear," he said gently, "that you told *me* the truth?"

She sat very still, staring at him. At last, "Ben, what do you mean? You heard me tell Leech what happened. There's— nothing else."

"What I mean, Adelaide, is this. I believe Adrian is innocent, and I mean to prove it. But I can't do it if things are kept hidden from me. Something happened when you were in Luela's room that you think looks black for Adrian, and with a great deal of courage and tenacity you're hiding it. You can fool Leech—but you can't fool me. And it is probably only a question of time before Leech, or somebody else, finds out what it is. If it is something that looks as though it implicates Adrian, isn't it better to tell *me*, when I think he's innocent, what it is, and give me an opportunity of clearing him, than to leave it to chance that Scotland Yard won't find out?"

She was swaying in her chair. "Don't, Ben—don't go on. It's no good—nothing's any good. . . ."

There was a pause. Benvenuto, with his arms folded on the table, stared at the girl and she stared back at him with vacant eyes. Suddenly he leapt to his feet, sending his chair spinning, and began pacing up and down the studio. Then he turned and faced her. He brought down his fist on the table with a crash that made the plates jump.

"Adelaide," he said, "you're a damned young fool. You're a criminal fool. I know you're tired, I know you're frightened, but I tell you this—if you don't tell me the truth now, at this moment, it may be too late. Answer me, am I Adrian's friend or not?"

"Yes."

"Do you trust me?"

"Yes, absolutely, but—"

"Do you think I or Ashby would give Adrian away even if he *had* done it?"

"No—but—Oh, Ben, you are bullying me, and I am so tired."

"I'm bullying you, and I'm bullying you for the sake of Adrian, and I'm going to keep on bullying you."

"Oh, Ben, don't make me say it."

"Say *what?* Say *what?* Shall I tell you? Or will you tell me?"

"Ben, you know?"

"Yes."

Adelaide dropped her head on her arms and sobbed. Through her tears Paul heard her say brokenly, "Adrian killed her. Oh, Ben, what can we do?—how can we save him?"

"Drink this brandy. That's it. Now take a deep breath and tell me about it calmly."

She sat up gallantly and wiped her eyes. Benvenuto gave her a cigarette, and there was silence for a moment while she lit it; then, in a voice still shaken by tears, she began.

"It started just as I told Leech—I talked to Luela through her bathroom door, and then while she was still in her bath the telephone rang. She called out and asked me to answer it, and then a man's voice asked for her. I said she was engaged and could I take a message—and he said would I ask her if she could see Adrian Kent at six o'clock. When I told her, she sounded very excited and said yes, she could."

"Was it Adrian speaking?"

"No, it was someone speaking for him. A minute after I'd rung off she came running in in her dressing gown, and went to her dressing table. We fixed up about the painting, and then I could see she was anxious to get rid of me—and I was anxious to go, for I didn't want to meet him, *there*. I said good-bye to her, and she could hardly turn from her mirror—and when I left her she was putting on her jewels for him. The next thing I knew was when Paul lent me a paper in the train."

Adelaide's voice broke, and there was silence in the studio. Then Benvenuto got up and went out of the room. When he came back he had a heavy overcoat on his arm, which he wrapped Adelaide in, very carefully.

"Listen," he said, "you're to go home and you're to go to bed and you're not to think about anything any more until you've had a good sleep. D'you see? And nothing is your responsibility any more—it's mine, and you've got to trust me.

"Here, Paul, take her home."

CHAPTER XIII
"THE BEAUTIFUL CITY WITH DIRTY FEET"

TAP-TAP-TAP! So they'd come for him. They'd found him after all, and now they'd come to take him away, him, Paul Ashby, and hang him by the neck till he was dead for the murder of Luela da Costa. *Tap-tap-tap!* By God! they shouldn't catch him—he'd see them in hell first. There was still time—he'd run for it. But the room had no window—no door except that one which trembled with the insistent knocking. If it was that damned little Leech he'd trip him up and run for it. But of course it wouldn't be—they'd never send Leech by himself. They'd sent him to torture Adelaide, though. *Tap-tap-tap!* God! he hadn't much longer—they'd break the door down.

Adelaide—would she be sorry when she heard?—would she cry, as she had for Adrian? *Tap-tap-TAP-TAP!* Could nothing save him? They were opening it . . . Oh, God! they'd got him!

He struggled, and woke to find Benvenuto shaking him by the arm.

"You lazy devil, get up. I've been banging on your door for the last ten minutes. Thought I'd better come in and see if you'd passed away in your sleep. Buck up and dress—we're going to Marseille in the car."

"Marseille?" said Paul half awake. "What the devil for?"

"I want to find our friend the Slosher. Explain later. How soon can you be ready? Adelaide is having coffee with me down at the café—join us as soon as you can."

"Ten minutes," said Paul, springing out of bed, and the door banged behind Benvenuto.

He turned on the bath, and splashing himself with cold water tried to get his thoughts into shape. Why on earth was Benvenuto interested in the Slosher now—when Adelaide had made plain Adrian's guilt? Or was that all a dream, too? He shook himself, and started to scrub vigorously. Of course it wasn't—he could remember the whole thing, and taking her home afterwards, she leaning on his arm. Was Benvenuto trying to get hold of something to put the authorities off the scent while he got Adrian away into safety? If that was it, he'd help, too. Adrian, poor devil—Paul was able to feel nothing but sympathy for this man he'd never met. Tough luck on his father; shock would probably kill the old chap. So thinking, Paul shaved and dressed as quickly as possible, and ran down to join the others.

He saw them drinking coffee on the quay, and Adelaide waved as he came towards them. He was sorry when he saw she had no hat; she couldn't be coming. Dressed in one of her usual white linen frocks, she looked very fresh and trim, her hair waving back from her face.

Her smile was almost as gay as usual when she greeted him.

"Forgive all this handshaking," she said. *"Touche la main* is the great national sport of France. We shake hands when we meet a friend, regardless of the fact that we'd met round the corner five minutes before. He sits down at our table, finds he has no cigarettes, rises to go and buy some, shakes hands all round, is absent two minutes, and the ceremony is repeated on his return. I shook hands thirty-five times in one morning with a woman who was doing her marketing at the same shops that I was, and she'd have been deeply offended if I hadn't. Do try to remember!"

"I will," said Paul fervently. "Useful little tip that. Do you mind if we practise it? I find I'm out of cigarettes."

"Bon voyage," they said, and he left them, his brain rather in a whirl, to find the nearest tobacconist's. How were they managing to be so cheerful when things had taken on such a sinister appearance? "Upon my word, I believe I'm more concerned for Adrian than they are," thought Paul, walking back from the shop; and then had an idea so startling that he stopped dead. Supposing *someone else* had used Adrian Kent's name on the telephone in order to throw suspicion on him? This was interesting. He lit a cigarette and stared out to sea. But who could have done it? Adelaide would have recognized De Najera's voice with its rich Southern drawl, and yet who

else was there? . . . Ah, he had it—the Slosher, his companion of the train. He hurried back to the café full of his idea to put it to Benvenuto, and somehow his enthusiasm evaporated when he found them calmly discussing painting.

Sitting down to his coffee, he determined to test his theory. "You know that chap you spoke to on the phone, who made an appointment for Kent," he said to Adelaide. "D'you remember if he had an extraordinary uneducated voice?"

"No, he hadn't in the least," she said, bewildered. "Why?"

Benvenuto shook his head at Paul.

"I'm afraid we can't hang my late fare on his accent, strong as it is," he said.

"That's disappointing. But didn't you say just now that we're going after the Slosher today?"

"Mr. Herbert Dawkins, to you," corrected Benvenuto. "I got his name from Leech this morning. Yes, at the moment he's our only line of action, for since you laid out De Najera last night we can't expect to glean anything from friendly intercourse with *him*. Still, I must say it was worth it." He smiled reminiscently. "Meanwhile Leech is keeping a firm eye on the chateau. You know, there's no doubt that Herbert is mixed up in the affair, more so than I can explain to you just at present, for I've no facts, and only an inkling as to how. Now, it seems to me more than likely that he'll be in Marseille to-day, for it was only yesterday he got that address in the Rue Galette from Mr. Paleidos."

"Seems like weeks to me," said Paul. Benvenuto nodded. "Me too. If you've finished your coffee I think we'd better be getting along."

They said good-bye to Adelaide and climbed into Benvenuto's car, a rakish-looking two-seater. Driving along the Marseille road they passed the spot where De Najera had doubled back the day before and continued inland for a time, the white dusty road, already very hot in the sun, winding up through the hills above the town. Paul caught a glimpse of the port of St. Antoine far below him, the church raised up over the houses like a hen brooding over her chickens, the bay lively

with boats. A big wine ship was coming in, its siren hoarsely summoning the town pilot. Along the road the olive trees
were a dusty grey, and through them Paul could see vineyards
heavy with grapes, and sometimes a stone-built farmhouse
with a shaded court in front where children played and hens
scratched about. It got hotter as they went inland, and the
peasants at work in the fields wore wide straw hats to protect
them from the sun. Topping a rise, a great plain spread out
before them bounded by range upon range of bare mountains.
They passed an ancient Provençal village, formal as an Italian
hill town, its red roofs packed closely round a square-towered
church, and beyond it a massive wedge-shaped mountain jut-
ted into the plain. The side facing them was perpendicular,
formed of different stratas of rock, and Paul imagined the sea
washing against it thousands of years before.

"Montagne de Ste. Victoire," said Benvenuto, taking off his
hat. "You're on holy ground—rapidly approaching the birth-
place of Cézanne. All this country looks to me as though it had
been created by him—indeed was, as far as I'm concerned. Five
minutes, and we'll drink to his memory on the Grande Place."

Aix-en-Provence proved to be a town of mellow and faded
magnificence, very quiet and forgotten. Paul caught glimpses
of enormous carved gateways and ancient courtyards where
fountains played, and determined he would come back one
day and stay for a bit. They drove down a fine wide Place with
a great fountain playing at one end, and had drinks in a café
in the shade of plane trees, watching the townspeople go by
with their market baskets, and students from the university
with books under their arms. It was very tranquil and orderly.

Half an hour's drive down the main road brought them to
the outskirts of Marseille, and Paul asked Benvenuto his plan
of campaign.

"Well, the only real clue we've got to the Slosher's whereabouts is Madame V.," he replied, "but it would be difficult
to watch her house all day, particularly as the Rue Galette is
down in the Vieux Quartier, and it's no place to hang about
in. I think the best thing to do is to go straight to the Gare,

for the station detective is a pal of mine and he might give us a lead. Fortunately the Slosher isn't one of these people one would overlook." Paul agreed, and on arriving at the station Benvenuto went in to make inquiries, leaving him in the car. He reappeared in a few minutes.

"Bad luck," he said. "Chap's gone off duty. However I've got his address and we shall have to go and hunt him up. Damn waste of time."

They started off again, crossed the Cannebière, the main street of Marseille, and drove into the suburbs; Benvenuto held his own with great skill amongst the Marseille taxi drivers, possibly the most temperamental in the world, and presently arrived at a small villa surrounded by a neat garden on the outskirts of the town.

He rang the bell and they were let in by a cheerful-looking woman with a shrill voice, who explained her husband was in bed, but if they would give themselves the trouble of entering she would go and speak with him. With many apologies on their part and much volubility on hers they seated themselves in a dark little parlour where heavy Provençal furniture smothered in knick-knacks and fringed mats stood uneasily against an execrable modern wallpaper.

Presently their hostess returned and begged them to mount to her husband's bedroom, where he would have much pleasure to see them if they would excuse . . . Passing through a tiny hall, where mingled odours of charcoal and garlic issued from the kitchen, they went up the stairs and into a bedroom, preceded by Madame. Here, lying in an enormous bed draped with mosquito netting, lay a fat Frenchman with fierce moustaches who greeted Benvenuto enthusiastically.

"*Ah, mon vieux, vous allez bien?*" he roared, grasping his hand, and Paul saw to his great delight that he was wearing a flannel nightgown. Then Paul's hand was crushed in his grasp while the great voice said:

"*Enchanté, m'sieu, enchanté—et qu' est-ce que vous voulez boire? Mais oui, mais oui, il faut prendre un petit verre.*"

The preliminaries over, healths drunk and compliments passed on the brandy, Benvenuto broached the subject of their errand, to find that the detective had been on duty the night before and remembered a monsieur who might be their friend arriving on the nine o'clock train from Cannes. The monsieur was carrying two suitcases, one large, one small, but *helas!* he regretted infinitely he knew not what had become of him after leaving the station. Benvenuto thanked him profusely, and with many handshakes they left him among his pillows and went down to the car.

"That's something anyhow," remarked Paul. "What do we do now—try the hotels?"

Benvenuto considered, and then said: "I think on the whole we'll try the station again first. The town is stiff with hotels and it would be a long business, whereas if we're lucky we might get hold of a taxi driver or a porter who remembers him and knows where he went."

Back in the station yard Paul sat in the car while Benvenuto strolled over to the taxi rank, where he soon had all the drivers round him, gesticulating and talking. After various suggestions had been made and discarded Paul saw him hand a note to one man and walk on one side with him. Presently he came back looking very pleased and said: "Smart fellow—remembers taking him to the Hotel George V. Attaboy"—and off they went again.

Leaving the car in a garage, they walked to the hotel, where things were simple, for after a murmured consultation with the hotel clerk and a further note expended, they were allowed to look at the register. Benvenuto ran his finger down the names entered on the previous night and stopped opposite one of them. A delighted smile overspread his face. "Percy de Winter, London," he said softly, and Paul bent over and read it, written with many flourishes. A conference with the clerk confirmed their suspicion—Percy was undoubtedly the Slosher, and he had, it seemed, left the hotel half an hour before, saying he would not be back for lunch.

Whilst standing in consultation at the hotel entrance they were approached by a very shabby, genteel, elderly Englishman.

"May I have the pleasure of showing you round this city, sirs?" he began, taking off his greasy hat and speaking in a sprightly tone which went badly with his threadbare clothes and furtive-looking face. They turned away hastily, but he was not to be put off.

"Very interesting, the old quarters of the town, sir," went on the voice insinuatingly. "Churches — antiquities — unusual cinemas — lovely women—"

Benvenuto drove him off with a curse, and then suddenly took Paul's arm and went back to him. He drew a fifty-franc note from his pocket which the man eyed hungrily. Benvenuto gave it to him and said, "This your usual pitch?"

"Yes, Captain, night and day. I have many clients among the English visitors."

"Well, look here. A stout man came out of this hotel this morning—an Englishman with sandy hair and a red face, wearing a grey check suit. Did you see where he went?"

The man eyed the fifty-franc note in his hand, coughed, and looked at Benvenuto meaningly.

"Your words of wisdom are precious, my friend, but you don't get more than another ten. Now then, what about it?"

"I am obliged to you, Captain. The tourist season is not what it was. Yes, sir, I remarked the gentleman, and noticed he seemed in a hurry. About half an hour ago it was, and he went in that direction"—pointing down the Cannebière.

"Thanks," said Benvenuto, and they left him, only to find him at their side a moment later.

"For a further fifty francs, Captain, I could give you some more information about the gentleman," he said confidentially. Benvenuto sighed and took out his pocketbook again.

"Well, sirs, I made acquaintance with the gentleman last night," the tout went on, "and as he was in search of amusement I took him to the Elysée Club, where he was very free with his money and did himself well on champagne. Towards the close of the evening he picked up a young lady, and I didn't see much more of him. I offered him my services this morning when he came out of the hotel, thinking he might care to see the town, but he refused, saying he was going to meet his little friend of last night. He did not mention where, sir."

The man appeared to be speaking the truth and they left him, though not before he had made another attempt to show them the sights.

"Ten to one it's the Cintra," said Benvenuto to Paul. "Everyone goes there, and it's a likely rendezvous with a *poule*. And look here, when and if we do run him to earth he's certain to recognize you. Don't cut him—but on the same hand don't be too eager, for I imagine you didn't exactly part like brothers. I flatter myself he won't know me, for I was pretty well camouflaged the other day."

The Cintra they found crowded, and noisy with many tongues. Pushing their way to the bar, they ordered brandies and sodas, and looked about them. Paul was the first to discover their quarry, and murmuring to Benvenuto he edged sideways through the crowd. The Slosher was sitting at a small table with a man and a girl, and the party seemed to be in the best of spirits. In fact the laughter was so loud that it was attracting general attention. The girl was quite young, and crudely painted, with coarse black hair plastered in curls on her cheeks. She was extremely smartly dressed, though when she laughed she displayed teeth that made Paul shudder. Her companion was a thin dark man in an exaggeratedly cut suit, a typical bar lounger. Paul was doubtful of his nationality, though he appeared to be acting as interpreter to the party. They were both laying themselves out to please the Slosher, who responded cheerfully.

"Wot abaht painting the town pink ternight?" he was saying expansively, as they got near enough to catch his words. The interpreter was unequal to this and said, "Pardon?"

"Seein' a bit of life," elaborated the host, raising his voice hoarsely.

"*Ah! mais oui*—yes, yes, *parfaitement,*" said his companion. He smiled and translated to the girl, who broke into a torrent of agreement.

"*Je connais une boîte beaucoup plus curieuse que celle d'hier soir, ou y trouve des jolies gonzes—et on y boit bien,*" she finished, looking at the Slosher eagerly. He was bewildered for a moment, but the man explaining, he proved entirely agreeable.

"Tell 'er," he said, pressing his companion's waistcoat with a podgy forefinger, "tell 'er if she's a good girl I'll give 'er a brace of hear-rings."

"Herrings?" queried the guide, again baffled.

The Slosher frowned as if he suspected a joke in bad taste, and then decided to laugh. He pinched the girl's ear coyly and repeated, "Hearrings, yer fool. Pearls—real 'uns."

"*Ah! Boucles d'oreilles,*" said the man, and translated the joke, whereupon there was general laughter and camaraderie.

"*Après midi, cinema?*" said the lady to her host, raising large and painted eyes appealingly to his face.

"She say she wish to go to cinema this afternoon," put in the interpreter superfluously.

The Slosher leant back in his chair and shook his head solemnly from side to side.

"*Je ne pooh pas,*" he replied. "*Je swee occupay,*" he added mysteriously.

The man and girl exchanged a fleeting glance.

"Meet yer both 'ere at six," he continued, getting up and paying for the drinks. "Cheerio, mate. *Au revoyer, chérie.*"

He turned and came face to face with Paul. "Why, Gor blimy where 'ave I seen *you* before?" he asked.

"Didn't we travel down together in the train the other day?" said Paul.

"Why, o' course, that's it. 'Ow are yer?"

They shook hands, and then a look of distrust crossed the Slosher's face. "I thought you said you was going along to the seaside?" he said.

"Yes, so I did," said Paul, "but I came over to-day to meet a friend of mine, Mr. Brown, who's just landed."

"Pleased to meet you, Mr. Brown," said the Slosher, shaking hands, his face clearing. "'Ave a cigar. This is some town, this is, 'ot stuff I can tell you. Now where's my little bit o' skirt gone? 'Ere, Fifine, come and say 'ow do to the gentlemen."

"Enchanté, m'sieurs," said Fifine, looking far from enchanted, and a moment later hurried after her companion who had strolled to the door and was waiting with a frown on his face and a cigarette dangling from his lips.

"Little bit of *orl* right," said the Slosher, winking at Benvenuto who nodded sympathetically. "Well, sorry I can't stop—pressin' engagement and I got to get a bite to eat first. So-long, all."

By this time the bar had emptied, and Benvenuto turned to Paul.

"Look here—can you lunch on sandwiches? They'll give us some here, and we've not much time," he said.

"Rather—I'll go and order some at the bar," said Paul.

When he came back Benvenuto had moved over to a corner table. He bent forward eagerly.

"Now for a council of war. If I mistake not, things are going to hum this afternoon. I'm determined on a quiet interview with the Slosher, and we must waylay him before he gets to Madame V.'s—for that's obviously where he's going after lunch—he's full of it. The Rue Galette is down in the Vieux Quartier and I warn you that place is no picnic. Want to come?"

Paul chuckled. "You bet I do. I'm told it's as fierce as the underworld of Chicago. It doesn't seem possible, cheek by jowl with this well-gendarmed city."

"Believe me, it is. Last winter I spent three months down there, painting, and more or less received the 'freedom.' I'd got no money and nothing they wanted. I didn't poke my nose into their business, and that being so, I found thieves and harlots extremely good company when off duty. The Senegalese are the worst. Last time I was over here I went into a gunshop to get some shot for my rifle, and while I was there

five fellows came in and purchased between them twenty re-
volvers, discussing meanwhile some gentleman of the name
of André. But to return—I'm afraid the plot is thickening
round the Slosher's head."

"How d'you mean?"

"Well, I'm pretty well convinced that his young woman is
the decoy of a gang. Poor Slosher—he may be a grand criminal
in his own country, but he's a sucking babe in this town. I don't
think their plans for trapping their rich Anglais will mature till
to-night—you remember she was very enthusiastic about some
place of amusement she intends taking him to—and there's our
chance. We must act this afternoon or there'll be no more jewels, and very possibly no more Slosher. When I've got hold of
him I propose doing a bit of blackmailing. We've got to get his
story of last Tuesday evening, and the threat I can hold over
him is my knowledge, or suspicion that amounts to knowledge,
of his theft of Lady Trelorne's jewels. Hence the haste—for once
he's disposed of them to Madame V. the thread is valueless.
Finished lunch? Well, let's go. I have a revolver (which doesn't
revolve, it's true) and you have a fist. Forward to Madame V.,
and for the love of heaven obey me exactly."

"Yes, Captain!" said Paul, and they started off down the
Cannebière, a wide street of hotels, shops, and cafés, with a
tramway down the centre, crowded and noisy. It terminated
on the Old Port, and while they were held up at the corner by
a stream of traffic Paul looked about him. Sea and sky were a
burning blue, the sun blazed down baking the cobbles so that
they hurt his feet, the noise was terrific, the air full of the tang
of fish, salt, and gasoline fumes. A wide cobbled causeway ran
round three sides of the port, backed by tall houses huddled
unevenly together and sun-dried to a dusty white. Fishwives
were throwing pails of sea water over their stalls. It glistened
on the bright green of seaweed and the yellow skins of lem-
ons which decked trays of strange shell fish. Plaques stuck
in them announced the price and the different varieties—*pi-
ades, piadons, moredues, violets, moules, portugaises*. The
harsh accents of the fishwives rose above the noise of traffic

as they called their wares or shouted across at each other from throats apparently of brass. Enormously strong, rather short and broad in the beam, they were dark and swarthy-skinned, and seemed to Paul, as they clattered about in wooden clogs with baskets of fish and pails, to be the embodiment of this harsh and vigorous town. He stared about him, fascinated, till Benvenuto pulled him by the arm through the traffic to the other side, where boats were moored up against the causeway. Here they could walk with comparative safety, picking their way among ropes and barrels, and eluding the boatmen who sought custom for a trip round the bay. Another five minutes brought them to the beginning of the Vieux Quartier, where every building seemed to be a tenement or a sailors' lodging house and washing hung like flags from the windows. Along the pavement were rows of *bistros* where sailors and dock hands sat drinking, their chairs sprawling across the pavement, and there were many Negroes among them, bright scarves tied round their necks. The interiors looked dark through the sunshine, but Paul caught glimpses of crude paintings on the walls, the gleaming brass rails of bars, rows of bottles, and dark faces bent over cards. It was smelly and noisy, coarse and strong, and very exciting. Between the houses narrow streets ran sharply up hill, some of them rising in stone steps, where women sat in the doorways and hung over balconies, and lines of washing stretched across between the houses. Painted signs stuck out over the doors, in French and English and Arabic. "Seamen's hostel," Paul read as he went by, "First-class English House," "Au Clair de la Lune." Suddenly Benvenuto turned up hill.

"Rue Galette," he murmured. "If anyone grabs your hat let it go. Bérets are cheap, but so is virtue."

Receiving many stares from the dark doorways, they strolled past No. 52 without incident, and found it was a *bistro* at the bottom of a tall house. There was a plaque on the door—"Madame V. Corsets. *5me étage.*" They walked on to the end of the street, turned and came back, and suddenly Benvenuto pulled Paul into a doorway. Coming towards them was the girl Fifine, her hands on her hips, whistling. She had not seen them and they crouched back as she went by, and then suddenly Paul felt hands pulling him backwards into the house. Not daring to struggle, he looked behind him to see an old hag with a painted mouth smiling horribly at him. Benvenuto thrust ten francs into the hands, muttering something in an argot Paul did not understand, and he was released.

"Can't go out for a minute—curse the girl—but what did I tell you? Unfortunate Slosher!" said Benvenuto in his ear. "Still, this isn't a bad observation post for the moment, for he must pass this way to get to Madame V.'s."

As he spoke a taxi turned up the street that was only just wide enough to take it, and as it went quickly past them they could see the Slosher inside.

"Damn!" said Paul with emphasis, and Benvenuto broke into a string of curses.

"I never thought of the fool coming up here in a taxi—didn't think it could be done. Come on, after him." They saw the Slosher alight, hand the taxi man a note, and enter the *bistro*, and then Benvenuto pulled Paul back into the doorway. For the girl, who had been whistling all the time in the street, suddenly stopped doing so, and three men emerged from a house and walked quickly across into the *bistro*.

"Hell! he's trapped. They won't attack him till he comes out, for money is money and jewels are hard to get rid of. Come on—we'll have to do our best and Lord help us."

Fifine had apparently done her bit and was walking off. They waited till she disappeared and then walked down towards the *bistro*, which was empty except for the three men, one of them a Negro, who were seated at a table drinking. They walked straight through and met the barman, a small green-faced diseased-looking pimp, who stopped them.

"I have an appointment with Madame V.," said Benvenuto in French.

"Elle est occupée," returned the barman.

"Yes, I know, but it is my friend with her and I have some important information for him."

"On ne passe pas."

It was getting difficult, for the gang were all looking at them and talking in low voices. Suddenly Benvenuto leant forward and whispered something in the barman's ear. His sickly face immediately became wreathed in smiles, and he made way for them to reach the staircase, making a sign to the three men as he did so.

"Bit of luck," whispered Benvenuto. "Fifth story—top of the house. Now follow me, and if you make a single sound, even breathe, you're as good as dead." With which cheerful remark he preceded Paul up the dark staircase.

Very slowly and quietly they climbed five flights without encountering anyone, and found themselves in a long narrow landing at the top with two doors facing them. Benvenuto bent down and examined the lock on the first door very carefully, and listened with his ear to the keyhole, then, making a cheerful gesture to Paul, he crept along to the next door. After repeating the proceeding he took what appeared to be a small tyre lever from his pocket, and inserting it between the door and the lintel he levered very gently at the lock until the door swung quietly inwards. They slipped inside and found themselves in a passage with a thick carpet on the floor. Benvenuto closed the door behind them, and went towards another at the end of the passage. This proved to be unlocked and he opened it very slowly, looked inside, and beckoned to Paul to follow him. They found themselves in a large bedroom ornately and vulgarly furnished, dim daylight coming in through the shutters. Another door, opposite the one they had entered by, obviously led into the second room which communicated directly with the staircase. They crossed over to it, thanking heaven for a thick flowered carpet on the floor; they heard the sound of voices, and it seemed to Paul an eternity before Benvenuto had turned the handle, pushed the door inwards, and released the handle without making a sound. He peered round the door, his revolver in his hand, and motioned to Paul to do likewise. They saw a large room with a window straight ahead of them, and in front of this an ormolu table was drawn up.

Sitting up to it, his back towards them, was the Slosher, and on his left another man, enormously fat, with a microscope in his eye. So Madame V. was a man! The table was covered with jewels which flashed and glittered as the men handled them.

Benvenuto covered the two men with his revolver, walked into the room and said:

"Mr. Dawkins, I presume."

CHAPTER XIV
ROUGH-HOUSE

THE SLOSHER had turned round, and was looking at them with the air of a paralyzed pig. The jewel merchant clasped his fat hands in front of him and smiled in a noncommittal sort of way, as if to say, "This is no affair of mine."

Benvenuto advanced further into the room.

"It's all right, Mr. Dawkins, I'm not going to shoot you if you keep *quite* still," he said, taking a chair, while Paul stationed himself behind him.

"Now listen to me," he went on. "We want some information from you and you don't leave here until we've got it. We have no connection with the police"—here the Slosher took on an easier attitude and gingerly turned his chair towards them—"but on the other hand I can, if I choose, put them on your tracks in ten minutes. Meanwhile I have three of the toughest thugs in Marseille downstairs in the bar, and unless you tell me what I want to know you will never leave this place alive. D'you understand? Your fat body will be rotting down a drain this evening instead of drinking champagne on the proceeds of the Trelorne jewels. Oh, yes—I know what I'm talking about."

The Slosher blinked.

"You fair took me by surprise, as the saying goes. Oo are yer, anyway?"

"Never mind about that. The point is I've got you by the short hairs, and unless—"

"Anything I can do to oblige," the Slosher cut in hastily.

"You will tell me exactly why you went to the rooms of the Signora da Costa in Bishop's Hotel last Tuesday evening about six o'clock."

The Slosher gave a spasmodic jump.

"I never done it—wajjer mean? I wasn't never in 'er bloody rooms, s'welp me Gawd I wasn't."

"I am not asking you whether you smothered the lady," said Benvenuto soothingly. "We will not touch on such a delicate matter, and even if you did I couldn't expect you to admit it. No. But you were there, and now's your chance to explain why. Quick, Mr. Dawkins."

"I take me bleedin' oath I never went near."

Benvenuto smiled.

"Does Loty's bath powder mean anything to you? Or *this*?" With a stride he had reached the table, and from the tangle of pearls and bracelets he picked up a small diamond brooch and held it in front of the Slosher, who quailed.

"You seem to know a 'ell of a lot. I'll come across; that's ter say, you get me out of this 'ome of rest and I'll come across."

Benvenuto thrust his revolver nearer. "You'll tell me now or you're a dead man," he said threateningly.

"Orl right, orl right, don't be so 'asty. Yer see, it was like this 'ere. The lidy you mention 'ad come over from Paris with a packet of snow—that's ter say, cocaine. A big packet it was, and a friend of mine 'oo'd 'ad a row wiv 'er—"

"Yes, yes—her brother."

"Well, it *was* 'er bruvver, now you mention it. 'E'd 'ad a row wiv 'is sister and wanted to get one back on 'er, like. Likewise 'e wanted the money, and 'e 'ated 'er like 'ell 'cos 'e said she was double-crossin' 'im and not goin' fifty-fifty, if yer get me. 'Er part of the job was to smuggle the stuff across from Paris to London, see? Jolly smart she was at it, too, and done it lots o' times before. Well, as I was sayin', this 'ere bloke and me, we fixed it up as I was to take a room in Bishop's 'Otel, nab the stuff, sell it in London, and give 'im two thirds of the doin's. The stuff was done up in Loty's bath-powder boxes, four of 'em, wiv a little real powder on the top. He tips me the wink from Paris, and I dresses up and takes the room the same day as the Signora arrives. I made all me plans to sell the stuff quick, and I 'ung around until 'er room was empty, as *I* thort. While I was 'anging around I managed to pick up this little lot from a room near," he gestured towards the table. "Couldn't keep me 'ands orf 'em like—saw the door open and slipped in easy as kiss me 'and. Well, then I went back to No. 62 and the key was in the door, and I'd seen the maid go out. In I went and what should I 'ear but the Signora splashin' about in 'er bath. 'Owever, I'm used to the work yer know," he smiled modestly, "and I took a chance. Didn't 'ave much trouble in findin' the stuff—there it was in a dressing case in the next room where 'er clothes was 'angin' up. I 'ad me little bag and popped 'em in, likewise that there brooch, like a bloody fool, never could say no to diamonds. I wos just going to slip out when strike me pink if there wasn't a knock at the door, and under the bed I was in a twinklin'. 'Come in!' yells the Signora, and a girl comes in, leastways judgin' by 'er ankles she was a girl, and they 'ad a set-to about art or some rot and me sweatin' like 'ell under the bed wiv the biggest scoop I ever 'ad. Well, after a bit the girl goes orf—"

"You're forgetting about the telephone call."

"'Ere, was you there too? You're right, there was a telephone call, and the girl answered it and said some blighter wanted to come and see the Signora."

"What was the name?"

"'Ow the 'ell can I remember? *Name?* I'd got somethin' better to think of than bleedin' names, wiv me sweatin'—"

"All right."

"Orl right be damned. The next thing was, the Signora finishes 'er bath, if you please, and comes into the room too, and says good-bye to the girl, who goes orf. I'm blowed if she didn't start singin', and then—"

The Slosher stopped and seemed to be considering. The fat dealer was still seated in his chair gazing at the ceiling with a slightly amused air, and twiddling his thumbs.

Paul, standing beside Benvenuto, had listened to the story with fascinated interest.

"And then?" repeated Benvenuto, leaning forward intensely.

But the Slosher did not reply. Outside the door were the sounds of feet shuffling, and suddenly the handle rattled sharply. The various actors looked at each other. Benvenuto was the first to move. Rising leisurely, he crossed over to the dealer, poked him in the stomach with his revolver, and said quietly, "Ask who is there and what they want."

"*Qui va là?*" said the dealer obediently, in a voice so high and squeaky that Paul wanted to laugh, in spite of an inner conviction that they were in a tight place should the gunmen be outside. The reply was unexpected, and was rumbled out in such a mixture of French and Italian that Paul could only catch its drift with difficulty.

"It is I, Julius Cæsar," said the voice. "We came up to see if all goes well. The fat English is still there, yes?"

Benvenuto closed his hand over the dealer's mouth, pressed the gun yet further into the yielding flesh, and turned his head towards the door.

"Go down, my children," he said in a very fair imitation of his victim's high treble, "and wait for ten minutes. All goes well."

It was a critical moment. Benvenuto's suggestion seemed to be causing a difference of opinion outside the door, and voices were raised in argument. It was obvious they weren't going to risk the chance of a fortune if they could help it. Paul suddenly realized the danger they were in, and looked round for something heavy to use in self-defence. The Slosher, meanwhile, not understanding French, was at a total loss as to what to think of the situation. He was rapidly replacing the jewels in his little black suitcase, and wearing the expression of a man who knew not who was his friend and who his foe.

The consultation outside came to a climax with a heavy blow on the door, and a voice, this time not belonging to Julius Cæsar, said, "Open."

Benvenuto, still with a firm grasp on Madame V., said to Paul softly, "Shove furniture across the door and keep low in case they fire," and then to the dealer, in French, "Your private entrance, quick, or I'll shoot."

The dealer hesitated but for a moment, met Benvenuto's fiery eye, and a sob shaking his fat body he gestured towards the bedroom door with a small ringed hand.

"Come on!" This time Benvenuto had to shout, for blow on blow battered at the solid door, and a revolver shot through the lock lost itself in a heavy wooden armoire which Paul had managed to drag in front of it.

First went the dealer, tripping neatly forward, then Benvenuto, using the revolver barrel as a timely spur in his back, then the Slosher clutching his suitcase. The weird procession was closed by Paul, his last glance backward showing him the armoire still standing at the post of duty.

Through the bedroom, through the bathroom, and then a short pause as the leader with trembling fingers opened a French window which led onto a balcony. They passed along the narrow ledge which was protected by a handrail from a sixty-foot drop to a courtyard below, and then through a door which was opened by Madame V. with a key. They found themselves in an attic from which a staircase led downwards, and all descended, each glancing nervously backward from time to time. But the pursuit, if any, was not in evidence. Down, down, flight after flight, with closed and mysterious doors lining the landings, and at last they were on the ground floor. Facing them was a heavy front door, and the dealer (Benvenuto with a firm grasp on the back of his neck) opened it by pushing back a catch. In a moment they were in the street and following Benvenuto who, having glanced rapidly from right to left, shifted his grasp from the dealer to the Slosher and set off quickly down the hill.

As Paul passed Madame V. he saw tears rolling down the fat and powdered cheeks. Was it a man or a woman? He had a moment of compassion.

A couple of hundred yards brought them to a populous thoroughfare; five minutes more and they were on the port near the Cannebière and dropped their pace to a quiet walk.

"Good exercise, that," panted Benvenuto. "Splendid for the liver. D'you know—I almost feel I could do with a drink."

Three empty glasses were on the table. Three men, sitting back in their chairs, presented a friendly spectacle to the outward eye, each smoking respectively a cigar, a pipe, and a cigarette. The centrepiece of the scene was a small black suitcase placed conspicuously on the table, at which they were all staring ruminatively.

Benvenuto was the first to break the silence. "Well, Mr. Dawkins, as you were saying when you were so rudely interrupted—" he began, when the Slosher sighed dismally.

"Orl right," he said, "I'll come across wiv the rest of it, but couldn' we 'ave another drop o' the old nonsense first?" He placed his hand over the region where his heart might be presumed to lie. "I feels quite faint after all that there." And he sighed again. His face had certainly taken on a purplish hue, and Benvenuto looked at him reprovingly.

"You should try Banting, Mr. Dawkins," he said. "A rusk and a dash of lemon juice for dinner would do wonders for you. Meanwhile, if you feel some liquid refreshment would make your story flow I think you might have it. Here—*garçon!* But if it doesn't—and quickly, too—we go hand in hand to the nearest gendarme, taking this little lot," pointing to the bag, "with us. You realize that, don't you?"

"I'll come across," repeated the Slosher earnestly, "specially after your getting me out of that there joint."

"Very well, then. *Garçon!* Curse the waiter—see if you can wake him up, Ashby, will you?"

Paul jumped up, and went to the back of the empty café to summon the waiter from a room beyond. He hurried, for as he rose from his chair the Slosher bent over the table towards Benvenuto.

"Well, it was like this—" he was beginning, and Paul didn't want to lose a word of the story. He had picked his way through half a dozen tables and chairs when a shout from the Slosher arrested him. "Look out!—'ere comes them bleedin' thugs!" he bellowed, and Paul was in time to see Benvenuto, who had turned to look behind him, bashed on the head with a water bottle by the Slosher, who thereupon grabbed the case of jewels and ran for the door with surprising agility. Paul tore down the room after him, his progress impeded by the tables and chairs in his path, and as he passed Benvenuto, saw him slip to the floor with a groan, blood and water pouring down his face. Paul reached the door in time to see the Slosher jump into a moving taxi, flinging a note to the driver as he did so. The taxi put on speed, and Paul, looking wildly round, saw there was no other in sight and not a gendarme for miles. He ran a long way down the road before he realized the chase was hopeless—a French crowd will not concern itself with cries of "Stop thief!" and the taxi had disappeared into a maze of side streets. Back to the café Paul ran, cursing himself at every step, to find a scared-looking waiter bending over the unconscious form of Benvenuto. Paul wiped the blood from the side of his head and forced some brandy through his lips. Presently his eyes opened.

"Dear me, Ashby," he said weakly, "you have triangular eyes," and returned to unconsciousness.

CHAPTER XV
IN WHICH ADELAIDE IS BITTEN BY A MOSQUITO

"So I TIED his head up in table napkins, and took him round in a taxi to the nearest chemist," finished Paul.

Adelaide's eyes were blazing with fury at the story of the Slosher's treachery.

"Miserable worm," she said. "Oh, I could kill him for that, when it was entirely due to you and Ben that he wasn't shot to bits by Marseille gunmen."

"Purely Ben's doing," said Paul modestly. "I did absolutely nothing but a bit of furniture removing. As a matter of fact Ben's been jolly lucky, for the chemist said that if the bottle had landed two inches lower it would have got him on the temple and probably killed him, instead of laying him out for a few minutes. As it is, he's got nothing worse than a sore head."

Adelaide nodded. "I had the utmost difficulty in persuading him to stay in the studio and have his dinner sent round."

They were sitting in the Café de la Phare having after-dinner coffee, while Paul recounted to Adelaide the day's adventures. It was very hot, and a full moon hung over the port, turning the night into a brilliant and phosphorescent day. All St. Antoine was out to enjoy it, and fishermen were taking parties of people across the bay in their motorboats. Outside the next café, sailors, home on leave from Toulon, were dancing together, spinning round very fast to a curious Provençal tune played by a pink-shirted man with an accordion.

"Enter bottle-scarred veteran." Paul turned with a start to see Benvenuto, the side of his head artistically decorated with sticking plaster, looking down at them gloomily.

"Ben, oughtn't you to be in bed?" Adelaide looked critically at him as he sat down beside her. "Paul has been telling me of your bloody, bold, and resolute deeds—and I'm feeling so proud of being an English Girl."

"Never felt finer in my life. I've just been interviewing Leech, which is always interesting. And talking of blood—" He bent forward, and Adelaide jumped as his hand came down on her shoulder. "Got it," he murmured, and stared down at a large mosquito, spread-eagled on his hand. When Paul asked him to have a drink he didn't answer, still staring at his hand, then abruptly he jumped up. "Will you children come along and hold a committee meeting? It's too hot to go back to the studio—how about going along the mole and sitting round the lighthouse?"

They agreed eagerly, and strolled round the port and along the mole, to find the lighthouse deserted. Seated on the stone bench that encircled it, they lit cigarettes, and enjoyed the night for a few moments in silence. Out here it was cooler and very quiet. There was no sound but the sea lazily washing the stones below them and the notes of the accordion coming faintly across the water. A fishing boat starting out for the night's catch hailed them as it went by, and they watched it disappear up the path of the moon. Paul's eye was caught by the white mass of Les Palmiers at a little distance up the coast, standing out sharply against the dark blue of the sky, and he brought his thoughts back with a jerk to the discussion before them.

"Did you get any news of De Najera from Leech?" he asked.

"Yes," said Benvenuto. "You won't be had up for manslaughter this time, for he was gracing the town with his presence this afternoon, and quite all right apparently. Leech tells me he called on you when you were out, my dear," he said to Adelaide.

She shivered. "Thank goodness I was. I went up into the hills to do a painting. I wonder what he wanted."

Benvenuto laughed. "I think I can guess," he said. "But let's get down to business. Look here, Paul—you're a lawyer—I suggest it would be good practice for you to present the case to us up to date. I've got various theories germinating, and it would clear things up in my mind to hear the facts as we know them expressed from your point of view."

"Right—I'll do my best. But first of all I'd like to hear what you found out about De Najera's alibi from that fisherman yesterday—you never told me, if you remember."

"Neither did I. Well, I had a talk with old Gallo, who's a great pal of mine, and it so happened he was down on the shore painting his boat at about seven o'clock last Tuesday morning, and he remembers seeing De Najera put out from his private harbour in the speed boat. It stuck in his mind because it was a bit early for the gentleman to be about, and he's certain it *was* De Najera on account of his yellow jumper and white hat. He was alone, he said. Then at about ten-thirty he saw the boat come back and turn into the harbour, De Najera still alone in it. As we know, it was seen later in the afternoon by dozens of people, and by a pure bit of luck we know it was the valet disguised as his master who was in it. With this knowledge it seems fairly obvious what happened in the morning."

"Why, of course," assented Paul. "They both started out from Les Palmiers, one of them lying in the bottom of the boat covered with a sailcloth or something. Then De Najera probably changed into ordinary clothes if he wasn't in them already, landed somewhere along the coast near Marseille, took a train or taxi into the town, and sent the valet back alone. How's that?"

Benvenuto nodded. "Very pretty. And, so long as it was un-suspected, a very nice little alibi indeed. If we're right it will be quite easy to prove. Meanwhile I think we can take it for granted that he can have had a good twenty-four hours away from St. Antoine, beginning at about 7 A. M. on Tuesday. Now carry on."

"Well," began Paul, "we know the history of the afternoon at Bishop's Hotel up to, approximately, six o'clock—that is, five minutes after Adelaide left, when the Slosher's story came to an end. At six-thirty the maid entered the suite to find that Signora da Costa had been murdered. Let us say that five min-utes elapsed between the departure of the murderer and the entrance of the maid—and possibly ten minutes for the murder itself. That leaves fifteen minutes unaccounted for; probably less.

"Who entered the Signora's room between six and six-fifteen?

"First we must consider Adrian, for he's obviously the perfect suspect from the police point of view. He had a motive, or at least what the police would certainly consider a motive, knowing as they do that Luela was threatening him with an accusation of theft. Further, he has disappeared, which is in itself extremely suspicious. Worse than all, he had a telephone appointment with Luela for six o'clock, although thanks to Adelaide the police do not know this."

He paused. The other two were silent until Benvenuto, in a low voice, said, "Go on."

"Suspicion next falls on the Slosher. He was, on his own showing, still in the room at six o'clock. He had in his possession a big haul of jewels stolen from Lady Trelorne's room, to say nothing of what must, I imagine, have been several thousand pounds' worth of cocaine, and a diamond brooch belonging to the Signora. Therefore he was a desperate man in a very tight place. What more likely than that in order to escape he crept out from under the bed, possibly at a moment when the Signora had turned to get a dress from the dressing room, seized the eiderdown from the bed, flung it over her head, smothered her without a sound, laid her body on the bed, and slipped quietly away? He is, we know to our cost, a strong brute and a treacherous one."

"I'll tell the world he is," murmured Benvenuto, ruefully rubbing his head. "And you make a strong case against him. But go on."

"Next—we have De Najera, and here is a definite motive, according to the Slosher's story. He and his sister had been partners in the illegal and highly dangerous business of cocaine smuggling. They had fallen out, apparently because the Signora had 'double-crossed' him, as Mr. Dawkins put it, and De Najera wanted money and he wanted revenge. He employed the Slosher ostensibly to steal a packet of cocaine from her; but isn't it quite probable that this was a blind—that he really intended murdering her and was proposing to use the Slosher, caught red-handed in a burglary, to divert suspicion? Further, isn't it at least possible that to make assurance doubly sure he telephoned, or got someone to telephone for him, making an appointment in Adrian Kent's name for the fateful hour? If so, it was an ingenious idea, for Kent is known to have been her lover, to have quarrelled with her, and to have been threatened by her. The most damning evidence against De Najera is, of course, the fact that he troubled to establish an alibi for himself on that day.

"Fourthly and lastly there is the possibility of some unknown person or persons—either someone who had a grudge against the Signora, or one of her dope-smuggling colleagues—who knew of the valuable booty concealed in her rooms.

"Now I propose we try to defend each one in turn.

"Take Kent first. The only thing in his favour, as far as I am concerned, is your belief in his innocence. The fact of his disappearance is what chiefly troubles me."

"H'm. He's a curious chap—I wish you knew him," said Benvenuto. "As I've told you, I know him pretty well, and he's never to be relied on to do the obvious thing. In my opinion he is the sort of chap who, if he had committed the murder, would have given himself up. If he hadn't, and knew that suspicion had fallen on him, he would be quite likely to go into hiding in order to avoid being questioned and so on, believing that the real murderer would be caught, and not realizing that he was making things look doubly black against himself. Not only that, he was suffering from extreme contrition at the quarrel he had had with his father and at the worry and anxiety he had caused the old chap. He's a highly nervous and sensitive fellow, and his first thought on learning that he was suspected of murder would probably be to keep it from his father at all costs, and to save him the horror of seeing his son standing for trial. If you remember, in that letter you told me about he said he was going away 'until this business was all over and done with'—meaning Luela's trumped-up case about the jewel—and that gives one an idea as to what his reaction to the really serious charge would be."

"I suppose that's possible," said Paul slowly, when Adelaide broke in.

"Oh, Ben," she said, "I've been so terribly afraid all the time that he *did* do it in a fit of madness, and that he killed himself afterwards."

Benvenuto didn't speak for a moment. Then: "You know him as well as I do, Adelaide," he said, "and it looks—pretty bad—if you, too, think he may have done it. And yet—I can't believe it. Go on, Paul—clear your next man."

Paul considered for a minute.

"The great point in the Slosher's favour," he said, "is, of course, the telephone call, which certainly indicates that someone came to the Signora's room at the appointed hour. It cuts both ways, of course, because the Slosher had overheard the conversation and knew someone was coming. Also he realized, no doubt, that a hue and cry after Lady Trelorne's jewels would soon start and that the hotel would probably be searched—and his fears *may* have incited him to try and get away at all costs. But it would have been a bit risky, to say the least of it, to attack her when he knew someone might arrive at any moment."

"Quite so. He was confronted with the devil and the deep sea all right. And remember—he hasn't the figure for playing hide-and-seek under a bed. But go on."

"Well, there are, it seems to me, three reasonable explanations:

1. "The Slosher committed the murder. In which case the Unknown, that is, Kent or someone using his name, would, one would have thought, have given the alarm, though this might not apply (a) if the visitor were De Najera or (b) if it were someone who took to his heels when confronted with a corpse, and hasn't come forward for fear of being suspected.

2. "The Slosher managed to slip away unnoticed while the Signora was in the bathroom or dressing room, and before the visitor arrived. Or,

3. "He lay hidden under the bed while the murder was committed, and escaped afterwards. He may not have seen the murderer, or even realized at the time that the Signora was dead. Remember his view was a bit restricted—an ankle was all he saw of Adelaide.

By the way, d'you know anything about his past record?"

"Who? Oh, the Slosher." Benvenuto had been gazing abstractedly out to sea, and pulled his attention back with an effort. "Yes, I learnt a few things from Leech this evening. He's an ex-pugilist—got turned out of the ring some years ago, and seems to have run to fat and crime ever since. He's been in clink twice—once for robbery, once for robbery with violence. Also he's known to be mixed up with an extremely shady racing gang in London—a man of parts, you perceive. I told Leech a garbled version of our encounter with him in Marseille, and he is off after him. Now let's get on to a more subtle type. Your next suspect is—"

"De Najera. And, while I'm temperamentally opposed to putting up a defence for him, I must admit that up to the present we've got the very flimsiest of evidence against him. True he is known to have had a grudge against his sister, and a sufficient one to incite him to rob her; but then he may have felt that the cocaine was his by right, and it's a far cry from wanting to get even with a person to wanting to put an end to their existence, and risk your own neck in doing it. Against this we must balance the fact that he is, I imagine, a man of violent passions and a cunning type. He certainly looked as if he had murder in his eye—and in his hand—when he made for me on the roof last night. But a knife, though rather disconcerting to an Anglo-Saxon eye, is, I believe, part of the ordinary make-up of an Argentine, and also we must remember that he'd been drinking a lot during the party, and wasn't quite himself for various reasons. The great point against him is, of course, as I said before, the fake alibi—and I humbly submit that the next item on our programme should be to look into that."

"I entirely agree," said Benvenuto, "and I was about to suggest that to-morrow we go into Marseille again, and visit the aërodrome."

"Please can I come too, Ben?" said Adelaide. "I don't much want to lose sight of you two again after what you've been up to to-day, and besides, I want my hair cut."

Benvenuto looked at her dubiously.

"I suppose it is a bit long," he said, "but if you think you're going to have a private view of Marseille gunmen you're wrong. We're going to spend a sober and uneventful day making a few discreet inquiries, so perhaps it would be better for you to come along with us than to stay here and be wooed by Hernandez. By the way, did you tell Paul about your bit of research last night about aëroplanes?"

"Oh! Paul, I forgot." She looked at him contritely. "And it was so exciting. I feigned a girlish enthusiasm for flying, and told him how I longed to go up. Actually I've flown a good deal, but he didn't know that, and he rose beautifully and said he would be honoured to take me on my first trip. So then I got quite ecstatic and said how marvellous it would be, but how could it be done? and he confessed to having a private plane of his own which he uses for going across to his place in Spain, and which he keeps in an aërodrome along the coast. He didn't say where, and I didn't like to seem too inquisitive, thinking that the best plan would be to go up with him one day soon. After that—well, things began to get rather difficult, as you know."

Paul congratulated her on her tactics, and then the council of war became gradually moribund. One by one they dropped into silence, watching the pale beauty of the night, and occupied with their own particular thoughts.

From the town, along the mole, came a small group of men and women, and with them a musician, striking now and again a few chords on his guitar. They climbed down into a boat painted pink and blue and, one taking the oars, rowed out across the bay.

"*L'Embarquement pour la Cythére,*" murmured Benvenuto. The voices of the singers came to them across the water:

> "*Chaque soir à la brune*
> *Quand au ciel monte la lune,*
> *Au loin dans des Savanes on entend*
> *Un chanson que fredonnent les amants. . . .*"

As the song faded softly in the distance Paul found Adelaide's hand resting in his own.

Benvenuto yawned and got up.

"For your own sakes I will leave you," he said.

"Why for our sakes?" asked Adelaide quickly.

"I might recite one of my own poems," Benvenuto replied gloomily. "Good-night, my children."

CHAPTER XVI
WINGS

THE RAIN SWEPT with summer violence down the Cannebière, giving it for the time a likeness to some English provincial town. Or so Paul thought, as with his Burberry buttoned up to his chin he hurried Adelaide across from the car to the door of the coiffeur's. Inside it was warm and dry, full of the smell of scented soapsuds and singed hair. Adelaide peered through the plate-glass doors as she slipped off her mackintosh, and grimaced at the wet streets.

"You won't know me at lunch time," she laughed at Paul. "I intend having a positive orgy in here all the morning and shall emerge with every nail gleaming and every hair in place. *C'est entendu* then—I meet you both at the Café Bristol for *apéritifs* at half-past twelve—and we'll go and wallow in *bouillabaisse* at Pascal's afterwards."

He said good-bye and left her reluctantly in the hands of an obsequious gentleman with permanently waved hair, but felt glad as he crossed over to the waiting car that she was to spend the morning in so scented and civilized an oasis.

Benvenuto looked at him critically as he got into the car.

"I was wondering which of us most nearly resembles a merchant prince," he said. "I rather feel I do." He looked into the driving mirror and carefully placed a bowler hat over his plastered head. "How's that?"

"Charming," replied Paul, regarding him in some astonishment. "But may I ask—"

"Got a card on you?" interrupted Benvenuto.

Extracting one from his case, he handed it to him, and watched him take out a fountain pen and add to the name of the club it already bore, *"Directeur du Commerce Civil Aëronautique d'Angleterre."*

Regarding it with some satisfaction, Benvenuto said, "Most impressive. And I think for the time being, with your permission, the card is my own. You, of course, are Our Mr. Brown, and we represent an English firm desirous of arranging an air route between London, Paris, Marseille, and Nice with a view to supplying the Riviera with salmon, pheasants etc., and taking back flowers and fruit. We may require a hangar at Marseille and so, of course, wish to inspect the accommodations available."

Paul laughed. "I don't feel it has the makings of a commercial success," he said, "but it certainly ought to get us round the aërodrome."

They drove through the town, and leaving the outskirts behind them came presently to a big flying ground on which stood numerous sheds and hangars. Benvenuto drove through the gates and up to the manager's office, leaving Paul in the car while he went in. The rain had subsided somewhat, and he got down and looked about him with interest. Through the open door of a hangar he could see mechanics at work on a machine, cleaning and polishing the gleaming metal, while in the distance across the muddy landing fields a big liner was taking off, the roar of its engine filling the air. Paul watched it bumping across the ground, the figures of the mechanics small and insignificant beside it, saw it rise into the air while its engine roared louder still, and then sail away in what seemed a curiously effortless flight over the distant trees and buildings, and gradually disappear into the grey clouds. He turned, to see Benvenuto and someone who was obviously the manager descending the steps of the office. Benvenuto's personality combined with the card had worked wonders, and the man was being very polite and talking volubly. Paul was introduced as the secretary, and they started on a tour of the ground. Along one side was a row of small hangars which the manager explained were hired out to private owners, some of whom had their own mechanics, some employing those attached to the aërodrome staff. Several of them were open, with mechanics at work inside, and Benvenuto regarded them with interest. He lingered outside one shed to admire a very smart plane of the latest type, on which a man was working.

"Ah, yes," said the manager. "It belongs to a Spanish monsieur, *très riche, très sport,* who has a house near Barcelona where he flies on visits to Madame his mother."

They passed on, inspecting a hangar which was free and ready for occupation, and Benvenuto took elaborate notes in his notebook. The manager was politely enthusiastic about their commercial enterprise, and gave them all necessary details. Promising to let him know if the scheme matured, they shook hands and left him, got into the car and drove away.

Presently Benvenuto turned up a side road and circled round to the back of the flying ground. At a little distance over a field they could see the fence encircling it, and beyond, the backs of the row of small private hangars. He drew up to the roadside, stopped the engine, and took out his cigarette case.

"Five to twelve," he said. "In five minutes exactly the mechanics will go to lunch, if I know anything about the French—and there is our chance to do a bit of investigation. The hangar with the monoplane in it is the third from this end, and I feel pretty well convinced it's De Najera's. If we can get inside we may be able to make certain, and also find out a few details about tank capacity, etc. Damn the rain!—it's worse than ever. I hope to God it won't keep those mechanics in the sheds."

A few moments later a hooter blew, and they could hear the sound of heavy doors being pulled to and locked. They got out of the car, and standing on the step could see some men running over the landing ground in the rain toward the entrance gate. Benvenuto replaced his bowler with a béret and they started across the muddy field. When they reached the fence and looked through there wasn't a soul about, and they scrambled over, and walked along to the third hangar, keeping a sharp look-out. Each hangar had a small door at the back, and after making sure there was no sound from inside, Benvenuto brought out a bunch of keys from his pocket and inserted one after another in the lock.

"I don't want to break the lock if I can help it," he said. "It would attract too much attention to our visit. I'm afraid these are all too small. Got any keys on you?"

"I don't think so," said Paul. "Here's the key of my room in the hotel—try that." This proved to be far too large, but after groping about he found another in the pocket of his mackintosh, which he handed to Benvenuto, who was so long fiddling about at the lock that Paul began to think they would have to break in. At last, however, the door gave and they stepped inside. Benvenuto slipped the keys into his pocket and cursed the rain as the water ran off their clothes.

"I hope to God this will dry up before the chap comes back from his lunch," he said. "We're flooding the place out. It's bad luck because it's not the sort of contingency one reckons with out here. Most unusual at this time of year. Was it wet when you left England?"

Paul nodded. "Rained like fury the night before I left, and probably hasn't stopped yet. I say, what a beauty!"

The monoplane in front of them lay impressive, shining, and competent. Benvenuto took it in from propeller to skid with an expert eye, climbed into the cabin, and then, looking down at Paul, said, "Note down a few readings while I sing them out, will you?

"Cabin monoplane, L'Hirondelle. Six months old. High lift wing. Horsepower, on a rough calculation from the French, 375. Got that? Two seats, pilot and mechanic. Aerial charts have been removed. That's food for thought. Mileage, roughly, 11,000. Can you beat it? Tanks. Here we are. Service tank, capacity 100 gallons, down to twenty according to the gauge. Reserve tank No. 1, same capacity, full. Reserve tank No. 2, same capacity, full. Reserve tanks 3 and 4, same capacity, empty. *Most* curious."

He descended abruptly and seized Paul's notebook and pencil.

"Now, the total gasoline capacity of this plane is 500 gallons, and the fuel consumption half a pint an hour for each horsepower of the engine. Any schoolboy, therefore, will tell you that it is capable of twenty hours' flying without descending or refuelling, taking it that he'd use twenty-five gallons an hour. Actually he'd not use quite so much. But twenty hours, mark you! Fly to London? He could fly to New York."

He stamped his foot irritably. "To the devil with these calculations. We can work them out later." He turned to examine the hangar. A long bench with a row of tools above it; spare landing wheels slung to the roof; empty cans; and many complicated garnishings of modern flight. In a corner a couple of leather coats hung on nails caught his eye, and he promptly examined every pocket.

"Nothing."

He turned away but as he did so his sleeve caught in a button of one of the coats, and it slid to the ground, disclosing a pile of papers carelessly stuck on a nail in the wall.

"Gasoline receipts. Good. Stick 'em in your pocket, Paul. No, wait a minute. Last Tuesday—a hundred gallons." He had flicked off the top sheet and was examining it closely.

"A hundred gallons, Paul, on that day. We're getting on."

But he did not seem to Paul, who was getting nervous about the return of the mechanic, to be getting on. He stood still, looked at the ground, gave a deep sigh, and filled his pipe. Suddenly he roused himself, and murmuring, "All is vanity," took Paul's arm and they walked towards the door.

At the door Benvenuto stopped, still grasping his companion's arm, and stared at him. Paul felt slightly embarrassed, and was about to suggest moving on when Benvenuto turned and walked back to the plane, saying, "Those reserve tanks, you know . . ."

He carefully unlaced the canvas covering of the fuselage behind the pilot's seat and, bringing out an electric torch from his pocket, examined the tank tops with minute care. The cap of each one of the four reserve tanks had a bar across it fastened with a small but strong steel padlock and chain, making it impossible, short of forcing the locks, to unscrew the caps. Paul, watching with interest, was told to fetch a spanner from the bench.

"No time for scruples," said Benvenuto, and taking the tool he got a leverage on the chain of tank No. 4, snapped it, and removed the round brass cap.

He looked quizzically at Paul. "The fate of a certain gentleman of our acquaintance depends on the brand of gasoline," he remarked, and bending over the aperture he lowered his rather large nose into it and sniffed. There was a pause while he hung suspended over the tank and then he turned with a seraphic smile on his face.

"Smell it—I beg you'll just smell it," he murmured.

Paul smelt. Certainly it was not in the least like gasoline. A sweet, rather stimulating smell came from the tank.

"It's cough mixture—or—no, toothpaste," he said turning in perplexity to his companion.

Benvenuto laughed. *"La sorcière glauque!"* he said exultantly. "Never tasted absinthe, Paul? It's forbidden in France— sent too many people mad—and, smuggled over from Spain in concentrated form very simply by our friend De Najera, it must be a paying commodity. Very paying indeed, I should say, judging by the price it fetches in the more dubious dives of Paris. Really, I admire the man."

"But," expostulated Paul, "he's a wealthy chap. Why—"

"So would you be if you were a successful absinthe and dope smuggler," returned Benvenuto shortly. "Let's get to hell out of here—I don't want to be shot up by his mechanic."

They hurriedly left the hangar; Benvenuto, Paul noticed, didn't trouble to relace the fuselage or even close the door, and when he asked him why, replied, "The game was up for De Najera when I broke the chain on the tank. Sure to be noticed. Why trouble to hide anything now?"

He relapsed into a gloomy silence.

As the car shot back down the Marseille road Paul thought to himself that this fresh evidence of De Najera's criminal activities would be valuable to them when he was arrested for murder. What was even better, they had proved beyond a doubt that he could have reached London, killed his sister, and returned to St. Antoine well within the period of his alibi.

CHAPTER XVII
CLIMAX

BENVENUTO STOPPED the car in the Cannebière.

"We're late," he said. "It's getting on for one o'clock. You go along to the Bristol and meet Adelaide, and I'll join you there in a few minutes. I've got to send a wire."

Paul hurried down the road, and reaching the Bristol looked for Adelaide among the crowded tables. He did not see her, and walked past a second time anxiously scanning every face. But she was not there, and he sat down at a table to wait. He ordered a Vermouth, and while he sipped it kept a watchful eye on the crowds passing along the pavement. Everyone seemed to have come out after the rain, and mixed with the townspeople were African and Moorish troops, spahis in flowing robes, and peasants from the country wearing shawls and white linen caps, the children dragging at their mothers' hands while they stared at the shops and traffic. At any other time Paul would have enjoyed it, sitting there with his drink and watching the people. But at that moment no face interested him that was not Adelaide's, and his eye slipped from dark skins to light ones, from the flat, coarse profile of an African to that of a trim bearded French bourgeois, without registering what he saw.

He looked at his watch. A quarter-past one; it was absurd to get oneself into a state—a thousand things might have detained her. But he was on the point of getting up from his table to see if he could find her at the coiffeur's when Benvenuto walked in, looking thoughtful and rather gloomy.

"Sorry I've been so long," he said. *"Garçon! Donnez moi un Pernod."* And he relapsed into silence, staring in front of him.

"I can't think what's happened to Adelaide—she's not turned up yet," said Paul.

"Hasn't she?" Benvenuto answered abstractedly. "She'll be along in a minute or two."

"I think I'll just go up to the hairdresser's and see if she's still there—it's a long time since she was due."

"Right." Then, just as Paul was leaving, he called after him. "Oh—it's no good doing that—all the shops shut from twelve till two. Much better sit down and wait for her."

Paul returned to his seat moodily. If all the shops shut at twelve, where on earth . . . really, Benvenuto might take a little interest. He looked as if he were trying to solve the secrets of the universe, thought Paul irritably. They sat in silence for a few moments and then an elderly waiter came up and addressed Benvenuto.

"Pardon—c'est M'sieur Brown, n'est ce pas?"

"Ah, bonjour, Georges. Ça va bien?"

"Toujours bien, m'sieur—et vous?" He had produced a little note from his pocket, and Paul nearly snatched it from his hand. Controlling himself with difficulty, he watched Benvenuto open it carelessly, and then sit up with a start.

"Good God!" He handed a tip to the waiter and turned quickly to Paul. "Read that," he said.

It was scribbled in pencil on the back of an envelope, and read:

DEAR BEN: I've gone to lunch with Hernandez. It seemed the best thing to do—explain later. Meet you at the Bristol about three. Have a good lunch but don't come to the Verdun. Love—A.

P.S. England expects—etc.

Paul was glaring at the little note with mingled emotions, when Benvenuto spoke.

"In spite of her injunction I think we will stroll round to the Verdun," he said. "I don't like the sound of it much. I can only imagine the chap has got his suspicions of us and has taxed her with something—and she's engaged in throwing dust in his eyes across the lunch table. All very damn fine, but I wish she hadn't gone." He turned round to call for the bill, and a moment later they were hurrying down the Cannebière. Suddenly he uttered an exclamation, and Paul looked quickly at him to see his eyes wide open, staring with the peculiar intentness that he was beginning to recognize as a danger signal.

Benvenuto seized his arm and hurried him still faster down the road.

"Ten to one it's all right," he said, "but I've just realized what may happen. Suppose he asks her to go for a trip in the plane after lunch—the signs of our visit are sufficiently obvious to put the wind up him, and he may try to make a getaway."

They broke into a run, Paul's heart thumping as though it would burst. At this very moment she might be miles away up in the air. . . .

At the corner of the Rue Paradis the Verdun came into view, and they looked to see if the Hispaño was outside. It was not, and in two minutes Benvenuto was questioning the head waiter.

Yes, the m'sieur and the young lady had left in a big car about a quarter of an hour before. In which direction he did not know. If M'sieur liked he would call the waiter who had served them.

Benvenuto said he would like to speak to him, and Paul fumed at the delay while the man was fetched from the kitchen. At last he appeared and Benvenuto, thrusting a note into his hand, questioned him in French.

But yes, he remembered perfectly. The Spanish m'sieur had wanted his bill rather hurriedly after he had been called out to speak with a man who was asking for him. Yes, the man who had called was possibly a mechanician, and had driven away with the m'sieur and madame in the big auto.

They hurried out into the street and hailed a taxi. Benvenuto told the man the direction and bribed him to go as fast as he knew how.

"It would take even longer to get the car—I ran it into a garage before I met you," he said as he climbed in.

The drive through the crowded streets was maddening, and cross streams of traffic seemed to hold them up at every moment. Paul, sitting on the extreme edge of the seat and peering through the glass window in front of him, treading in imagination on the accelerator and taking off the brakes, would have been both annoyed and incredulous had anyone suggested he was not hastening their progress. He banged on the window in exasperation when the driver wasted precious moments in a rich stream of Marseillaise invective directed at another taxi which had cut in front of them. At last they got away into the less crowded streets and were soon leaving the town behind them. Paul suddenly realized they were taking a different road from the one they had followed in the morning, and was about to expostulate when Benvenuto pulled him back.

"Let him alone," he growled. "There are two roads and this is probably shorter."

Paul sat back feeling thoroughly impotent, only to spring up in his seat a moment later.

"Look!" he said, clutching Benvenuto's arm.

Far above them was a small plane, rising rapidly and heading in the direction of the sea. They stared at it, then met each other's eyes. Paul was very white.

"It's De Najera. Hold on, Paul. She may not be in it. We'll know in a second. If she is—we'll get him."

They swung into the gates, nearly colliding with a taxi coming out, and saw in front of them the empty Hispaño-Suiza drawn up just outside the manager's office. At that moment the manager emerged and walked down the steps, pulling on his gloves in a leisurely way, to receive a violent shock as Benvenuto leapt out of the taxi, Paul at his heels, and addressed him.

"Was that De Najera's plane that went up a few minutes ago?" he demanded.

Recovering from his surprise, the man drew himself up.

"By what right, m'sieur, do you question me regarding my clients?" he began, when Benvenuto interrupted him savagely.

"Your precious client is an absinthe smuggler, carrying on his business under your nose. Had he a lady with him when he went up?—answer me."

A startled look crossed the man's face.

"The Señor arrived with a lady and has taken her up for a pleasure trip—he told me himself. It is monstrous what you say, m'sieur, impossible. . . . I shall complain to the police."

"You'll soon have ample opportunity, m'sieur—they will be here in a few moments. Come on, Paul"—and leaving him aghast on the steps, they tumbled into the taxi, Benvenuto giving hurried directions to the driver, and started back down the road. Benvenuto's face was grim as he turned to Paul.

"We're going straight to the gendarmerie—and within half an hour they'll have notified the police all over Europe. Don't look like that, man—he can't possibly escape. We'll reach her by to-morrow. Why, good Lord! it may be a pleasure trip as he said—he may suspect nothing, and they'll be back in half an hour to find gendarmes waiting with a warrant for his arrest. Here—have a cigarette."

Paul took one and stared at it in his hand. He seemed to have become numb all over. Perfectly calm he felt—as if some part of him had died. Afterwards he could remember nothing of that drive—the next thing he knew was that he was sitting opposite an official who was taking down notes from Benvenuto's instructions. The process was achingly slow, and Paul, coming back to an intense consciousness of what had happened, sat there in torment as the description went on. "Brown hair—brown eyes—about five feet four . . ." the pen travelled over the paper.

"Not a hair out of place—every nail gleaming," she had said laughing, and he repressed an idiotic desire to say the words aloud.

Presently Benvenuto rose, and the official followed them to the door assuring them that everything possible would be done. Benvenuto thrust a hand through Paul's arm as they walked up the street.

"We'll stay here till they get news," he said. "There's nothing else on earth we can do, so let's go and get rooms at a hotel where we can be on the telephone."

At last Paul found his voice.

"Isn't there a British consul we could go to?" he said. "They might put a military aëroplane to work."

"Good idea—we'll go round and see them at once. I don't know where they hang out. Come over to the Bristol and we'll look it up in the phone book."

"I'll meet you both at the Bristol for *apéritifs,*" she had said. Paul clenched his hands and followed Benvenuto across the road.

They pushed through the chairs and tables towards the café at the back, when suddenly a voice said, "You *are* late."

It was Adelaide, drinking a cup of tea.

CHAPTER XVIII
ANTI-CLIMAX

"MY BLESSED CHILDREN, what *is* the matter? Aren't you glad to see me?"

The two men had dropped into chairs on each side of her, and she regarded their paralyzed expressions with amusement as they stared at her unbelievingly.

At last, "Glad to see her," murmured Benvenuto weakly. "She wants to know if we're glad to see her, Paul."

Paul removed his gaze with difficulty from Adelaide's face and met Benvenuto's eye. Suddenly they started to laugh as though they would never stop, and Adelaide looked at them with amazement, concern, and finally petulance.

"I've always been told women have no sense of humour," she said, "and really I begin to believe it. All the same, if it's such an exceptionally good one I do think you might try it on me. Ben! Paul!"

Exhausted, they lay back, and then Benvenuto addressed her with something like fury. "Oh, disgraceful and abominable woman," he said, "d'you realize that the police of every country in Europe are this moment writing down descriptions of you—and that Paul and I have been spilling our heart's blood because we believed you'd been abducted?"

She dimpled. "I very nearly was," she said, "and it's entirely due to my native wit and feminine intuition that I'm with you now—so don't be rough with me. Hadn't you both better have some tea and hear my piteous story? But—oh, Ben!—what about the poor policemen? Oughtn't we to go and reassure them?"

Benvenuto looked at her wearily. "I refuse to stir from this spot until I've had a drink and a sandwich," he said. "I'll write a note to the gendarmerie to tell them you've been found, and you'll have to come around and explain afterwards."

He scribbled a note while Adelaide poured out tea, and despatched a messenger with it, after which both men fell upon sandwiches and *brioches* with fury. Paul suddenly remembered he'd had no food all day—he'd not given it a thought before.

"Fire away," said Benvenuto with his mouth full.

"In your own words—take your own time," quoted Paul. By now he was feeling quite weak and childish.

Adelaide fired away.

"I'd better tell it you as it happened, from the moment I left the hairdresser's. I stayed there until twelve, and then of course I had to leave because they were closing for lunch. I was standing in the doorway looking at the rain—it was simply pouring—and wondering what on earth to do. Just then a car drew up opposite where I was standing and I looked up and saw that it was Hernandez's. I turned away quickly and was about to hurry down the street, rain or no rain, when he jumped out and came towards me. He looked awfully subdued and rather ill, and stood there in the rain with his hat in his hand. He said, 'Adelaide, don't go. I've been waiting for you all the morning, don't go. I must speak to you—I must apologize to you. I have thought of nothing else for two days. I am so miserable—please do not refuse me.' 'I'm sorry, Hernandez,' I said, 'I can't stay now, and I've got to meet Benvenuto. There is no need for an apology—I would rather not hear it. Good-bye.' Then he rushed after me. 'At least let me drive you to wherever you're going,' he said. 'You cannot walk in this. It is more than I can bear if you leave me like this. I shall kill myself.' It seemed so silly standing there in the middle of the pavement in that awful downpour, being jostled by people with umbrellas. He still held his hat in his hand, and he looked so funny and bedraggled with the rain trickling down his face. I didn't mind his threatening to kill himself, but somehow I couldn't stand watching him get a cold in the head, so I walked back and got in the car. It was so difficult to realize he was possibly a murderer, with raindrops running off the end of his nose, if you see what I mean.

"So when we got to the Bristol I looked at him and said severely, 'You'll probably get pneumonia if you go about like that—you'd better come in and have some hot rum.' Then he looked so pleased I was sorry I'd said it. However, there was nothing for it but to go on now that I'd started, and we were soon inside in a corner of the café drinking hot coffee and rum, and looking as if we'd both been shipwrecked.

"He started a long and impassioned apology about the other night—said he'd drunk far too much and didn't realize what he was doing. His hands were shaking, and he kept breaking into Spanish, which I don't understand, and was working himself up into a terrible state. I noticed people were beginning to turn round and stare at us, and I tried to interpose a few soothing words, but it was no use. Apparently he'd been turning over in his mind what I'd said the other night about seeing him in London, and he asked me why I'd said it. I opened my eyes innocently and said I really thought I'd seen him, but that seemed to make him worse and he swept on and said he was surrounded by an atmosphere of suspicion—and what were you and Leech doing in his house the other night? Apparently his servant had seen us when we went out, and had told him, and he was beginning to believe we all suspected him of something. I thought this would never do, so I did my level best to disabuse him of the idea—and succeeded only too well, for the next thing was he asked me out to lunch. I said I couldn't possibly come because I was meeting you two at half-past twelve, and he begged me to leave a note for you and come with him. He said he wouldn't believe I had forgiven him unless I did, and began to work himself up into a state again, about our all being in league against him, so finally I agreed and wrote you that note and gave it to Georges. You see, Ben, I really thought it better not to antagonize him while you were still making investigations, and I didn't dare to do anything that might hinder our clearing Adrian. It was a perfectly hateful business—I simply loathed eating his food, and I was so miserable the caviar tasted like sawdust.

"However, the lunch was quite a success, I suppose—I was very bright and encouraged him to talk, hoping he might let drop something useful, but he would enlarge on the beauties of Spain and the Argentine. I could see we were approaching dangerous ground—another minute and he'd have proposed again—so I was terribly relieved when the waiter came and said somebody called Miguel wanted to speak to him. He excused himself and went outside. He was away quite a time and I lay back and looked out of the window, and wished I were sitting over a nice honest *bouillabaisse* with you, instead of eating everything that was geographically and seasonally improbable. However, I cheered myself up with the thought that I was being terribly knowing and helping you two like anything, really.

"When he came back he looked rather excited, I thought, but he only apologized about being away so long, and said he'd been speaking to his mechanic who knew where he generally lunched, and had come along to tell him that he'd finished working on his plane and it was in perfect shape. Then he remarked that the weather had cleared up and looked like being a nice afternoon—would I care to come up for a short trip?—and that we'd have plenty of time to get back so that I could meet you at three, if we hurried. Well, of course I didn't know how successful you might have been in running his plane to earth this morning, so I was quite enthusiastic at the idea, having a private vision in my own mind of meeting you both afterwards and your looking very discouraged and saying you'd entirely failed to find out where the machine was kept, and my remarking, casual-like, 'Oh, I've just been up in it.' Sensation. 'What a lucky thing for us that we've got Adelaide to help us.'"

She smiled mournfully at them. "I take it you'd actually been there first?"

Benvenuto smiled back at her. "We did manage to catch a glimpse of it as a matter of fact. But go on—I can't bear the suspense."

She sighed, and continued: "After he'd paid the bill we went out, and there was the mechanic waiting with the car. He scowled when he saw me, and I thought it rather funny for a minute. However, he touched his hat and opened the door for me and then climbed in at the back, and I thought no more about it. Hernandez by this time seemed in an awful hurry and simply tore through the town. I was rather nervous at the way we dashed through the traffic, but thought he was trying to avoid making me late for meeting you, and felt mildly grateful to him. However, he stopped once, outside a big bank in the Rue de la République, and went in for a minute or two. When he came back he was stuffing a note case into his pocket, and he smiled at me and explained the bank would be shut when we came back. For the rest of the drive he didn't speak and I sat back and felt very excited and ever such a detective. When we got to the flying ground he parked the car with a lot of others outside an office, and a man who was standing there, who, I suppose, was the manager, took off his hat and spoke to him. He bowed to me, and Hernandez explained he was taking me up for a little trip. Miguel, the mechanic, had gone across to a shed on the field and we followed him, and then he and Hernandez had a very excited conversation in Spanish to do with some part of the plane. I couldn't understand and didn't take much notice, so after looking at the plane I strolled over to the door and left them to it.

"It had got cold and was beginning to rain again, and I stared at the muddy field and the grey clouds, and all at once I began to feel most peculiar. All my excitement had gone, and I began to get terribly frightened. Hernandez came towards me looking very white and shaking and began to hurry me into the plane, and all the while Miguel went on talking, his voice getting angrier and angrier. I'd got one foot up on the plane when he suddenly dashed forward and pulled Hernandez's arm, and then they both started to shout at each other. I listened for a bit, and although I don't speak Spanish I began to understand that Miguel wanted to go up in the plane instead of me, and that he kept on referring to the police. Suddenly I remembered Hernandez's violent haste—his visit to the bank—the way he'd examined some part of the plane and then tried to hurry me into it—now Miguel refusing to be left behind; and while they were still arguing with each other and getting more and more angry, I slipped down and tore out of the shed and across the field as fast as I could go. There was a taxi standing in the yard and I told the man to drive to the Bristol, and then fairly collapsed on the seat. When we'd got down the road a little way I told him to stop and then got out—and I knew my fears had been justified, for I could hear the roar of the engine. A minute later the plane appeared over the trees and made off—so it seems"—she looked at them comically—"Hernandez wasn't going to risk his skin in following me!"

CHAPTER XIX
"LOU CAT"

SHE LAY at anchor, rocking gently in the water of a sheltered cove. She was painted pink, the chilly pink of an ice cream, her line accentuated by a thin band of green, and on her bow was written *Lou Cat* in white lettering. She looked coquettish, conscious of her finery as she rode the glittering water, Paul thought, and he paused in his scramble over the rocks to admire her. The picture was completed by Adelaide, in a short white frock, as she jumped on board and began to handle the ropes in a seamanlike manner.

"I don't know that rig," Paul called to her as he continued his descent. The sail came down with a rattle and flapped in the breeze.

"It's a tartan—usual Mediterranean rig," she answered, her hands busy. "You won't like it if you're used to yachting in the grand manner. I prefer it myself—it's such a relief to have an upright boom that doesn't clip you on the head. I'll be captain this morning till you're used to it. Will you take the sheet?"

He clambered on board as she started the engine, and in a moment they were *chug-chugging* out of the little bay. Away from the shelter of the coast there was a light breeze, and soon she bent forward, close-hauled the mainsail and stopped the engine, and *Lou Cat* slipped through the water in an exquisite silence. The only sound was the water slapping the bow, the only colour an illimitable blue, and Paul was divinely happy, sniffing up the salt breeze and feeling his skin burn in the sun. He did not want to speak—he felt himself and Adelaide existing for the moment as part of the boat, the sea, and the clean wind. Presently when he looked at her she was sitting still and straight as a figurehead, the tiller under her hand and her eyes fixed on the distant horizon. Conscious of him, she brought them back to his face with a smile.

"This is more like it, isn't it?" she said. "It's nice to do something normal again. I'm always happy in *Lou Cat*—Ben taught me to sail her four years ago when I first came down here."

"Are you certain he won't mind our taking her out—I mean, oughtn't I to have asked him?"

She laughed. "Of course he won't mind. Didn't you see him this morning?"

He bent forward. "Well, yes, for a minute. I wanted to tell you about it. You see, I didn't get much chance to talk to him yesterday—he got very silent and absorbed, and I thought probably he was tired. So first thing this morning I went round to the studio; as you know, there are a million things to discuss since we were at the aërodrome yesterday—calculations to be made about De Najera's possible journey to London last Tuesday, and so on. Also, I should have thought that this was the right moment to compile our suspicions against him and hand them to the police, because although Ben told the French authorities in Marseille yesterday about the absinthe smuggling, he didn't say a word about suspecting him of murder. Of course, that isn't their affair, I know; Scotland Yard is the place to inform, and I naturally thought Ben would be taking some steps in the matter. Instead of which, when I get round to the studio I found him sitting opposite a collection of eggs and oyster shells, a loaf of bread and some wine bottles, painting away like mad at a still-life. The room was full of smoke— he must have been at work for hours, and he'd hardly speak to me. Meanwhile I'm afraid De Najera will get clear away in that plane of his to some country like Paraguay or Chile where there's no extradition."

Adelaide regarded him with wrinkled brow, and shook her head slowly. "You can depend on it, Ben hasn't been idle," she said. "Either he's got an idea incubating in his head or else he's taken action of some sort and is waiting for results. It's no good trying to probe him when he's in one of his moods. The only thing to do is to leave him alone till he emerges of his own accord. In the meantime"—she shook her head in the wind and broke into a smile—"let's have a day off. I say, wouldn't you like to bathe soon?"

"Rather. Shall we put ashore or bathe from the boat?"

"There's an island about a couple of miles along the coast—no one ever goes there, and I know a strip of shore out of the wind where we could tie up." She held her hand up to the breeze. "It's freshening a bit—we ought to do it in about a quarter of an hour if you can hang out till then. Hot, even out here, isn't it?"

Paul stretched himself along the deck and looked up at her in perfect content, slowly took out his cigarette case, lazily gave one to her and one to himself.

"As leading ladies say on first nights, this is the happiest moment of my life," he murmured, watching blue smoke vanish into the blue air. "It's the sort of thing one dreams about on a wet, grey day in London—only better. I've never had the imagination to dream of such a day as this or such a boat, or—or you," he added, only so low that he thought perhaps she hadn't heard.

The coast was changing, the grey rocks of St. Antoine were left behind, and instead high cliffs of deep red, capped with pine trees, rose from the water, casting purple shadows on to the intense blue. Rounding a point, a chain of small islands three or four miles from the coast came into view. Paul, propping himself on an elbow, looked at them with interest. "What a marvellous place," he said. "Does anyone live out there?"

Adelaide shook her head. "There's no water, and in rough weather it's difficult to land. There's nothing on them but what you see—rocks and a few pine trees—and they're very seldom visited. I landed once with Ben, when we were out sailing last year. Ben's a wonderful sailor—the fishermen round here think he's crazy, the weather he goes out in." She laughed. "We were out once in a mistral, the big wind they get round here, and when we got back to the town we found the natives offering up prayers for us."

"Tell me more about Ben," he said, sitting up and clasping his knees. "Have you known him long?"

"He used to dandle me on his knee—when I was five and he was twenty," she added, her eyes twinkling. "During the war I didn't see much of him—I was only ten when it ended. He was in the Secret Service, you know; he did simply brilliantly and got covered in decorations—he'll never talk about it. I know he was offered a marvellous job in the Foreign Office after the war, but he refused, and took up painting, and has wandered about all over the world since then. He's always had this passion for elucidating mysteries, and has had the most amazing adventures in the most obscure places. He's always promised me he'll write them down for me one day. Of course, if he hadn't been such an independent creature he'd have been a terrific success—in the F. O. or the Diplomatic Service or the Police or anything he'd chosen to take up. But he never would—he's got a perfect passion for flying his own flag. As things are, he's making himself a reputation as a painter, and sells awfully well in Paris and in the States, although, as I told you, he didn't take it up till after the war. When I ran away from my school in Paris—four years ago—and came down here to try and paint, Ben was here too, and he took me under his wing, pacified my irate guardian, and persuaded him to let me do what I wanted. We've been tremendous pals ever since— we both come here every year. Then, two years ago, Adrian turned up and we always went about together, all three. Oh, Paul, I wish—I wish I knew what had happened to him!" She sighed and then shook her head. "Sorry. I said we'd have a day off. And here we are at the islands—we'll run into the biggest one, it's the best beach. Stand by to go about."

Quite a high sea was running as they tacked, and their faces were drenched with spray before Adelaide skillfully piloted *Lou Cat* into a kind of rocky fjord that cut into the island, ending in a sandy beach. Here there was no wind, and Paul took the oars for the last few yards until the boat grounded on the sand. Adelaide jumped out and made fast, splashing through the surf in her bare feet.

"Bring the bathing things," she called. "Isn't this a wonderful place? There are a lot of these fjords along the coast—*calanques* they call them here."

Paul followed her and stared about him. It was curiously impressive, like some roofless cathedral, for water action had twisted and tortured the walls of grey rock into high pillars, some resembling organ pipes, others in the shapes of men and beasts. Adelaide's voice had wakened a dozen echoes, and Paul felt a little awed as he stood there. The *calanque* continued some way inland, turning at an angle so that the end was not in sight, and what looked like a stony path was overgrown with bushes and stunted pine trees. Adelaide, seated on the shore, was pulling her frock over her head, and Paul retired behind a bush to get into his bathing suit. When he emerged she was already in the water, her scarlet costume bright as a poppy, and one brown arm flashing up into the sun as she swam swiftly out towards the open sea. Paul was a strong swimmer, and overtaking her they went side by side down the *calanque* to a rocky ledge. Together they climbed a natural stairway, and looked down from twenty feet into the clear deep water.

"Can you dive with your eyes open?" she said. He nodded, and in a second she was a red bird skimming through the air, a moment later a goldfish in the translucent depths. It was a good dive, and Paul pulled himself together—she was watching him. He went in neatly and for cool moments of silence saw the green world slide past his eyes, saw the smooth stones of the ocean bed, and fish that flickered and vanished mysteriously, before he shot up into the dazzling sunshine.

When they were lazily swimming back she said, "I'd like to live here forever."

In the boat was a bottle of wine and some cakes they had brought with them, and they lay on the sand and drank from the bottle, turn and turn about. The sun and wine were making him relaxed and sleepy, Paul felt—and it was fine. Here he was, alone for the first time with Adelaide; she was terribly attractive, they were on a desert island. He wished he could express what he felt about everything, especially about her; he would give anything to tell her. How did one begin? He could think of nothing but a classical quotation, and cursed himself for a clumsy fool. Why wasn't he able to flirt graciously with her?

He had just decided to begin by saying he wished the boat would sink and they would be marooned, when she said, looking up at the sky, "What I like about you, Paul, is that you don't try to make love to me."

"Damn," he thought, and then aloud, "Perhaps it's because I haven't the courage."

"You know," she went on, ignoring his remark, "there are awfully few men I could come out here alone with who would behave nicely, like you do, and not spoil everything by flattering me, and making me use all my wits to stop them being what the Americans call 'fresh.' And all without making enemies of them, if you see what I mean."

"I say," said Paul indignantly, "how perfectly horrible for you."

"On the contrary I find it most agreeable," she said, and gave a peal of laughter at his bewilderment. "I believe somebody has poisoned your life," she went on solemnly, making him embarrassed to a degree, "and I think it's monstrous."

He sat up. "You're making fun of me and I deserve it; I must be an intolerably boring companion. But honestly I don't know much about women, except that I think they are wonderful."

"You don't deserve anything of the kind and I'm awfully sorry. Really we have a good time, don't we, Paul? And—I only wanted to make you talk to me."

He bent forward eagerly. "You know, I believe I *could* talk to you. . . ."

Dressing again behind a clump of bushes, he decided to explore the *calanque* a little until she was ready to go. It looked desolate and mysterious, and he thought he heard an animal moving away through the undergrowth as he strolled up the path. The sun beat down on his head, the stones slipped and rolled under his feet, and he subsided under a pine tree, lit a cigarette, and felt sleepy. There was a heavy scent of some strong herb in the air and a buzz of insects. A great pile of grey rocks beside him, that had tumbled at some time from the high walls, seemed to throw back the sun's rays with re-doubled intensity.

He leant against the bark of the tree. What a delightful morning he had had—and what a charming companion she was; as intelligent as she was beautiful. As easy to talk to as a man, he thought, lazily watching a bright green lizard that was crawling slowly down the sunny rock. And how near he had been to putting his foot in it and trying to make love to her. He shuddered at the recollection, and then drifted into thinking of the talk they had had. It was curious, he thought with half his mind . . . the lizard seemed to be growing longer and longer . . . He sat up and rubbed his eyes as a clear whistle rang through the *calanque*, and jumping to his feet ran down the path to join her.

She was already on board and he untied the mooring rope and climbed in. In a moment they were heading for the open sea, the noisy little engine waking echoes across the water on each side of them.

"The breeze has gone," she said. "We'll have to go back on the engine. Oh, Paul, I'm so hungry—where shall we lunch?"

Half an hour brought them back to the little cove, and making fast the boat they scrambled over the rocks towards the town. They passed the American boy perched up on a ledge, intent on a canvas he was painting. He waved a brush to Adelaide and begged a cigarette as they passed. "The Mark of the Beast," she laughed, as they turned to leave him, and pointed to the rock beside him streaked with different-colour-ed paints. Paul stood still, staring at it. In one place a blob of paint was running down the hot rock—of what did it remind him? He followed Adelaide, puzzling over it. After all, it was too hot to think consecutively about anything—and then, just as they reached the town, it came to him. The green lizard on the island that seemed to grow longer as it crawled was noth-ing but green paint—and wet paint at that, fresh from somebody's palette. He remembered the movement through the undergrowth that he had thought was some animal startled by his approach, and determined he would go back to the island and investigate. Better not say anything to Adelaide—after all, it might be a mistake, it might have been a lizard and his eyes had played him tricks in the sun.

Meanwhile there was lunch to think of. Inside the little restaurant it was cool and dark. "Let's have some of these *hors d'œuvres,*" he said, pausing on the way to their table; "they look delicious."

CHAPTER XX
"DR. LIVINGSTONE, I PRESUME?"

As HE LEFT Adelaide at her door Paul half regretted his resolve. Before lunch it had been hot—now, for the first time in
his life, he realized why the sun is not always regarded as the
friend of man. He went down to the quay to see if he could hire
a boat, but the sun-baked port was deserted; for everyone but
himself it appeared to be the hour of siesta. The only sign of
life was an old woman mending some nets, her chair tipped
back in the shade of a pink house, and as Paul approached
her an ancient dog at her feet opened one eye and growled
half-heartedly at him, then stretched himself out and resumed
his slumbers.

"Bonjour, madame."

Her reply, accompanied by a toothless smile, was unintel-
ligible to Paul. He tried with French and Italian to make his
desire for a boat known to her, and deciding that she spoke
nothing but *Provençal* he sighed and went on his way. The
only thing to do was to take out *Lou Cat* again—he would have
to apologize to Benvenuto afterwards, but anything seemed
better than disturbing him at work. With a vague sense of guilt
he bought a can of gasoline and went on his way, to feel somewhat encouraged as he passed the paint-daubed rock where
they had seen the American.

Sea and sky were a milky blue. The boards of the *Lou
Cat* scorched Paul's hands as he climbed in and busied himself in setting off. He was glad to get away from the coast to
where the air was cooler, and put his feet over the side into the
water. The town, the port, the white rocks diminished slowly
but did not lose definition. The island, when it came into view,
was black against the sun. "When I get there," he thought, "at
least I can bathe," and remembered his morning with Adelaide. He fell to thinking of his search—and even more of what
he had already found, and between the two reached the island
before he realized it. The sea was calm now; he swung into

the *calanque*, and shutting off the engine drifted down towards the white beach. It was best not to disturb the possible inhabitant. Following his path of the morning, he came upon the rock where he had seen his green lizard. There was the emerald paint now drying and tacky to the touch, and with revived interest he determined to explore the island, and began to pick his way carefully through the loose stones and bushes. The path seemed more clearly defined and looked as though it had been recently used, and Paul followed it with rising spirits—though it might have been made by sheep, he reminded himself. With intense disappointment he presently came to a piece of rising ground from which he could see the sea on the other side, and bare rock and a few trees all round him. The island was deserted, and he decided to bathe and go back to the town. But the emerald paint still worried him, and he sat down to think it over, and lit a cigarette. Glancing up from his match, his eye was caught by a square dark patch between two low-growing pine trees, and peering forward eagerly he saw that it was a doorway nearly concealed by leaves, the doorway of a rocky shelter.

He got to his feet, walked gently forward and looked in. Certainly there was someone there. As his eyes got used to the gloom he saw a basket, a saucepan, some coloured blankets, and on a mattress, his head resting on the blankets, a young man, fast asleep.

Paul stood still. He felt exhilarated at his success, and at the same time shy, for the young man, unshaved, almost bearded, dressed in a faded *tricot* and an old pair of flannel trousers, was certainly Adrian Kent. He looked very young, was thin and bronzed, and had fair curly hair. The face was curious and sensitive, almost beautiful, Paul thought, the features finely carved with bold yet delicate curves in the mouth and nostrils. He looked strangely aloof and calm, yet somehow pathetic lying there in his sleep. By his side was a book, and half hidden under it, a revolver. Paul stooped and picked it up, noticing as he did so that the book was the *Poems of John Donne;* for some reason this made him doubly sure of the man's identity. He slipped the gun into his pocket, having no wish to be shot before he could make his errand known, and felt for Major Kent's letter to his son, which he had carried with him since leaving England. He half thought it out. Should he just leave it and go, or wake up the fugitive, he wondered, looking at the figure on the bed. The question was decided for him, for the youth opened his eyes, lay staring for a moment, put out his hand for the gun, and then jumped back like a cat and remained still, breathing fast.

"*Qu'est-ce que vous voulez?*" he demanded at last, breaking the silence.

Paul thought that to announce himself as "a friend" would sound too melodramatic.

"Sorry to break in," he said. "I think you must be Adrian Kent," he continued pacifically.

"No!" said the young man, preserving his tense attitude, his eyes blazing out of the shadow. "Never heard of him. My name is Short, and I've been here for a long time, painting."

Paul usually tended to believe what people said, too much so, perhaps, for a barrister, and a doubt began to creep into his mind as to whether, in spite of the unusual face, the resemblance to the photograph, and the man's obvious fear, he might not be making a mistake. After all, it was difficult to tell—the shadow was deep, the man was bearded.

"Well," he said, "I'm sorry. I'm looking for a man called Kent. You see, his father is ill, and I have a letter from him." He looked keenly at the other's face, where conflicting emotions became only too apparent. "Benvenuto Brown is a friend of mine," he added.

"Oh!" The young man looked enormously relieved. "In that case—" He realized that he had given himself away, and after a second's pause straightened himself and came forward courteously. "Please come in. I am Kent but I—I get so used to being alone. I suppose Ben sent you over. Will you have a whisky?"

"Thanks," said Paul, who was thirsty. Inwardly his astonishment grew. So Benvenuto knew where Adrian was hiding—had probably brought him there and was supplying him with food and drink—the very whisky in his hand. His embarrassment grew—it was impossible to explain anything to Kent without arousing his suspicion. He took the gun from his pocket, and laid it surreptitiously beside the book while his host bent over a soda-water syphon.

Paul coughed and took out the letter. "I met Major Kent before I left England," he said, "and he asked me to give you this if I came across you."

"Thank you very much," said Adrian gravely, and hurriedly glancing at the envelope put it into his pocket. They seemed mutually unwilling to enter into details of how Paul had got there, but while Paul was uneasy and anxious to be gone, Adrian Kent sat on a wooden box as though it were an armchair, and dispensed hospitality easily and gracefully.

"Please have another drink. It is very hot—I was reading Donne and went to sleep."

Paul found himself discussing the Elizabethan poets with this strange, burning-eyed young man, and as he did so his gaze wandered round the shelter he sat in. It was a natural chamber in the rock and had the semblance of three walls and a roof, the lower part of the walls jutting out in shelves. On these were arranged, very neatly, the few clothes, books, and cooking pots of the occupant; on one side a heap of canvases, with tubes of paint and brushes in a row, on the other a group of sea shells arranged with sprigs of flowering herbs. It was very orderly, almost feminine. Paul looked at his watch and jumped up, anxious to be gone while the conversation remained impersonal.

"Time I was going," he said.

The young man laughed. "Time!" he said. "There is no time here, only light and darkness, hunger and food. I had forgotten time. Must you go? I am glad you like Donne. He was the best of them all."

He said good-bye at the door of his shelter, and when Paul looked back he seemed to have forgotten his very existence, and was leaning against a tree, broodingly examining some leaves he held in his hand. . . . Paul felt more mystified about him than before he had found him.

Once out of the *calanque* and the boat heading for St. Antoine, he tried to sort out his impressions of Adrian. In retrospect the conversation between them seemed ridiculously improbable; there had been no mention of the crime—no suggestion that Adrian was a fugitive from the police. It was the kind of conversation that might have taken place in a man's rooms in Oxford between two strangers who, meeting for an hour, would discuss nothing more personal than their intimacy with the poets; the kind of conversation made possible under a social system whose problems of life and death, of safety, shelter, and the advent of the next meal, do not present themselves.

Adrian was perhaps twenty-two; he was alone, in hiding, possibly in danger of his life, certainly in danger of arrest; he was living with a gun under his hand, dependent on one man for food and drink to keep him alive, cut off for an indefinite time from his family and friends. Was it the consummate artistry of a guilty man that had made him treat Paul in so impersonal a manner—or was it his nature to feel more interest in John Donne than in his own safety or the well-being of his father? Paul was not sure. One thing was certain: an intense emotion of some kind had shown for an instant in his face when Paul announced that his father was ill—though it had found no expression beyond his seizing the letter and placing it, unopened, in his pocket. Had his mind become unhinged by his solitude? Paul gave it up, and hoped for enlightenment from Benvenuto.

CHAPTER XXI
A YOUNG MAN OF TEMPERAMENT

AT HALF-PAST three Paul was mounting the studio stairs, nervous as to what his reception would be, and extremely nervous of explaining to Benvenuto that he had found Adrian. He felt—illogically, he knew—like a spy about to convict himself. It would have been easier if only he had not used *Lou Cat*.

A savoury smell greeted his nose as he got higher, and at the top he met Benvenuto emerging from the kitchen with a spluttering pan of bacon and eggs.

"Good man," he said, "just in time to share my breakfast, lunch, and tea. Come along in. Afraid I was a bit terse this morning. My creative powers were better than my temper—at least I hope so."

Considerably relieved, Paul followed him into the studio, and earnestly refusing offers of food he stopped opposite a canvas on the easel. Here were the eggs, the oyster shells, and the wine bottle sublimated into a still-life of remarkable beauty. The colour was pallid and cold, the form suggested rather than stated, the brush work nervous and sensitive. It gave Paul an impression both restrained and austere, and he eyed it with delight.

"I think it's fine," he said.

Benvenuto grunted. "They're always so damn fine while you're doing them. You think to yourself, 'At last I've got it'—and in the end, of course, you haven't. Still, it has its points." He sat down at the table, his head on one side looking at it. "Well, have you been giving detection a rest?"

"As a matter of fact, since I saw you, I've found Adrian." Paul blurted it out half defiantly.

Benvenuto paused with his fork halfway to his mouth. Then, after consuming a mouthful of egg and bacon, "Nice chap, isn't he?" he said.

The remark for some reason enraged Paul—really, this taking things for granted was going too far—and he burst into an explanation of how he and Adelaide had borrowed *Lou Cat* and gone to the island, of how he had seen the paint on the rock, and realizing later its significance, had gone back to investigate, without suspecting for one moment that Benvenuto knew of Adrian's hiding place.

Benvenuto nodded. "Unless a man is temperamentally a good liar," he said, "it always seems to me a pity to load him up with information that he may have to conceal. There seemed nothing to be gained by telling you where Adrian was. I've been able to keep him supplied with everything he needs, and I gave him a small dinghy which he's got hidden somewhere and could use in the event of my being eaten by a shark. Actually I don't believe he'd notice if I didn't appear for a week or two. He's always pleased to see me, but I often find he's completely forgotten to eat the food I take him. I've given up taking him fish—he invariably uses it as the subject of a painting, and leaves it about in the heat until it has to be returned hurriedly to the sea from whence it came. He's doing some magnificent work—did you see any of it?"

Paul shook his head. "What an extraordinary chap he is. He betrayed not the slightest interest in the progress of events—and instead we discussed the Elizabethan poets. He's a complete enigma to me."

Benvenuto sat back from his meal and lit his pipe. "Nero fiddled while Rome burned," he remarked, "and doubtless was denounced by his friends for callousness, bravado, or affectation. Actually, I expect he had got hold of a phrase that had been eluding him for weeks. A man of temperament is always misunderstood, and has the most abstruse motives ascribed to him when actually he is moved by perfectly simple ones. Shelley read his poetry to a girl friend through her prison bars, and aroused probably the most intense feelings of exasperation in the unfortunate lady's breast. Yet he was only offering her something that seemed highly important and significant to him, regardless of the mere accidents of time and place—which is, after all, the best that any of us can do. It all depends on the point of view. If a man has got anything to express, in painting, music, writing, however it takes him, he has got to keep himself in a frame of mind that is impervious to the ordinary complications of existence. It may be irritating, even harmful, to the people with whom he comes in contact, yet in some circumstances he must leave the baby to cry for its milk and the butcher for his bill. I shall never marry, because I know I should be tempted to change the child's napkins and take the dog for a walk. Adrian, on the other hand, could marry with perfect impunity to himself. He'd go on painting quite calmly if the house were on fire, simply because he hadn't noticed it, though, mark you, if his attention were once attracted to it he would be capable of the most heroic deeds of rescue."

Paul looked at him doubtfully. "It sounds an enviable frame of mind," he said, "but it's distinctly lucky it's not more general. Tell me, how did you get him to do anything as practicable as seeking shelter on the island?"

"I'll tell you," said Benvenuto. "The beginning of it all was on Marseille platform, on the night of Wednesday, the day after the crime. I'd had a wire from Adrian asking me to meet him—he came down from Paris on the day train, and I went over in the car, got there rather early, and hung about on the platform. It so happened that the train was crowded and came down from Paris in two parts. I met the first half, and Adrian wasn't in it, but among the passengers at the barrier I caught sight of our friend Leech. I went over and talked to him—I hadn't seen him since I'd helped him over a case a year or so ago. 'Hullo!' I said. 'What the devil are *you* doing here?' He drew me to one side and explained he was down here after a chap suspected of a murder in a London hotel. This chap, it seemed, had eluded the police, and Leech was told off to hang about along the coast here, which he was known to frequent, and keep an eye on him. Also he said he was after a jewel thief, who was, of course, our friend the Slosher, as I learnt later. He said he was going on to St. Antoine the next day, in the guise of an ordinary tourist. I said good-bye, after recommending a hotel, and went back to wait for the rest of the train, which turned up half an hour later complete with Adrian. He was

looking thoroughly worn out so I took him to the station restaurant for a meal, and bought a copy of the *Daily Mail*, which
comes down from Paris on that train. I gave him a cocktail,
and opened the paper to give him time to recover from the
journey before asking him how things had turned out. You can
imagine I was a bit taken aback to read an account of the murder of Luela in Bishop's Hotel, and it immediately occurred
to me that this was the case Leech was working on. I didn't
say anything about it to Adrian, but asked him how he'd got
on in London and if he'd been able to pacify Luela. He shook
his head gloomily, and said they had had a terrific dust-up
over lunch the day before and parted on the worst of terms.
I asked him how he'd passed the time before the boat left in
the evening, and he was completely vague about it—said he'd
wandered about, and thought he'd been in the park because
he could remember a lot of pink flowers covered with dust,
and that he'd seen no one he knew. He said he felt terribly
upset because Luela had sworn she'd have him up for theft,
and he couldn't bear the idea of the disgrace it would be to his
father. Obviously he had no idea what had happened, and I
thought the best thing to do was to show him the *Daily Mail*,
which I did. He seemed absolutely dazed when he'd read it
and kept staring at me and saying, 'Luela—poor Luela! Oh,
God!' The idea of his own danger never dawned on him at all
until I'd explained it all carefully to him, and even then he was
extremely scornful of the idea that he could possibly be suspected. I managed to persuade him in the end that Leech was
actually in Marseille looking for someone who was almost certainly himself, and though I didn't think he held a warrant for
his arrest there might be one issued at any time. Then he really
began to get in a panic, *not*, I am convinced, from the point of
view of his own. safety, but simply because of what it would
mean to his father, and he agreed at once when I proposed
taking him straight away to the island that night. I promised
him I'd make it my business to work in his interests, and once
I'd got him on the island I believe he left the whole responsibility with me and has never bothered his head about the thing

again. I go over in *Lou Cat* every second night and take him paints and food and tell him how things have been going, and he always listens attentively and thanks me for all the time I'm wasting when I might be painting, but I know he's always glad to talk about the books he's reading or the way his latest canvas is working out, or some other subject that seems to him really important. He doesn't appear to mind the solitude at all."

"I don't know," said Paul. "I think he's got a bit nervy all by himself. He was quite ready to shoot me when I appeared, and I don't believe I'd have got him to talk to me at all if I hadn't explained at once that I'd got a letter for him from his father."

"Eh—what's that?" Benvenuto's voice was sharp.

Paul looked at him in surprise. "It was only when I got out a letter I had from his father that he—"

Benvenuto jumped to his feet, the familiar danger signals alight in his eyes. "Ten thousand devils! Come on. I hope to God it's not too late."

In a moment, it seemed, they were running hatless through the town; completely at a loss, Paul followed Benvenuto, purely, he thought to himself, through force of habit. In ten minutes they were seated panting in *Lou Cat*, and for the third time that day the bowsprit was pointed toward the island.

CHAPTER XXII
CONFESSION

BENVENUTO SAT silent and frowning, the tiller in his hand, while the yacht cut her way through the water. Paul was silent too, mystified, suspicious, and unhappy, a thousand questions on his lips which his pride kept him from uttering.

"I hope to God it's not too late." What could the words mean?—what significance could that letter have, the very mention of which had sent Benvenuto rushing from the house? The most painful, yet the only reasonable, answer that presented itself to Paul's mind was that Benvenuto had been making a fool of him all along, using him for his own convenience, hiding from him the fact that he was in truth an agent of Scotland Yard engaged in keeping Adrian Kent under surveillance. Paul was revolted at his own thought, his every instinct denied it, while the cold and logical side of his mind insisted that it was the most probable explanation. Benvenuto—whom he had trusted and admired, whom he had grown to look upon as a real friend. It was intolerable and impossible. Paul grew hot all over as he considered it. Yet, all the afternoon a growing suspicion of Adrian had been forming in his mind, a suspicion which had not been dispelled by Benvenuto's explanation of his character, and which had been definitely strengthened by the account of the events which led up to Adrian's flight to the island. Everything pointed to his guilt—the motive, the opportunity, the subsequent flight—and he, Paul, had allowed his judgment to be warped by Benvenuto's professed faith in his innocence. God! what a fool he had been. He looked at Benvenuto, half determined to have things out with him, and felt his anger die down. Benvenuto's humorous, sunburnt face looked worn with anxiety, his keen blue eyes were fixed on the rapidly approaching shores of the island. He was so obviously unaware of Paul's confusion of mind, so obviously concerned with some urgent problem of his own, that it was impossible to interrogate him, Paul felt, and he resigned himself as philosophically as possible to waiting for whatever his third visit to the island might reveal.

As the boat entered the *calanque* he looked towards the shore with feelings of excitement and, for some reason that he couldn't account for, of dread. But the scene was unchanged, the deserted beach, now half in shadow, stretched peacefully before them, and as Benvenuto cut off the engine, complete silence enveloped them. *Lou Cat* grounded in the soft sand, disturbing the tiny waves that were lapping the shore, and Benvenuto jumped out and started running over the beach. Paul made fast and followed him—to find, what? Visions of Adrian with a bullet through his head flashed before him as he ran panting through the undergrowth, and then, as another thought struck him, he quickened his pace still more. Suppose that letter somehow conveyed to Adrian Benvenuto's treachery, if treachery it were, in keeping him on the island? But of course it couldn't be so—it was written before Adrian came down here. Still Paul pressed on, for the fact remained that Adrian was armed and Benvenuto wasn't. The afternoon sun, slanting down through the rocks, blazed on his head as he ran, the prickly undergrowth tore at his clothes, but he did not notice. Benvenuto might have been fooling him—that didn't matter now.

At last—there were the two pine trees, and Benvenuto disappearing between them into the shelter. There was no sound but Paul's own heart thumping—and a final spurt brought him breathless to the door in the rocks. For a moment he could see nothing, then as his eyes accustomed themselves to the shadow he realized the room was empty except for Benvenuto kneeling on the bed, looking at two sheets of paper he held in his hand. He read them in silence, his breath coming fast after his run, and gave something like a groan as he finished. He looked at Paul standing in the door, and after hesitating a moment handed the letter to him.

This is to confess that I, Adrian Kent, murdered Luela da Costa in her room at Bishop's Hotel, London, on the evening of Tuesday, July 29th. We had quarrelled and I killed her in a moment of passion. No one else is implicated in any way.

The second sheet read:

DEAR BEN:

Please give my confession to the police. It is no good their trying to catch me, or you either.

It has been the worst of all, deceiving you.

ADRIAN.

"My God—do you think he's killed himself?"

Benvenuto jumped up from the bed. "No, I don't—but we'll make sure the boat's gone." He hurried off, his face drawn and white, and went down the path away from the beach. A few moments brought them to the opposite shore and Paul joined Benvenuto as he stood examining the tracks of a boat that had been dragged out from the shelter of some bushes.

"As I thought—and he's got a good start because he's got a better engine than *Lou Cat's*. There's no time to be lost," he said as he turned to go back. Catching sight of Paul's face, a faint smile broke through his troubled expression.

"Expecting me to take out my truncheon? Believe me, Paul, I'm not a policeman but all the same I've got to catch Adrian."

Paul followed him down the path. "Are you going to bring him back here?" he asked.

"No, I'm not. He can't stay in hiding any longer."

It was nearly six by the time they were back in the town. The voyage home had been silent, for Benvenuto, beyond telling Paul that he believed Adrian would make for Marseille and take the night train to Paris unless they could intercept him, had been wrapped in his own thoughts. Back in St. Antoine they started to hurry to the garage, and everything contrived to delay them. From the terrace of the Café de la Phare Adelaide hailed them, and Paul looked longingly at her sitting there, cool and beautiful, a cocktail in her hand and an empty chair opposite.

"Don't tell her," said Benvenuto sharply in his ear, then, "Can't stop, my dear—we've got to go into Marseille. See you later."

She looked at them disconsolately. "Oh, Ben, and I am so consumed with curiosity."

"What about?" He paused a moment.

"Why, the elegant closed limousine that disgorged some person unknown into your flat. I thought you were having a party and hadn't asked me."

"Oh, my God—I hadn't realized it was so late! Come on, Paul."

To Paul's surprise he went on to the garage, and there, while the mechanic filled the car with gasoline and oil, he hurriedly scribbled a note and sent it round to the studio. They got in and drove quickly through the town. Soon they were climbing the now familiar road, Benvenuto driving into the eye of the setting sun, and keeping up a good speed in spite of the blinding glare, the bad surface, and the tortuous route. He looked at the clock on the dashboard from time to time. "I don't believe we can do it," he said.

Mile after dusty mile rushed by. Paul had ceased to think, his mind so torn by conjecture that it no longer functioned, and he felt himself identified with the engine that bore him swiftly onwards. Benvenuto's urgency had somehow conveyed itself to him and he felt the need of nothing but speed and still more speed as he stared ahead, his eyes smarting with the dust and sun, the wind blowing past his face, while the car lurched and skidded round corners. For one mile the sun would be straight in their faces, for the next, as the road went off at an angle, it would stream through the plane trees planted regularly along the ditch, staining the road with zebra-striped light and shadow, until Paul was mesmerized into thinking he would ride on like this for ever, chasing something that perpetually eluded him.

He was brought back to reality with a start by a loud report and the shriek of brakes as Benvenuto drew into the roadside. The two men stared at each other in dismay for a moment. Then, "Damn!" said Benvenuto, "that's a burst tire." He opened the door and got down. "We'll have to get the spare on as quickly as we can, but I'm afraid that's torn it."

While he hurriedly jacked up the car Paul unscrewed the spare wheel, but a precious ten minutes had been lost before, hot, greasy, dusty, and bad-tempered, they resumed their journey. Paul had a momentary vision of a whisky and soda, iced, with a slice of lemon, so vivid that he said the words aloud. Benvenuto groaned, his eyes fixed on the road ahead.

"Mint julep," he replied briefly.

At last the outskirts of Marseille came into view, and tram lines and traffic forced them to slacken speed. The clock on the dashboard showed them the train was due to leave in five minutes.

"But I don't know if it's right," said Benvenuto. "There's the railway over there—and just ahead is Marseille Blancard, the suburban station. The trains for Paris go straight through it."

Paul kept his eyes glued to the railway line—there was no sign of the train. They passed Marseille Blancard and then heard the shriek of a whistle as a long train with every window alight thundered through the station. *"Grandes Expresses Europeans. Wagon Lits. Restaurant Car,"* Paul read, and then in white letters on a black board, *"Paris."* So he'd got away. Paul, to his surprise, felt a lifting of the heart.

Benvenuto paused but for a moment before he ran the car into a side turning and reversed it.

"I'm sorry, Paul," he said. "We shall have to try and make Avignon before the train gets there. We've got an hour—and a fairly good road. Eighty kilometres—now for a race with the P.L.M."

Off again in the gathering dusk, lights beginning to twinkle in the roadside cafés, slow tramcars alive with hordes of home-going workmen blocking the road. At last they were out in the open country, making good going along the now empty roads, but slowing down of necessity through villages where the peasants were all out for their evening promenade in the cobbled streets. Many had brought their chairs out into the road and were seated there, the men smoking, the women with their hands busy at work, chattering with their neighbours who collected in groups round them. It was impossible to hurry, and Benvenuto's hand was perpetually on the horn, though the loudest warning made little difference to the strollers. In France the street is a social club to which the natives feel they have prior rights over the bustling noisy *étrangers*.

Through Aix, where the going was easier, for the streets were empty of pedestrians and the traffic well ordered; through Orange with its Roman gateway and crumbling walls, mysterious in the half light; through smaller towns of which Paul did not know the names, and then at last they crossed the Rhône and drew into Avignon. A few more minutes and they were at the station, and Paul leant out and shouted to a porter as they drove up the yard.

"Encore dix minutes m'sieur," he replied, and strolled off when he saw they had no luggage.

"Ten minutes to spare," Paul breathed. "What a marvellous run!"

Benvenuto got down stiffly, mopping his brow.

"Time for a swift one—and two platform tickets," he said.

They consumed two bottles of weak French beer and arranged that Benvenuto should search the front of the train while Paul took the back, and they'd meet afterwards under the clock. Seven minutes for their search; Paul felt nervous when at last the train was signalled, and envied the innocent passengers around him who had moved their bundles and suitcases to the front of the platform and were full of preparations to embark. He left Benvenuto and took up his place nearer the end of the platform. Suppose Adrian offered resistance—or worse, denied all knowledge of him and refused to move from his seat? Paul shrugged his shoulders resignedly; it was likely to be a difficult encounter, particularly if he had to use force in a carriage full of French bourgeoisie. The idea of Benvenuto finding him in his half of the train never occurred to him, somehow. The line of passengers bowed down to their luggage like trees in a wind, porters with bags slung over their shoulders stood to attention, the hissing of the engine and interminable lines of lighted windows flashed past him and came to a standstill, and in a second Paul had boarded the end compartment. The first coach was easy, no one seemed to be alighting at Avignon, and Paul pushed his way through the corridor, passing in review a double line of faces, pale in the lamplight, in each carriage. Then his troubles began, and his progress was impeded at every step, as he came into contact with the oncoming passengers who surged towards him, weighed down with their luggage, anxiously searching every compartment for a resting place for the night. He was further confused by those trying to get out, most of whom were engaged in thrusting their bags and boxes through the corridor windows to porters waiting on the platform below. The train was hot and stuffy, and Paul was pushed and buffeted and his feet were mercilessly trampled, but he persisted doggedly, and did not let a single face escape him. Once or twice a trick of light or a young man's face imperfectly seen brought his heart to his mouth, but each time he found, half with relief, half with disappointment, that his search was still unrewarded. The corridors were gradually clearing and he was making better progress, when all at once the shouts of *"En voiture"* and the blowing of whistles on the platform warned him of departure, and running to the end of a corridor he had to jump for it as the train moved slowly out of the station. Looking up to see what progress he had made he realized he had searched more than half the train—perhaps, after all, Benvenuto's deduction had been wrong, and Adrian had chosen some other means of escape.

He hurried back to his rendezvous under the clock, and saw from a distance Benvenuto standing there, and—yes—another figure beside him, lighting a cigarette from a match in Benvenuto's hand. They awaited him silently.

CHAPTER XXIII
IMPACT

SEATED IN the dickey, while the car bumped along the dark country roads, Paul considered rather miserably the state of mind of the two men in front of him. Adrian's youthful face had looked wretched and hopeless, very white under his sunburn, as Paul saw him into the front seat. Benvenuto he could make nothing of—for his action in hunting down his best friend seemed totally opposed to his character as Paul understood it, and for the past two days he had preserved most of the time a moody silence, making his motives doubly incomprehensible. Until the moment of Adrian's capture Paul had felt a secret hope he would get away—or failing that, that Benvenuto would help him towards escape. Now—they were bound for St. Antoine, where Leech might already have returned, thought Paul as he stared into the darkness, and Adrian's fate as a self-confessed murderer left no room for doubt. He tried to put himself in Adrian's place—tried to imagine this was the last ride he would take along country roads with the cool night air in his face, the last time he would see the dark Mediterranean glittering in the moonlight, as the car swung back on to the coast road. And all because of a few moments of madness that had shot up somehow in the midst of his ordinary life, when he had been shaken by passion—

Paul shuddered and found his imagination could not follow Adrian's feelings any further. The night seemed to him to have become sinister; the moon, which had been so beautiful two nights ago while they sat on the lighthouse, now seemed to cast a cold and deadly pallor over the landscape; the rocks and pine trees, outlined very black against the clear sky, looked threatening as the car climbed on and on. They were mounting up to the top of some high cliffs, and Paul knew that from the crest he would see the lights of St. Antoine below him. The road twisted and turned in tortured angles, sometimes tunnelling right through the rocks—the most dangerous road in Europe, he had heard.

Suddenly he leapt in his seat as the sound of a grinding crash came from above somewhere out of sight, and heard men's voices shouting, and then saw the glare of flame. The car rounded a bend and came to a standstill, and Paul found himself running, Benvenuto at his side, towards the two cars farther along the road. One was drawn into the roadside, its headlamps shining upon the second, which had crashed into a wall of rock and had burst into flames. Two men were dragging something away from it, something which hung limply in their arms as they staggered away from the tongues of fire, something which they laid down upon the road just as Paul and Benvenuto reached them.

"I'm afraid he's done for." The voice was English, and Paul, looking up quickly, saw that the speaker was Detective Inspector Leech. The little man knelt down in the road and did what he could for the thing which lay before him. Benvenuto knelt down beside him. "I'm Brown," he said. "Let me see what I can do."

"It's no good, Mr. Brown," said Leech huskily. "He's dead, poor devil. I've been after him all the way from Monte Carlo, and he knew 'twas only a question of minutes before I got him. Lost his head, I suppose—it's a nasty road in the dark when you don't know it—and took that corner too quick." He got to his feet and turned to Paul. "A lucky thing for you two gentlemen you didn't meet him head on."

Benvenuto was still kneeling over the body, fumbling with the clothes on the chest. He rose slowly.

"There's nothing to be done—he was killed instantly. Justice has been done for you, Leech. Would you like me to send the doctor out from St. Antoine, while you stay by the body?"

Leaving Leech and his chauffeur standing in the road, Paul and Benvenuto walked slowly back towards their own car.

"I didn't see him very clearly," said Paul, "but was it—the Slosher?"

Benvenuto nodded.

"Yes. Nasty business. Poor old scoundrel—he didn't get much of a run for his money, did he? Well, after all, the very least that awaited him was a long term of imprisonment. It was a swift finish."

They had reached the car and Paul suddenly remembered Adrian. He was still sitting there, sunk back in a corner, his face in shadow. What was Benvenuto going to do? Paul wondered, as he climbed into the dickey; he hadn't said a word to Leech. As they drove on every detail of the roadside was vividly illuminated by the wreckage of the car, there was a strong smell of burning rubber and oil, and they passed through a zone of scorching heat before rounding a bend into complete darkness. They were descending the hills to St. Antoine, and another quarter of an hour brought them to the town. Benvenuto drove through the back streets and stopped at the door of his own house, where he got down and came round to speak to Paul.

"I'm going in for a minute—if you'll wait in the car I'll drive you down to the café."

He took Adrian into the house and joined Paul a few minutes later.

"God! what a day. And it's not over yet, believe me. Look here, what you'd better do is this: Go and get some food—if you're as hungry as I am you need it—and then in half an hour call for Adelaide and bring her along to the studio. You've been most forbearing, Paul, and I'm grateful to you, and I hope that to-night matters will clear up. We're going to have a difficult time, and I shall want your support. Here we are— see you later."

CHAPTER XXIV
CRIME

HIS HEART BEATING uncomfortably, Paul stood with his hand on the studio door, and looked down at Adelaide standing beside him.

"I'm frightened, Paul," she said.

He slipped his hand into her arm, opened the door, and drew her into the room.

Three people were sitting round the fireplace: Benvenuto on one side, his pipe in his hand, Adrian opposite him, and a third man, whose back was towards them. He rose with the others, and when he turned round, Paul, in a flash of realization, felt he understood at last the significance of Benvenuto's actions. He had brought Adrian back to St. Antoine for a last meeting with his father—for the man who came towards Paul with his hand outstretched, his face worn with grief, was Major Kent. He seemed to have aged by ten years since Paul had seen him last, and looked very frail and ill. After a few words of greeting Major Kent looked expectantly at Benvenuto, who was standing by the fireplace. Adelaide had seated herself next to Adrian and was talking quietly to him, and as Paul sat down beside her she, too, raised her eyes to Benvenuto.

He looked round at the circle of faces, and Paul thought he was nervous for the first time since he had known him. He lit his pipe and then, still standing, with his elbow propped against the fireplace, he addressed them.

"I feel I owe you all an explanation," he said. "You see, up till now I've been obliged to keep my own council, but now I think the time for that is over, and so, because for different reasons it concerns each one of you, I am going to ask you, first of all, to listen while I give you my version of what happened on Tuesday, July 29th, in Luela da Costa's room in Bishop's Hotel."

He paused for a moment and puffed at his pipe while four people watch him tensely.

"At one o'clock," he went on, "Adrian went up to her suite and knocked at the door. Luela answered it herself—she had sent her maid away so that she could talk to Adrian in complete privacy. She had waited a long time for this meeting—she had indeed been obliged to resort to threatening Adrian in order to get him there at all. She was still passionately in love with him—perhaps even more passionately in love with her own fast disappearing youth—and she was counting desperately on winning them both back that day. Adrian meant more to her than just a lover; she had had many of those in her life. He meant youth, and gaiety, and the continuance of the kind of life she valued, and if only she could win him back he would be a living proof, a complete assurance to herself, that she still had her power to attract.

"She had arranged a delightful lunch for him, choosing his favourite food and wine, she had dressed herself beautifully, and she exerted all her charms to please him. An hour went past; lunch was over, she began to feel nervous, slightly hysterical, her confidence slipping from her. She started to make love to him, descended to prayers and entreaties that he would come away with her, offered him everything she had in the world; and realizing finally the hopelessness of her pleading, her desires turned to fury, and she heaped recrimination and abuse on his head with all the bitterness her passionate nature was capable of. Seeking some kind of satisfaction for her rage, she attacked his one vulnerable point—here at least she had power—and swore she would drag him through the courts as a jewel thief who imposed on women for what he could get out of them, and bring disgrace and unhappiness to his father, whom she knew he cared for more deeply than he had ever cared for her. At last he escaped and rushed away, to wander about London in a state of complete misery and indecision. He thought of going to his father's house, but pride and the fear of hurting him kept him from this.

"We will leave Adrian and go back to Luela, lying in floods of tears in her room. She was disturbed at last by the telephone, and pulling herself together she answered it. It was

Adelaide, asking if she might come round and see her about some paintings that Luela had written to her about. Anything was welcome as a distraction—she could not lie in her room all day, it would send her mad—so she arranged with Adelaide to come round. She decided she'd have a bath—it would make her feel better and repair the ravages of her tears—so she placed a key in the outer keyhole of her door in case she was not ready to open it, and went to the bathroom. Perhaps ten minutes later the outer door of her suite was quietly opened, and one Herbert Dawkins, alias the Slosher, a jewel thief and habitual criminal, slipped into her room. He had been sent there by Luela's brother, De Najera, to steal a big packet of cocaine which she had smuggled to England. The unfortunate man had waited until he believed the suite to be empty—he had seen the maid go out, and had watched the door. Tempted by the open door of another suite and unable to resist a haul, he had relaxed his watch at Luela's door for a few minutes while he lined his bag with the Lady Trelorne's jewels. When he re-emerged in the corridor he saw that a key had been placed in the keyhole, and concluded Luela had gone out and forgotten it. All was quiet on the other side—it wasn't until he'd slipped in that he heard the splash of water from the bathroom. He decided to continue his search, found what he sought, pocketed it, and was about to slip away as he had come, when there was a knock. He was safely under the bed, in a good deal of agony of mind, before Adelaide came in. Luela, finishing her bath, talked to Adelaide through the bathroom door, and then—the telephone rang. Adelaide asked for a message, and then told Luela that Adrian Kent wanted an appointment with her at six. Imagine Luela's excitement—she had won, after all, he was coming back to her. She hurried Adelaide away, she went to her mirror and slipped from her shoulders the dressing gown which covered her. Anxiously she looked at herself in the mirror, gradually her confidence returned, and she smiled and sang to herself as she held her diamonds against her smooth skin. Seized with a whim, she decked herself with jewels as she stood there naked, and then, putting on her silk wrapper, she went to her dressing room to choose a dress to wear. Nothing could please her—one dress after another she took down and looked at. So intent was she that she noticed nothing of the Slosher, crawling warily from under the bed in the room behind her, tiptoeing across the carpet, slipping out of the door.

"At last she was disturbed by a knock, and hurriedly replacing the purple wrapper she wore by a scarlet silk one, she ran into the bedroom.

"'Come in,' she called, her heart beating, a smile on her lips, ready to forgive her lover. The door opened, and a man stood there. He walked slowly in, looking at her, and closed the door behind him. The smile had died from Luela's face, and was replaced by astonishment, perhaps by fear and hate.

"'You!' she said at last. 'I thought it was Adrian.'

"I cannot tell you what these two said to each other during the next few minutes. I only know that at last Luela, inspired by God knew what feelings of disappointment, lust, arrogance, tore off her silk wrapper and stood defiantly before him in the pride of her beauty.

"I think there was only one instinct in the man—to hide her from his eyes—to get her out of his sight, forget she had ever come into his life. He stood at the end of her bed, and hardly knowing what he did, he put out his hand blindly for something—anything—to cover her with. He advanced towards her holding in his hand the silk eiderdown, and she, fear beginning to creep over her, backed away from him until she reached the bed. In an instant he had thrown the eiderdown over her, covered her, pressed her backwards. She struggled under his hands, but by now a kind of madness had seized him and he pushed her down and down, the thick silk covering over her body and over her face, hiding her from his eyes, until at last she lay still. I don't know what he did then—whether he tried to wake her, to make her speak. I think he simply crept away out of the room, hardly knowing what he had done, locking the door behind him, putting the key in his pocket with a kind of instinctive caution. Perhaps he knew she was dead—I don't know. He hadn't gone there to kill her—he'd gone there to plead with her, to bribe her . . ."

"She had been my mistress when Adrian was a child." Benvenuto looked at Major Kent, who stood facing him, and gave a sigh that was almost of relief.

CHAPTER XXV
—AND PUNISHMENT

THERE WAS silence for a moment. Adrian's face was hidden in his hands, Paul and Adelaide sat in paralyzed stillness, while Benvenuto and Major Kent faced each other. Then the old man, as if in answer to some unspoken word of Benvenuto's, sank back in his chair and went on, his voice suddenly quiet and expressionless.

"I saw in the morning paper that she had arrived in London, and I knew from my son's letter that he was going to see her. I decided I would make one more attempt to find him, for although I had little hope of appealing to her humanity or decency—I had learnt too much about her before we parted fifteen years ago to expect that—still, I thought, I might be able to find out from her his whereabouts. I rang up her suite at the hotel and someone answered for her, and gave me an appointment at once. Apparently, as it turned out later, she thought I was my son, and was waiting for him when I arrived.

"I tried to talk to her quietly, without bitterness; my son's letter had told me that he had ceased to love her, and I begged her to leave him in peace. I offered her money, suggested I should settle an income on her for life, and finally asked her to give me my son's address. She heard to the end, smiling, and then prompted by heaven knows what malicious instinct to hurt me, and through me, Adrian, she told me he had come back to her, sworn that he loved her passionately, and that they were going away together. She laughed at me when in my horror I offered her everything I own to give him up, told me that I had grown old and had forgotten what love meant, boasted that the years had not touched her, and in a final burst of arrogance and defiance she threw off her wrapper and flaunted herself in front of me. She was vile—vile—"

For the first time the old man's voice was shaken, then pulling himself together he lifted his head and faced Benvenuto.

"I have only been waiting to see my son again before giving myself up."

Benvenuto was about to speak when Adrian jumped to his feet. "Don't listen to him, any of you. He doesn't know what he's talking about, you're not to believe him. It was all my fault, and I shall—"

"Sit down!" Benvenuto's voice was stern, and Adelaide put out her hand and pulled Adrian down beside her.

"But Ben—what are you going to do?" she asked, her voice very low.

He was looking over her head at the wall, and Paul, following the direction of his glance, saw that a clock was hanging there. Then he looked down at the four faces round him.

"I am in a sense going to put myself on trial before you all," he said abruptly, and each one of them was startled into attention.

"In the eyes of the law I have no possible justification for the part I have played in investigating the murder of Luela da Costa, so I want you four people to sit in judgment on me."

"This investigation is one of a good many with which I have identified myself since the war ended; in some of them I have given over to the police the results of my inquiries, in others I have remained silent. I suppose I shall go on to the end of my life mixing myself up in affairs that don't concern me, simply because four years of war left me with a very lively respect for human life.

"You will tell me that the obvious and proper course to have taken would have been to enter the police force, which exists for the purpose of protecting human life. It is the machinery for enforcing a very wise and very sound judicial system which we have built up in our own interests, and for which I have as great a respect as any of you. It succeeds in making us the most law-abiding people in the world, and under its rule the majority of us live in peace and security, able to sleep at night with a reasonable conviction that we shall not be murdered in our beds. I very much doubt if this state of affairs could exist unless the punishment of willful murder were death, or at least life imprisonment, which instils into most people a deep-rooted conviction that murder, as a means of satisfying greed or lust, is a game that simply isn't worth the candle. The result is that the majority of murders are committed by people who are mentally, physically, or morally diseased, and so are better out of the way. There remains the minority—the rare murders which are committed by the sane, the essentially gentle and law-abiding specimens of humanity who are under the influence of obscure, even ethical motives. In some cases a wisdom above law and a merciful ruler may extend pardon, but not before the agony of a prolonged trial and the resultant suspense and suffering have done their work.

"Surely, to all of us who are not servants of the law it is the spirit, and not the letter of the law, that matters. If that is so, surely it is possible to conceive of a situation in which an ordinary thinking man might arrive at a better understanding of what is justice than a judge and jury, who are bound to apply general principles in individual cases?"

Now he was directly addressing Major Kent.

"Everything that you have told us to-night I knew, before I sent you that telegram which brought you out here. How I came by that knowledge I will explain to you later; it is sufficient for the moment to say that it would have been extremely difficult for me to offer proofs of what I knew, and further, that no one beyond the five people in this room share this knowledge. You told us just now that you have been waiting to see your son before going to the police with your confession. I want you to realize that at this moment the police hold no shred of evidence against you, and it is extremely improbable, indeed practically impossible, that they can ever find any. Such evidence as exists points to one man, and he—"

"Do not go on."

It was Major Kent speaking. "Believe me I am grateful for what you have done for me, and grateful to all of you for what you have done for Adrian. But my mind is made up, and nothing that you can say can make any difference. Suspicions exist—and the only thing that I can do is to give myself up to-morrow—" The quiet voice stopped as a loud knock sounded on the door. Each one of them turned with a start, and after a hardly perceptible pause Benvenuto called, *"Entrez."*

The door opened, and Leech stood there, behind him two uniformed gendarmes. They came in and stood in a group round the door. Leech looked straight at Benvenuto.

"Sorry to intrude, Mr. Brown, I didn't know you had company. I just came in, knowing you was interested in the matter, to tell you we know who committed the murder in that Bishop's 'Otel case." He paused for dramatic effect, and there was a breathless silence in the room.

Paul jumped to his feet.

"Who d'you mean?" he demanded hoarsely.

But Leech was not to be hurried.

"Of course, nothing's proved yet, but there's evidence that makes it as plain as a pikestaff. I had my suspicions all along. Herbert Dawkins, alias the Slosher, it was, him as you saw dead on the road this evening. When I came to search the body, bless me if I didn't find the missing diamond brooch with initials L. da C. on it, and alongside of it the actual key of her room. It beats me, the way they'll carry incriminating evidence about on them, even the most experienced ones."

"Extraordinary," interjected Benvenuto.

"You may well say so, Mr. Brown. Well, he's no great loss to the world. He's been suspected of murder before, but we could never fix anything on 'im. I must be getting along now."

Major Kent rose from his chair and took a step towards the little detective, and then Paul placed himself between them.

"Congratulations, Leech," he said, shaking him warmly by the hand. "Pretty good evening's work, that. He looked a thorough-going scoundrel, that fellow, and I can't say I'm surprised. Well, he saved you some trouble at the end, didn't he? *C'est la Justice*, eh?" he added, addressing himself to the two men in uniform.

"C'est la Justice Divine," said the fatter of the two gendarmes, taking off his hat.

"That's true enough," agreed Leech. "And now I must be O. P. H., so good-night all."

"Good-night," said Major Kent.

CHAPTER XXVI
JUMPING TO CONCLUSIONS

THE NEXT DAY towards dusk Paul and Adelaide climbed Benvenuto's stairs, for he had asked them to dine with him, promising to take them in retrospect through his investigations. Pleasantly tired, they sat down on the big settee, while a fat peasant woman laid plates and glasses on a check tablecloth. The day had passed like some agreeable dream, Paul thought, for Adelaide had painted him, sitting on the rocks in his blue *tricot*, and at frequent intervals they had bathed. Impatient to hear Benvenuto's story, they also felt remarkably hungry, and while there were obvious preparations for dinner and an appetizing smell, the principal character was still missing. Soon, however, his footsteps were heard on the staircase, accompanied by a song to the effect that

> *"He was her man*
> *But he done her wrong,"*

and Benvenuto opened the door and greeted them.

"Food is what we need," he cried. "Rosette, the soup!" and they sat down to dine in the cool twilight.

"I can't tell whether my wine is red or *rosé,*" expostulated Adelaide. "Do turn on the lights, Ben."

He got up and turned the switch, flooding the large room with amber light, and at once was answered by a subdued twittering that came from a house across the narrow street. The sound grew, swelled, and mounted into a burst of watery bird song, and as they sat silent, listening, Paul half expected to see eggs and bacon on the table before him, such a morning exuberance was in the air.

"Poor silly things," said Benvenuto at last. "Those birds are kept in cages on the shutters of a fisherman's house across the way, and each evening when I turn on the light they think the sun has risen. They jump to the wrong conclusion, in fact, and what right have we to laugh at them? Haven't we all been doing the same thing for the past week?"

"Speak for yourself," said Adelaide, holding out her plate.

"Well," said Benvenuto, serving her to *bouche de la reine*, "there would have been no mystery at all if you hadn't jumped to the conclusion that a certain telephone call was from *Adrian* Kent, and not from Major Kent. You expected the name of Adrian, and you heard it, my dear, or thought you did."

"And you jumped to the conclusion that I'd made a mistake, I suppose?" said Adelaide.

Benvenuto smiled. "Perhaps you'd better hear the whole story. I started off in birdlike innocence myself, jumped to a false conclusion, and saw what I expected to see. I think I shall have to give up reading detective fiction—it tends to make one so horribly conventional. I ought not to have been led away by the fact that De Najera was an obviously perfect villain, but I was, and wasted a lot of time disabusing my mind of the idea that he was our particular villain. Still, I must say in my own defence that there did seem to be a reasonable amount of evidence against him."

"Indeed there was," Paul agreed. "The false alibi alone was enough to make anyone suspicious."

Benvenuto nodded.

"The trouble with us was that, a murder having been committed, we allowed it to overshadow everything else, and forgot that business was as usual in other branches of crime. We both of us felt about De Najera that we were dealing with a criminal, and we were perfectly right. His elaborate alibi was obviously covering one of his little absinthe smuggling expeditions, and no doubt the valet masquerading as his master was a precaution that De Najera had taken many times before. It was unfortunate for us that I happened to spot it at the very time when darker deeds were afoot—though I think even without the incident I should have been obliged to suspect the man."

"Why d'you say 'obliged'?"

"Simply because he *was* such a perfect suspect, both from the point of view of his own character, and our knowledge that all was not well between him and Luela. Never at any time did I feel an inner conviction about his guilt, but I didn't dare to disregard the apparently logical chain of thought which directed suspicion against him. From the moment that I heard Adrian's story, a fugitive idea began to float about in the back of my mind, something flimsy and unsubstantial that had no foundation in evidence or in logic. It was far too slight to be called a 'suspicion,' and was directed against no one, yet it had sufficient vitality to rob me of a comfortable degree of conviction in my suspicions against De Najera. In almost every investigation I've ever made I have had this same experience—of something which begins to roam about in my subconscious mind, and worry me, in contradiction to any amount of apparently satisfactory evidence. I can only describe it as the ghost of an idea, that is, as Chesterton says, the 'right shape,' and though I don't know myself what shape it is, yet by contrast it makes other apparently well-fitting pieces of a puzzle appear the wrong shape. The only thing to do, I've found, is to carry on with one's investigations, follow up every clue that offers itself, and keep one's mind on the alert for anything—a chance word, a turn of a head, even a smell, that will suddenly drag this elusive wisp of an idea out into the broad light of day. In the present instance it was borne forth on the wings of a mosquito, but I'll come to that later."

"I think I see," said Paul. "It must be rather like having a word on the tip of your tongue that you can't for the life of you bring out—or finding one day that you can't whistle a single note of a tune which actually you're perfectly familiar with."

"Exactly. Now, to get to business. I heard Adrian's story and took him to the island. I talked with De Najera, and, putting two and two together, produced a spurious four on the strength of his false alibi. I heard your story, and the creature in the back of my mind which had come into existence as I talked with Adrian raised its head again. If I hadn't been a fool I should have realized then that what my subconscious mind was trying to tell me was this: the controlling emotion behind this crime might be not hate nor greed, but devotion—the devotion of an old man for his only son. However, by that time I was in full cry after my conventional villain, and was duly rewarded by lighting on a very pretty little situation during one day in Cannes—when De Najera was discovered holding a secret meeting with a professional thief fresh from England, giving him an introduction to a jewel fence, and subsequently proceeding to change a large quantity of foreign money in a fairly suspicious manner. Although at the time all this did little but confuse the issue, it helped, in a roundabout way, to lead us to the truth in the end; I must admit I wasted a lot of valuable time in trying to concoct a theory by which De Najera might have employed the late Slosher to do the bloody deed for him, and yet be receiving money from him, and it was then that the idea of theft as a motive for the murder first entered my mind. Against this was the fact that Luela's jewels were intact, apart from the missing brooch. Even the brooch wasn't a certainty, and its value was negligible compared with the other jewels; though its value as evidence was great, as it turned out later. To make confusion worse confounded—why had De Najera established an alibi if he hadn't done it himself? I decided to continue along the safe paths of research and wait for an inspiration.

"The next problem that confronted me was the behaviour of Adelaide. Never, never attempt to earn your living on the stage, my dear," he smiled at her. "Your dismay on first catching sight of Paul in the café was sufficiently obvious to set my inquisitive mind working, though I naturally didn't connect it in any way with the crime. Actually, I take it, you thought he was a detective engaged in tracking you down in your character of the Missing Woman? I thought so. Anyhow, later in the evening when De Najera made his drunken and melodramatic denunciation of Adrian in the café, it struck me you looked really unnaturally alarmed even in the circumstances, and beat rather too hasty a retreat. The following night when Paul and I dined with you after our adventures in Cannes, I determined to find out if you had in some mysterious way got yourself involved in the affair, and when I told you of Adrian's danger and asked you to do a bit of espionage, your reaction was such that you destroyed both a perfectly good wine glass and any doubt in my mind that you were ignorant of the whole matter. When you went off to dress, Paul and I spent a pretty sticky half hour talking about the weather and theories of relativity, while with great cunning we concealed from each other the fact that we each thought your behaviour a little fishy."

Benvenuto looked at Paul who blushed.

"The rest of that evening was really too full of incident for any entirely successful soirée—in fact, in the words of the poet, the dance, *as* a dance, was a failure, so far as I was con- cerned. To begin with, I was more than a little worried by you, particularly when I realized that Leech was keeping a watchful eye on you. Then, when Paul and I searched Luela's rooms, I came across a faded photograph which maddened me by a vague resemblance to someone I knew—hardly a resemblance even. For an instant it woke an echo in my mind, which died away even as I looked at the thing, and try as I would I couldn't recapture it. I put it in my pocket feeling thoroughly annoyed, and knowing I had let a clue escape me. Next I came upon the Loty bath-powder boxes, innocent enough appurtenances to any bathroom, but a little too numerous, a little too clean and fresh. It was when I discovered that they were empty, and that their labels had been steamed open instead of torn in half, that the idea of smuggling entered my head. It was while I was sitting on the unfortunate Luela's bath stool that I got the first glimmerings of truth about De Najera's position in the affair.

"The rest of our adventures in the château that night did little towards clarifying things, though just before Paul jumped the parapet and knocked out his foe I was interested to hear De Najera say to you, Adelaide, that since the death of his sis- ter he had become a very rich man. I couldn't decide whether this counted for or against him, because although the remark suggested a most conventional and correct motive for the mur- der, the fact that he didn't mind calling attention to his benefits seemed a just about equally strong factor in his favour.

"It was when we got back to the studio that the band really began to play, with Leech conducting. I had already decided too in my own mind who was the missing woman, before Leech began to cross-examine you, and was much relieved you were able to parry his questions. One small fact that emerged from the interview was that you mentioned Luela wearing a purple silk wrap, whereas the one found beside her bed was scarlet. This helped me later on, when I came to reconstruct what took place in her room after you left. When Leech had finished with you and made his farewells, I'm afraid I handed out some rather rough stuff, and hope you've forgiven me, my dear.

"I admit I was rather staggered when you made your announcement about Adrian's telephone message, and the true solution didn't occur to me until the next night, when I got my great inspiration. It may have helped, subconsciously, to bring Major Kent nearer to the forefront of my mind, but at the time it only seemed to point to De Najera's guilt, he being the only person I could conceive of as being likely to think of casting suspicion on Adrian. If De Najera had really been contemplating murder Adrian would have been the ideal red herring, as Paul pointed out during his summing up at the lighthouse. It was quite extraordinary what a number of things pointed to the wretched De Najera, and when I was sitting over the fire with a pipe after you two had gone that night I nearly managed to persuade myself, against my inner conviction, that he was indeed the murderer. However, there was something wrong somewhere, I thought, and I decided once more to keep calmly along the paths of research. As it turned out our progress was far from calm the next day, if you remember."

"I wouldn't have missed it for worlds," said Paul fervently.

"Nor I." Benvenuto smiled reminiscently. "And now let's go and have some coffee by the fire. I've talked so much lately that I'm thinking of going into a retreat for a month with a vow of silence."

"Please go on," said Paul and Adelaide together as they settled down with coffee and cigarettes.

"The next day, apart from its dramatic qualities, disappointed me. The Slosher's story told me little that I hadn't already vaguely suspected, and if it were true, as I believed, I felt it definitely tended to divert suspicion from De Najera, without offering me anyone to put in his place. The villain might of course be the Slosher himself—I had no hesitation in believing him capable of murder—but somehow, although he was a badly frightened man in a tight place, he didn't give me the impression that he was concealing his own guilt. I felt he had about as much histrionic power as my boot, and if he'd been harbouring a guilty secret I should have known it. The gangsters tactlessly cut him off in his prime at the very point in the story that interested me, though, as it turned out later, he could have told us nothing more exciting than how he effected his exit. The powder boxes were explained; the meeting between De Najera and the Slosher in Cannes was explained; the money changing was explained; a little more light was cast on the ways of living and the characters of De Najera and his sister; but the false alibi was still puzzling.

"Do you remember that same night when I joined you at the Café de la Phare with my head plastered up, and pretending that the Slosher's bottle had been a mere nothing to a hardened veteran like myself? I will now admit that every few minutes my head was going round like a roulette wheel, and I felt more than a little muzzy, though I heroically managed to conceal the fact. Like a man with a high temperature I became obsessed by one idea—not *who* killed Luela, but *why* was Luela killed—why was Luela killed—why was Luela killed? I couldn't get rid of a vision of her, dead, and this somehow got mixed up with a large mosquito on Adelaide's shoulder. I thought, rather stupidly, how very like a mosquito she had been, sucking Adelaide's blood. No, not Adelaide's, of course, Adrian's. If you remember, I reached out my hand and squashed the damn thing, and it made a bloody smear on my hand. I looked at the blood, and my head cleared a little. Why, I thought, as I stared at it, why, fundamentally, did I kill that mosquito that a moment before I had confused with the dead Luela? Because it was biting Adelaide, of whom I'm very fond, and sucking her blood. Whose blood was Luela sucking? Adrian's. Who would, might, kill her because she was a mosquito, a vampire bat, out of disgust, protection, and love? His father. In an instant I heard the telephone call as though I were there in the hotel bedroom. Would Signora da Costa receive Major Kent?

"Round went the roulette wheel in my head, and my mind went spinning after it, trying desperately to find something to tell me that I lied. What had I done in trying to save my best friend? I had hit on a solution that would be the most terrible punishment his worst enemy could devise. I had no proof, I insisted to myself; it was not, could not, be true. I asked you to lay the case before me as we sat round the lighthouse, and tried to put myself in imagination in the place of each suspect as you held him up to me.

"I am Adrian Kent, I thought. I loathe this woman whom I once thought I loved. Through her I have lost everything I used to value, my way of life, the companionship of my father. Now she threatens me, and through me him, by saying she will have me up as a common thief. . . .

"I am De Najera. She has cheated me, I thought, she has been disloyal to our partnership, she may betray me to the police. I want revenge, I want money, I want to silence her. . . .

"I am the Slosher, crouching under the bed with enough jewels and cocaine to keep me in comfort for the rest of my life, if only I can get to the other side of that door. I must get out of this, I must get away, nothing shall stop me. . . .

"The whole thing was so much sound and fury, a tale told by an idiot. You see, I *knew*. Hatred and fear, revenge and greed and fear—it was none of these, it was devotion at the back of it all.

"What was I to do? I had no proof. And suppose Adrian's father had killed her—why should I help to bring it home to him? Why shouldn't I leave it to the authorities to find out if they could? Yet I couldn't leave things as they were, with Adrian on the island and Leech looking for him, with unexplained mysteries surrounding De Najera and the Slosher. A kind of faint illogical hope came to me as I thought of these two, and I determined to go on, just as though I didn't know. Suddenly I thought of the faded photograph, and leaving you two at the lighthouse I hurried home to look at it. It might, I thought, establish a link between Major Kent and Luela in the past. I held it to the light and round went the roulette wheel. It was Adrian it reminded me of—but wait a minute. Could I be sure? Wasn't I seeing what I expected to see—jumping to conclusions? I didn't know, I only knew I had no proof but my inner certainty, and on that I could not act. I stumbled into bed, feeling dizzy and pretty miserable.

"It's difficult to say how things would have turned out next day if it hadn't rained." To the exasperation of his two listeners Benvenuto stared at the fire absent-mindedly before continuing.

"When we burgled the aëroplane shed, the rain, if you remember, was coming down like fury. We stood outside the little door at the back of the shed fumbling at the lock and cursing, and when I'd tried all my keys unavailingly I asked you, Paul, if you'd got any on you. You said you hadn't except your hotel key, which we tried and found too big, and then to your surprise you found another in the pocket of your Burberry and handed it to me. I noticed as I took it that it was a hotel key with a brass number plate on it, rather a neat affair, such as you get in a decent hotel, with the number 62 cut out of the tab. 62! In a flash I knew I had found the proof. It was the key of Luela's bedroom, the key she had put in the outer lock of her door when she was expecting Adelaide, the key the murderer took away with him, for Annette on her return had opened the door with her own key. That same evening Major Kent, on his way to a detective agency in a desperate attempt to find his son, had a heart attack, and fell down your staircase. I had heard your story of your meeting with him, and in my imagination I saw you, after parting with him, pick up a key on your staircase, slip it in your pocket, and forget it till this moment. Trying to gain time, I fumbled at the lock of the shed, not daring to ask you where you'd got it for fear of arousing your suspicions. If I were right, and I *must* be right, I held damning evidence in my hand. At last I opened the door and we went in out of the wet. I put the key in my pocket while you were looking at the plane, and stood staring at the water running from your clothes. Then I realized you had taken the thing from the pocket of your Burberry, and when, in answer to a question that I tried to make sound casual, you told me it had rained the night before you left England, I knew there was no escape. All the time we were examining the plane I was torn with indecision, and when we found the absinthe tank I knew I had accounted for De Najera's false alibi, and so destroyed the last bit of evidence against him. Directly I got back to Marseille I wired to Major Kent to come.

"After that—well, I was faced by two problems. What to do finally, after I had spoken with Major Kent; and how to conceal from everyone my suspicions until the time when he arrived. As it turned out, Adelaide and De Najera provided a quite sufficient distraction to engage Paul's attention for the rest of the day, and I must say my own problems didn't enter my head for an hour or two.

"My visit that night to Adrian was brief, for after unpacking my basket of food and wine, I left him hurriedly, afraid to talk with him. I passed a melancholy night, trying unsuccessfully to persuade myself that I had constructed a fabric of lies out of a diseased imagination, got up early next morning and threw all my energies into that canvas over there. It had the double advantage of absorbing me and frightening Paul, who, coming round after breakfast to talk about the crime, beat a hasty retreat down the stairs on catching sight of the Artistic Temperament. While painting that picture the details of the crime sorted themselves out in my head, and I began to know what I would, and finally did, say to Major Kent. If he came by plane he would probably arrive that afternoon; meanwhile you and Adelaide were out for the day and all went well. However, I soon discovered I was living in a fool's paradise when you came in and said you'd found Adrian and given him a letter from his father. The rest you know—and it's odd, when one comes to think about it, that throughout all our investigations you were carrying in one pocket a letter of confession from Major Kent to Adrian, in another the only real piece of evidence—the key."

Adelaide bent forward.

"Ben—I know I'm stupid—but I don't see why that key was such important evidence. After all, the Slosher had a key, *and* Luela's brooch, in his pocket when they searched the body."

Benvenuto looked at her blandly.

"My child, I put them there myself."

CHAPTER XXVII
ON THE RAFT

"In Salamis, filled with the foaming
Of billows, and murmur of bees,
Old Telamon stayed from his roaming
Long ago, on a throne of the seas."

PAUL REPEATED the words to himself as he lay on his back in the morning sunlight The raft rocked gently on the water, the planks were hot beneath him, while the rays of the sun dried the salt water on his body, turning him at every moment, he reflected proudly, into the nearer likeness of a native of the coast. The morning was a rhapsody in blue, a blue which burnt across the sky, echoed in the placid sea, and spread in a veil over the distant mountains.

Paul stretched himself luxuriously; this must be the height of human felicity, he thought; what more could a man want? Raising himself on an elbow, he looked down at Adelaide lying beside him, a sleeping caryatid, he thought, with her arms above her head. She opened her eyes and smiled lazily at him, and suddenly he found that he did want many things, and had no words to ask for them. He turned away and stared at the shore, where the bright houses of the port seemed painted against the mountains and scattered bathers on the beach so many spots of pigment As he watched, a figure separated itself from the rest, and climbed a high rock, dived neatly, and reappearing a moment later, struck out towards the raft. Suddenly brave, Paul slipped his hand over Adelaide's.

"There's somebody coming," he said.

"Oh, Paul!" She sat up and rubbed the sun from her eyes; then, looking across the water, "I believe it's Ben."

The swimmer was still a long way off, thought Paul . . . and Adelaide's face . . . so very close to his own . . .

When Benvenuto arrived at the raft he half swung himself on to it and shook the water from his eyes. Then he paused.

*"What happy hours a man attend
That hath a cultured female friend,"*

he murmured, slipping back unseen into the sea.

THE END

WHAT DREAD HAND?
THE SECOND BENVENUTO BROWN MYSTERY

CHAPTER I
DRESS CLOTHES

JULIA'S NOSE detected perfumes by four different dressmak-
ers as she stood awaiting her turn at the long mirror. What
acres of flowers, she reflected, must be bottled for every London season. Her mind wandered to the flower farms of Grasse,
mountain paths at sunset heavy with the scent of lavender,
then returned with a start as she swept her skirt out of range of
a jewelled heel. The summer night was hot, the cloak-room of
the Metz was crowded, each mirror echoed an absorbed face
intent on the activities of lipstick or puff, feathers fluttered
in the air, and jewelled fingers plucked at flowing lengths of
skirt. Pink ladies, yellow ladies, green ladies, elbowed their
way past Julia as at last she took her place before the glass,
and if for a moment she looked at herself with satisfaction,
who shall blame her? The sleek white satin of her Molyneux
gown gave her the distinction of a lily in a bunch of over-
dressed carnations, and stressed the slenderness of her figure;
bright chestnut hair crowned her rather high white forehead;
slanting brown eyes held a suggestion of humour even while
they looked in the mirror; and three freckles which persisted
on her nose gave a faint air of the schoolroom to Julia at twen-
ty-three.

Really, she thought to herself as she turned from the mirror, really I do look awfully like the future Lady Charles Kulligrew. And remembering how she had kept Charles waiting,
she dropped a shilling in the saucer, threw a glance of sympathy at the kneeling attendant who was sewing up a damaged
flounce, and went out into the foyer.

Yet her confidence, even the confidence of wearing a perfect frock, began to slide away from her as she walked across

to Charles Kulligrew, standing at the foot of the staircase. It is absurd, she told herself hurriedly for the hundredth time, to be engaged for three months to this charming, intelligent and distinguished creature, to be quite sure that I know him really well and adore him—when he isn't there—and then, when I'm with him—She slipped her hand through his arm and started to talk, to conquer her growing shyness.

Lord Charles Kulligrew, who looked down at her, was chiefly remarkable at first glance for the attractive and penetrating eyes which unexpectedly humanized a face and figure suggestive of a nervous race-horse. Tall and dark, he walked with a limp, the result of a German shell splinter, and when he spoke his voice betrayed a slight but charming nervous hesitation. He was one of those people who seem unfairly endowed with a multitude of talents, any of which taken alone and fostered would have brought fame and fortune to an ordinary man. Oxford remembered him both for athletic prowess and a Prize Poem, while to the public he was famous for his book on his Aztec expedition. During the war he had served with great distinction in that most adventurous force, the Intelligence Service, but met with acute dismay any reference to his achievements in this as in any other walk of life. He had become engaged to Julia Dallas partly because he admired her beauty and her mind, partly because, knowing her from childhood, he had never found in her independence and high-handed gaiety the hero-worship and invitation which he saw in the eyes of other women. Now, to their mutual but unspoken dismay, the demands of a closer relationship seemed to have done nothing but obscure a light-hearted friendship—and, half unconsciously, they invariably tried to arrange some kind of a party when they were to meet.

"Sorry I've been such an age, Charles. Have you been amused? It's the most exciting kind of evening, isn't it? I've a feeling Martin Pitt's play is going to be a success. Did you get him for dinner? You've not told me who's coming."

"The party's to be small but distinguished," he smiled at her. "Professor Edward Milk, Miss Agatha Milk, Benvenuto

Brown—and ourselves. I tried to get Martin, but he's dining early with Terence Rourke. We'll probably see them inside if they haven't gone back to the theatre already. Look—isn't this the Professor and Agatha?"

Framed in big glass doors held apart by two commission-aires, against the background of Piccadilly lit by the evening sun, they could see a taxi-cab from which two people were alighting. The first, a very tall and bent old man, seemed confused between an attempt to help his sister down and to extract money from beneath the folds of his long caped coat in one and the same movement. The lady who stepped with determination on to the pavement conveyed somehow, in spite of the warmth of the evening, an impression of frost-bite surrounded by tulle scarves and jet. As thin as her brother, she seemed but half his height, and he bent down to listen to her as they entered the hotel, nervously fingering his white beard.

"Tuppence would have been quite sufficient," she was saying. "I do wish you could remember, Edward, that ten per cent. is the correct reward for the lower classes." She unwillingly gave him over to the custody of an attendant who led him to the cloak-room, following them with her eyes like an anxious hen. Julia clutched Kulligrew's arm.

"Such a nerve-racking moment," she whispered. "Last time I went to the theatre with the Professor, he took off his dinner-jacket with his overcoat in the front row of the stalls, and sat down blandly in his shirt-sleeves." Her face crumpled with laughter, and they went forward to greet Agatha, whose thin lips softened into a smile as she saw them.

"My dear children, this is a pleasure. I fear we are late, but Edward could not arrange to leave Oxford until this afternoon. He will be with us directly—he is removing his coat."

"You're so wise, Agatha, not to brave the cloak-room—there's such a traffic block."

"I washed myself before I left our hotel, my dear." Agatha's tone swept all the face-powder out of the universe. Then, suddenly softening, "I'm glad to see you are wearing white. Young girls should always wear white."

"Doesn't she look charming?" said Charles, and Julia went forward to greet Professor Milk, whose mild blue eyes looked at her affectionately.

"O matre pulchra filia pulchrior," he said, and then, turning to Charles, "Most kind of you, my dear Charles, to ask us up to this little gathering. It is a rare treat for Agatha and myself." He beamed vaguely round at the company. "I confess myself greatly stirred at the prospect of seeing Martin Pitt's play. A most promising boy—most promising—"

Kulligrew nodded. "Pitt is a great man, Professor, and has never won the recognition he ought to have had. I hear the whole of London is turning out for him to-night. Now, shall we go in and have a cocktail? Benvenuto Brown is joining us, but he rang me up and said he might be a bit late—he's painting a portrait—so we won't wait for him."

Julia took the Professor's arm and led the way along the softly lighted corridor to where Mario stood welcoming his clients at the door of the restaurant. "Good evening, Miss Dallas—good evening, sir—the window table, isn't it, Lord Charles? This way." He spoke with the urbanity only born of many years' association with the most expensive kinds of food, and led the party with slow dignity through the crowded tables, while waiters melted out of his path. He stopped at a round table by an open window which gave on to the Park, and as a final honour rearranged with his own hand one of the green orchids in the centre bowl. They sat down and Julia threw a grateful smile at Charles. He did everything so well—her favourite table—her favourite kind of flower. She looked round the crowded restaurant, whose decoration always pleased her with its slightly faded splendour, listened to the hum of conversation and the distant rumble of Piccadilly traffic, the one broken here and there by laughter and the other by the notes of motor-horns; let her eyes rest on glass and flowers and silver, bare arms loaded with jewels resting on the white cloths, bright dresses, and the rich reds and yellows of wine, and thought to herself there is really nothing so nice as London in the season. She turned to the Professor at her side.

"D'you remember bringing me here on my birthday, one summer holidays? We sat in the corner over there—and you told me who all the people were who came in. It was only when we came to Mr. Gladstone and the Queen of Sheba that I began to get a bit suspicious!"

"My dear, I remember you looked like a little princess, and that it was all very expensive." He smiled at the recollection of the early days of his guardianship of Julia, and stretched out his hand absent-mindedly to the cocktail in front of him.

"Edward!" Agatha's voice admonished him. "Your tablets."

"Of course, of course—very remiss of me—unusual excitement—" He fumbled in his waistcoat pocket and was about to place a pill in his mouth when a hand descended on his shoulder.

"Still doping, Professor? Sorry I'm late, Charles—had a hell of a day. Agatha, how are you? Julia, you look like a snowflake—can I come and sit next to you? Whew!" Running a hand through his already unruly hair Benvenuto Brown dropped into a chair beside her, dipped his rather long nose towards his cocktail glass and drank the company's health.

"Good man—I thought you'd forgotten us. How's painting—and how's crime?" said Kulligrew.

He looked round the table before answering, his good-humoured, lined face with its long upper lip creased into a smile. Somehow with his coming the party had become a party, and even Agatha, rather primly holding her glass, seemed to wear her scarves at a more jaunty angle.

"Deep depression in both," he said. "Country's too well fed and too well policed—no one buying pictures or committing crimes. Going to have a shot at murder myself in a day or two—I'm painting a woman who wants high lights on every pearl. What's this play you're taking me to see to-night? I don't know Martin Pitt—seem to remember seeing a play by him at some Sunday Society show."

Kulligrew nodded. "He's a most brilliant man and has never been properly appreciated. He was up at Oxford with me, and I got to know him pretty well, though he was fresh from school and I was just demobilized. Most interesting mind. The Professor knows him too—he'll be admittedly a great man one day; don't you think so, sir?"

The Professor looked up vaguely from his caviare.

"Yes, yes, a prophet in his own country—the mind of the masses is slow—think of some of our Australian poets—" He sighed and returned to his food.

"I owe a lot to Pitt," went on Kulligrew thoughtfully. "I can never disassociate him in my mind from Blake, Shelley, Pope—even Aristophanes—I suppose I'd read them all before I met him, but he seemed to make them his own, light them up from the inside and give them to you all alive. The first time I met him he was striding up and down Port Meadow outside Oxford, in the rain, holding his hat over a volume of poetry which he was reading aloud to himself. An extraordinary-looking creature, very pale and lightly made, with limp yellow hair and curiously vivid dark eyes which used to blaze with excitement when he read aloud anything that particularly stirred him. I went up and spoke to him that day. I said, 'I used to sit in a trench in the rain and try to think how that went on—I wish you'd read it to me.' He gave me a quick look and started at the beginning—'The daughters of the Seraphim led down their sunny flocks.' Evidently he considered my remark a sensible one, or he'd have turned on his heel and left me—his manners are non-existent. After that I seem to remember talking with him and reading with him for about four years—he's got a more intense appreciation of literature than anyone I've ever met."

"What's he like as a man?" asked Julia. "I've only met him once, and that was at a polite tea-party. He was introduced to me, but wouldn't speak a word and left shortly after. I thought him beautiful to look at, like some kind of a faun—but I couldn't make him out."

Kulligrew laughed. "He's very like a child in some ways. If you'd talked about something he considered a suitable subject of conversation for a woman, like onion soup or the best kind of shoe leather, he'd probably have responded and been perfectly charming—but he's got the most Eastern ideas of women's mentality, or professes to have. I think actually he's extremely shy of women—and of men too for that matter—and hypersensitive as to his effect on other people, so that he invariably seeks out highly abstract or excessively concrete subjects of conversation in an attempt to avoid the personal. This, of course, unfits him both for tea-parties and for intimate friendships. He's got a rooted objection to discussing for one moment anything which doesn't appeal to him as interesting."

"Bad trait for an author," put in Benvenuto.

"I don't know," Kulligrew considered. "It gives him great singleness of purpose and forbids other people inflicting their moods on him. I admit"—he smiled reminiscently—"it is rather irritating at times when he entirely disregards what one has been saying, and then proceeds to open up a train of thought far more interesting than one's own. I think he needs success to humanize him. He'd never admit it, but I believe that the fact that neither of his previous plays caused anything of a stir hit him pretty hard. I only hope to-night will be a success."

"The town is alive with rumours about it," said Benvenuto. "I suppose that's due to our friend Rourke—who's not only a man with extremely good judgment but one of these damned Irishmen who infect other people with their enthusiasms. You know Rourke, don't you?"

Kulligrew's expression was slightly troubled, and he looked round, almost uneasily, Julia thought, before he answered:

"Known him all my life; we went through the war together. He ought to be here somewhere—Pitt told me he was dining with him. Isn't that their table at the other end of the room?"

Following the direction of his glance Julia saw the yellow head of Martin Pitt, bent in conversation with a lady, the back of whose low-cut pink frock was towards her. Facing the pink lady sat a man who towered head and shoulders above the other two, and even across the distance which separated them, he conveyed a vivid impression of force and vigour to Julia. A mass of iron-grey hair was swept back from a surprisingly young face, and for a moment, across the babble of talk, she thought she heard his laugh, deep and rich. So that was Terence Rourke, the man who, although unheard-of two years before, had created a reputation as London's greatest play-producer. She looked at him with interest, but while she did so found time to wonder why Charles hadn't mentioned who was dining with Rourke and Pitt that night; in reply to a question of Benvenuto's he was explaining that the owner of the pink dress was Louise Lafontaine, Rourke's leading lady, playing the name part in *The Lily Flower*.

"Charming creature," said Benvenuto. "I saw her once. Specializes in vamp parts, doesn't she?"

Kulligrew frowned. "She's a woman who's been damned by her own success. She's created a reputation for undressing on the stage almost as great as Tallulah's own, but actually she's an extremely good actress, and Rourke has had the sense to realize it. You'll see her in an entirely different kind of part to-night."

"She doesn't appear to have changed her habits," remarked Agatha acidly, surveying the bare and unconscious back of Louise. Julia gave a small explosion of laughter that seemed in keeping with the freckles on her nose, and became quickly conscious that Charles was silent. She picked up her glass and drank her wine. She was being ridiculous; why, she was not even sure that Charles had ever known Louise well. In any case, Charles was thirty-eight—presumably she herself was not the only woman he had ever met. For a moment she tried to imagine Charles in Pitt's place, his head bent towards the dark curls above the pink dress, and felt at once, painfully, that the intangible veil of half-shy, half-friendly diffidence that she knew so well would not hang between Charles and that pink dress. It was her own fault, she told herself fiercely—she would break through it. She raised her eyes to Charles, but he was talking to Benvenuto.

"The play is called *The Lily Flower*," he was saying.

"'Thou low-born Lily Flower?'" quoted Benvenuto.

"Exactly," Kulligrew looked at him appreciatively. "It concerns a suburban family, and more especially the daughter

Lily, one of those entrancingly lovely creatures that are the miracle of London's suburbs. Have you ever stood outside a big store at about six in the evening and watched them emerge from their ribbon counters and their typewriters—a conquering army with slim bodies and faces like angels, going out to do battle for seats in a Putney bus or an Ealing train?"

"Indeed I have," returned Benvenuto, his fork suspended in mid-air. "They're the most dazzling beauties in the world; and apart from the few who break away and advertise a shampoo powder or get in the Follies, they're entirely unhonoured and unsung. This sounds interesting—tell us more about it, if you can spare time from this engaging soufflé."

"Have some more. Professor, your glass. I won't tell you the plot, it will spoil the show, and it is in any case merely an excuse—an emotional explosive which alights in the midst of this commonplace family and illumines each member of it for your benefit. It is psychologically that the play is interesting—the various reactions of Lily and her family to this event. You might call it a Study of the Effect of Suburban Life on the Soul. But you'll see for yourselves." He smiled at them.

Benvenuto looked at Kulligrew thoughtfully. "I shan't be happy till I've met Martin Pitt," he said. "You've described a most contradictory—But look—look—our friends must be rehearsing."

Round them people were standing up and gazing at Terence Rourke, who, looking magnificently like some cavalry leader at the head of a charge, a long incongruous sword in his hand, was making cuts and thrusts at a frightened waiter. Pitt and the leading lady hung desperately to his coat-tails, but, dragging them behind him, he advanced menacingly, his grey hair waving, the sword-blade glittering in the electric light. "A superb composition," Benvenuto murmured to Julia. "That's his famous sword-stick. I'd better calm him down or we'll have the gendarmes in." So saying, he left her, and walking swiftly across the restaurant put his hand on his friend's arm.

Rourke's fury seemed to leave him as quickly as it had begun, and after saying in a loud voice, "Napoleon brandy! Holy

Powers!" he allowed himself to be led up to Julia and introduced, kissing her hand and apologizing in the grand manner
for his behaviour.

"I hope you didn't wound the waiter," said Julia, rather at
a loss as to how to treat this melodramatic giant. "You seemed
careless of his feelings," she added.

"Sure, I'd be wounded myself if you thought so," he replied.
"The fellow thought I wouldn't know his damned poteen from
Napoleon brandy."

He appeared rather ashamed of himself, and slipping his
sword into its stick and tossing back his mane of hair, he
seemed to draw himself into the likeness of an ordinary diner,
and bowed very formally and gallantly to Agatha as Benvenuto
introduced him. She gave him a bird-like smile.

"I consider you were perfectly right, Mr. Rourke," she assured him. "Far too many people nowadays allow inferior ar-
ticles to be fobbed off on them."

Kulligrew had turned to greet Rourke's fellow-diners who
were approaching, and the next moment Julia saw the owner
of the pink dress smiling at him.

"Charles," she said, and gave him a small and beautifully
shaped hand.

"Won't you all join us for a moment?" he asked. "I want
you to meet my fiancée. Julia, this is Miss Lafontaine—Miss
Dallas."

Julia saw a smiling mouth and unsmiling dark eyes, heard
a clear and very controlled voice say, "I congratulate you
both," and then, "I didn't know you were going to be married,
Charles," as a smooth shoulder was turned towards her.

Julia talked to Pitt while Kulligrew introduced Louise Lafontaine to Agatha and the Professor, and while she contented
herself with conventional remarks about the coming play, felt
she would have liked to pat him soothingly on the shoulder.
He was obviously nervous and gave her his attention with an
effort, his curious and beautiful face very white, his eyes very
dark under his yellow hair. She was glad when Rourke summoned them both away to the theatre. She liked Rourke, she

decided, if like was a word one could apply to so spectacular a creature, and as she watched him say good-bye to the others, wondered why his manner to Kulligrew should be almost exaggeratedly frigid.

What Dread Hand? and *Crime de Luxe* by Elizabeth Gill are now available in paperback and ebook editions.

Made in the USA
Middletown, DE
09 June 2023

32339015R00115